GOOD GAME

Visit us at www.boldstrokesbooks.com

By the Author

A Talent Within

A Talent Ignited

Good Game

GOOD GAME

by

Suzanne Lenoir

2025

GOOD GAME

ISBN 13: 978-1-63679-764-9

THIS TRADE PAPERBACK ORIGINAL IS PUBLISHED BY
BOLD STROKES BOOKS, INC.
P.O. BOX 249
VALLEY FALLS, NY 12185

FIRST EDITION: MARCH 2025

CREDITS
EDITOR: BARBARA ANN WRIGHT
PRODUCTION DESIGN: SUSAN RAMUNDO
COVER DESIGN BY SUZANNE LENOIR

Acknowledgments

So many people have helped me get my stories out in the world. I have to start with my GCLS Writing Academy classmates, who have acted as sounding boards, beta readers, and cheerleaders. A big thank you in particular to Rita Potter and Nan Campbell for steering me in the right direction on *Good Game* after looking at a partial alpha draft.

Thanks to my friend Katie Lamm for being my sensitivity reader and making sure the quarter-Korean American character was believable. She did so while nine months pregnant. Welcome, Lyra!

Thanks to beta reader and fellow gamer Chris Sandusky for letting me call and talk about plot ideas, as well as reading ten different versions of the book.

Of course, thanks to Bold Strokes Books for letting me tell another, very different story. Cheers to my editor Barbara Ann Wright, and all the other skilled folks at BSB who make sure my novels are the best they can be. I will forever spell "okay" correctly.

Author's Note: The racist, sexist, homophobic online trolling Sam O'Brian experiences from time to time is included as a small sample of the abuse online gamers endure.

Dedication

For Brianne, who is willing to cosplay every single one of my characters. I love you.

CHAPTER ONE

W ho thought it was a good idea to bring a stripper to the office?

Lauren watched the video on her mobile phone. No surprise that it had ended up on social media. One guy sent it to a friend who sent it to a friend, and then, someone who didn't know what privacy meant uploaded it without setting their account to private, and bang. They had a viral video of their professional esports team watching a stripper perform in the team facilities. The video had circled the internet faster than a Taylor Swift tweet.

A marketing and communications manager's worst nightmare. And as the most recent marketing and communications manager of the Baltimore Barrage, Lauren's worst nightmare.

The dull pain above her left eyebrow that had begun the day the video was released had since blossomed into a constant, pounding headache of epic proportions, with no remedy in sight. The backlash had been immediate: calls for barring the Baltimore Barrage from the next few tournaments to not allowing them to compete in the finals if they qualified.

Since then, she'd also found videos of staff playing Ping-Pong with background audio that leaked personal information, including financial data and confidential documents. She'd already warned Will Cambell, the team owner, to let her review all in-house social media posts. Employees could text and upload photos to Instagram on their own time, but none of them should be from the office without approval. The rules would have been more complex than a normal business since the teams lived in team housing in the same office building.

Since taking the job, Lauren had assumed her biggest challenges would come from the players. So many were still teenagers with little guidance, but it turned out that most of the company staff were in their early twenties as well, and only three of them were women.

Today, Lauren sat in the glass conference room and listened to two middle-aged men—Raymond Evans, the team lawyer, and Nate, the finance guy—try to have a conversation with Will about the repercussions of the incident.

"You've got no choice, Will," said Raymond.

Will shook his head. "I'm not firing my best player over a lack of judgment."

"Zach hired the stripper and brought her into the building after hours with total disregard to company policy."

"That was guys being guys. People are too sensitive these days. It will blow over."

Lauren took the opening to speak up. "I got an email from Yesenia Avila at Augustan Gaming. They're concerned about the situation. They got word that SuperDrinks is canceling their sponsorship for all five of our teams for the rest of the season, not only the *Siege Encounter* team. Also, I got a call from GMBY Hardware saying they're pulling out of Indianapolis for now and will take a wait and see attitude on the rest of the year."

Will looked stunned. "They can't do that. We have contracts."

"And every one of those contracts was negotiated with a morals clause," said Raymond.

Lauren pointed at her phone. "You can clearly see half a dozen sponsor logos in the video. I wouldn't be surprised if we hear from several more before the week is out."

Nate sat forward with his hands steepled. "Several companies who overinvested in esports are selling their teams right now, Will. You don't want to crash and burn over this incident."

Of course, none of it penetrated Will's thick skull. Typical of him, Lauren thought. He'd been a successful player once, and he'd sunk a lot of his winnings into creating the Barrage company. Lauren wasn't a financial specialist, but even she could tell from Nate's warnings that the team was in financial trouble. Will appeared to treat the company as his personal platform, using it to maintain his relevance in the gaming community. But he was no business manager. Although, she couldn't tell him that. No one could.

"What about trying to capture a share of the untapped female market?" Lauren suggested. She'd raised this issue several times, but the stripping incident meant they might take her suggestion seriously now.

Frank Moore, the company operations manager, leaned forward. "I think we should hire Shogun Una from Japan. She's the top women's player."

"Where's she ranked globally?" asked Will.

Lauren scrolled on her tablet. "Seventy-six."

"Her ranking is way too low," said Alec, the *Siege Encounter* team manager.

Will made a scowl and walked over to the window. After a moment, he turned back to the group and pointed at Frank. "How about Gidget411? The Twitch streamer? She'd be way cheaper than Una, and it wouldn't matter if she can play or not. She'd bring millions of viewers with her."

Lauren knew her mouth was slightly agape in disbelief.

Luckily, she didn't have to say what she was thinking. Frank said it first. "Seriously, you want Gidget411 to be the face of the Barrage *Siege* team?"

"She has, like, twelve million followers," said Will.

"Made up of twelve-year-old boys and perverts," said Frank. "I thought she got banned for cheating?"

"Only six months and not from playing *Siege Encounter*," said Will. "Besides, who cares? She looks great on camera."

Lauren raised her hand. "I care." She twirled her pen to make her point. "There isn't enough spin on the Earth's axis to make her appealing to Augustan Gaming or your investors."

"But you can do it. Right?" He gave her a hard stare.

Of course she could do it, the same way she could stop a runaway bus. "Sure, Will."

"I think we should consider someone else first." Alec pointed at a chart on his tablet. "Let's focus on the upcoming tournament. We barely made it out of online group play yesterday."

"Who do you want to replace Zach with for now?" asked Will.

"Let's move Luke over from the *Call of Duty* team. He needs more hours on *Siege Encounter* to get a sense for the maps, but he'll make a solid backup," said Alec.

Will nodded.

Lauren spoke up again. "I know you're focused on what steps you need to get the *Siege* team in a good place, but we need to get ahead of all the bad press first. Try to save our sponsorships. Get some positive stories circulating online. Show the players with their girlfriends or families doing wholesome activities besides gaming."

A few chuckles greeted her comment.

Will looked at her. "You've been around pro players, right? You dated Seth Madden, didn't you? He was a good player in his day."

Seth was only thirty-one. Two years older than her. "I think he'd tell you he is still a good player." She wasn't sure why she needed to defend him. They had broken up almost a year ago. Perhaps all this talk about aging out at twenty-five was making her feel old at twenty-nine.

"Did you play any games?" Will asked.

"I did. *World of Warcraft. Dragon Age. Skyrim.*"

Will smirked.

No, they weren't highly competitive games. They were immersive role-playing games in amazing worlds. She'd spent hours online in college, but she rarely played since she had no time for it anymore. "I've watched plenty of exceptional gameplay."

"Well, then you know our audience isn't girls."

Her growing frustration made her feel warm. She worded her next statement carefully since she knew Will was already on edge with her. "I might be wrong, but girls could be your audience if they saw a woman on one of your teams."

"We can talk about this at another time," he replied.

Of course, always the same answer.

Will paired his device to the large screen TV on the wall and pulled up the online amateur rankings listing players who had received invitations to the inaugural tournament. Different categories in the list included the most wins, highest score, and best kill-death ratio. "Who is this guy?" He pointed at the top overall rated player.

"The Buffalo Bangers have already made him an offer," said Frank. "He'll sign after Sunday."

"So number two."

Frank shrugged. "Same. Dallas made him an offer."

"Okay. How about this one?" Will squinted. "*Seven*. Kind of a dumb gamer tag."

"Never heard of him." Frank typed something into his laptop. "His real name is Sam O'Brian. Says he's from Havre de Grace."

About an hour north of the city, where the Susquehanna met the Chesapeake. Lauren hadn't been up to the Susquehanna in a while, but she had fond memories of sailing there with her father.

Will rapped a knuckle on the screen. "Someone keep an eye out for him at the tournament. He's an amateur. We might score him cheap."

Lauren leaned forward. "Speaking of the tournament, we need to discuss the media schedule for the players."

Will discontinued casting to the screen. "It can wait." He sat and crossed his arms. "This is more important. I need you to order the new team jerseys." He stared at her, waiting for her answer.

Ordering jerseys hadn't been part of her job description, but it appeared she was expected to do anything Will wanted. So she'd do it. "Of course." She made a note on her calendar as a reminder. When she looked up, he was still staring at her. "Did you mean now?"

"Yep," he replied.

As she stood, she pushed her chair back a little harder than she meant to. The screech of the chair legs across the floor got the others' attention. She collected her things and exited the conference room. As she closed the door, she heard Will say, "Is it hot in here?" While a comment like that might have inflated her ego on a bad night at a bar, it only infuriated her here. She'd been in this position before. As the only woman in the room, she'd heard it all, and it came with the territory. Gaming was currently the domain of young men, and changing it from the inside out would be hard but not impossible.

Lauren ordered Thai and picked it up on her walk home from the office. She'd been extremely lucky to find an apartment so close. In the past, she'd made the mistake of living an hour from her workplace. Unless it was on a metro line, she'd never do that again. Hours in the car staring at other people's brake lights was torture.

She dropped her keys in the entry bowl, kicked off her heels, and walked through to the open kitchen. She got herself a water and some silverware and sat at the counter with her back to her living room. The smell of chicken satay hit her as she opened the clamshell, but before the first bite reached her mouth, her phone rang. Her mother. She propped it against her Thai iced tea and answered the video call.

"Hello, Lauren."

Looking at her mother was like looking at a reflection thirty years in the future, her blond hair streaked with gray and pulled back in a perfectly styled chignon. "Hello, Mother."

"How's work?" The first question was always the same. Never how are you? Anything going on in your life? Not that there was anything going on in her life.

"It's work."

"So when are you coming to see us? I thought you'd be coming over more often now that you live in Baltimore."

"Because you chose to retire in Chestertown, which might as well be like driving to Philadelphia from here." Lauren took a bite of her food.

"We're only across the bay. That's no excuse."

Now obligation crept into her mind. She wanted to see her parents. She enjoyed her time with them, but it was a long haul to Chestertown. It wasn't like running up to her childhood home in Towson. No use telling her mother what she already knew. She could drive down to Annapolis and cross over to the eastern shore and drive up to Chestertown, or she could drive up to Havre de Grace and cross and drive down. Either way, it wasn't a quick trip. Funny that she had thought of Havre de Grace twice today. "Where's Father?"

"On the boat with a few friends."

Her mother should have led with the boat. She missed being out on the water with her father. Some of her best memories were long sunny days sailing on the Chesapeake, just the two of them. "Who's helping him?"

"He hires a captain and a few college kids to crew."

"That's what you get for buying that enormous boat. What was wrong with the old one? At least he and I could crew it alone."

"Retirement is about relaxation." Her mother slid a martini into view. "He's relaxing his way, and I'm doing so my way. Now, how's work? Really."

Her mother had been the CFO of a medical device company. When a bigger multinational corporation had bought her company, they'd given her a lucrative buyout package. It was obvious from how often she wanted to hear the details of Lauren's labor that her mother missed working. Knowing her mother would never divulge sensitive information, Lauren dumped her latest work drama about Will, the stripper, and her ideas being shot down.

Her mother gave a little eye roll. "I never understood why you didn't stay in pharmaceutical sales."

"Because I hated it, and I had to drive endlessly all over Maryland."

"Seems like you still travel."

"In a plane to another city. Not the same."

"So why does this other company…" She seemed to have forgotten the name.

"Augustan Gaming."

"Yes, Augustan. Why do they wield so much power over your company? Augustan doesn't have an ownership stake, correct?"

"Augustan Gaming owns the game, *Siege Encounter*. They developed it, along with a dozen other billion-dollar games and a few dozen less lucrative games."

Her mother nodded and took a sip of her martini. She seemed interested.

"They've created a league. Like an NFL that they own and control. Companies can buy into the league and field a team."

"Like the Ravens?" asked her mother.

"Right. Except Augustan controls the game and the league. Companies like mine, the Barrage, buy in for several million dollars for the right to field a team in the league, but they don't control anything about the league itself. And most companies can field more than one team, meaning some play *Call of Duty*, others *League of Legends*, and now *Siege Encounter*."

"How many million?"

Lauren narrowed her eyes. "Too much for you," she teased. "Depending on the game and the league, anywhere from a couple to twenty-five million, perhaps."

"Twenty-five million? To play a video game?" Her mother took a larger sip of her drink. "That's why you're worried about the sponsorships," she said knowingly.

"Yeah, the team doesn't have any stake in the league itself. We have to have sponsors, sell merchandise, and get a share of streaming revenue from advertisement."

"What about the tournament winnings? Don't you get a share of that?"

"The players split the winnings among themselves. With what little Will pays them, the only incentive to get talented players is the tournament winnings."

Her mother looked like she was thinking about something. "I'm thinking this through, and I see a lot of risk in this venture."

"Especially when a team member hires a stripper at the office."

"Was she talented, at least?"

Leave it to her mom to not be surprised by anything in business. Her face warmed a little thinking about the video. "She did a good job. It wasn't her fault. But she danced in front of a half dozen sponsor logos."

"Everyone needs to make a living, even if it's an industry we hate seeing take advantage of young women."

Lauren nodded. This was similar to being eleven and being scolded. "I know, Mother."

The eye roll was immediate. "Don't use that awful formality with me, kiddo. You're father's mother might have required it, but she's not running this house anymore."

Lauren winced. Grandmother Johanssen couldn't remember her own name anymore, much less all the rules she used to force on Lauren's dad and uncle Mark.

"Despite the incident, what control does Augustan truly have over a completely separate company?"

"They can revoke our franchise tag."

Her mother's eyebrows rose. "Oh."

"Yeah." Lauren laid down her fork and sighed.

"I blame the boy for all your gaming interest."

Her mother didn't say his name, but Lauren knew she meant Seth. Her mother hadn't liked him. He was brash and cocky, exactly why he was doing well now that his gaming career was over.

Lauren shook her head. "That wasn't Seth. I mean, yes, he was a pro, and I was a little blinded by all the attention he held, but I love the creative and educational aspects of gaming." She paused, thinking about what she'd said. "At least, I did. I'm not sure the Barrage is the best fit for me. I just wish the industry would get girls involved earlier so they'd have a chance."

"Mother talk incoming."

Lauren smiled. That was her mother's way of saying she was about to give Lauren advice.

"You need to date again."

Not advice about work, then.

"I want someone who cares for you when we're gone."

Lauren rolled her eyes and laid a hand heavily on the countertop. "For God's sake, Mother. Please don't talk about dying. You're fifty-eight. And I don't need someone to take care of me."

"Give it a couple of years. You'll want it," her mother said dryly. "You don't have to start a family yet. You could always adopt later, especially if you date a woman again. What was that girl's name? The one I liked so much."

"Chloe," Lauren mumbled. "You only liked her because she drove that ancient Karmann Ghia."

Her mother held up her martini in a salute. "Who doesn't love a convertible?"

"On that note, it's time for me to go. Good night, Mother." Lauren smiled. "Love you." She didn't wait for a reply before she ended the call. She pushed her empty food container to the side and walked to the wall of glass that filled the living room wall. It would be nice to go to dinner with someone and take a walk around the city at this time of night when everything looked clean and beautiful.

But it certainly wouldn't be someone like Seth. Lauren had spent more time taking care of him than he ever did her. And she wouldn't date another pro gamer, not in a million years.

CHAPTER TWO

Sam pushed open the hotel room with her duffle bag. The double room was small but clean. The tournament had arrived faster than she had expected. When she'd gotten the invite, she'd thought it was a joke. So did her teammates, Olivia and Jarek. But a few quick Google searches had confirmed that their invitation was real. They were about to play in the inaugural *Siege Encounter* tournament.

Jarek stood over the mini bar, his hair in his slouchy dreadlock beanie, and his oversized backpack still on his back. "Do you think this stuff is expensive?" he asked.

"Yes," Sam replied. She dug in her duffle and pulled out a Ziplock container. "Here. I've got some fresh fruit, Cuban loaf, and green bean salad."

Jarek dropped his backpack and sat on the end of the far bed. "Why aren't you a normal person? Like Utz chips and Butterfingers?"

She dug in her bag and pulled out a container of brown squares. "And brownies." She waved them around, taunting him with them.

He lunged and took them from her. Anyone else would have been frightened. He was the size of a Raven's linebacker, but he was as sweet as a stuffed bear.

Sam heard the door mechanism unlock, and the door opened to reveal Olivia, their third teammate. Olivia dropped everything she was carrying and grabbed Sam in a tight hug. She was warm, with soft curves, and the hug felt surprisingly comforting. She wore some kind of floral scent.

"I'm so glad to meet you in person finally," she said.

"Me too." Sam stepped back and slid her hands into her pockets. She hated being all mushy. It was weird. It was as if she'd known Olivia her whole life, and yet, they'd only ever met each other online. This was the first time to meet face-to-face.

Olivia took one look at Jarek and said, "*Ay, bendito*, I had no idea you were so tall." Then, she gave him a hug as well. Jarek's expression of surprise mirrored Sam's own feeling when it had happened to her.

Jarek held out the container in his hand. "Brownie?"

"How was your train trip down from New York?" asked Sam.

Olivia sat on the bed next to Jarek. "In the cheap seats with me? Lots of fearful flyers and plenty of Miamians heading back to Florida. I thought I had tickets for the Acela, but nope. Amtrak needs a better website."

"You okay with all of us in one room?" asked Jarek.

Olivia looked around. "My apartment in Brooklyn is the smallest efficiency this side of Tokyo. This is plenty big." She pointed at Sam. "I'm going to sleep with her, though. Boyfriend made that kind of clear."

Sam smirked. What was it with straight guys? Girls weren't a threat, even if they were a lesbian? She would never make a move on someone who was taken, but still, it was the principle. She fished around for her laptop and turned it on. Something about this seemed surreal. They were about to play *Siege Encounter* in person.

They'd been playing since it had first launched the previous year. Similar in play style to *Call of Duty*, it had stripped down and simplified the weapons and made the play more realistic, if that was possible in a video game. The game was slower and more strategic, meaning it had taken a while to become popular, but she and Jarek loved it. She was tired of gaming kiddies bouncing around like glitched reels and guys using the sniper rifle for instant kills while running.

Both games had their pros and cons, but she liked the pace and the communication required of *Siege Encounter*. "Now that we're all together, we should talk strategy for tomorrow's games."

Olivia moved next to her and ruffled her hair. Sam swatted her hand away. "Always thinking ahead."

"You talk strategy." Jarek grabbed an empty shoulder bag from his suitcase and loaded his keyboard and mouse into it. "I need to take our stuff down to the exhibit floor for them to check."

Olivia unzipped her suitcase and handed over her equipment, as did Sam. Rules were rules. All gaming peripherals had to be checked for cheat software. When the door closed behind him, Olivia flopped back on the bed. She turned her head toward Sam. "So, Captain, my Captain, what do you think our chances are of winning?"

Sam hated the idea of competing in person. She'd only tried a few times, and each time, she'd wanted to hide behind a mask of some sort. She was fine online, with her friends around her to block out the trolls, but in real life, how would she handle it?

Go back to the kitchen. Girls don't belong in gaming. Why don't you play Pokémon? That's more your speed. I f**ked your mom last night. I'm coming for you.

This was her chance to prove all those jackasses wrong. This was why she'd been playing games her whole life. To win. She pointed at the spreadsheet on her screen. "I've done an analysis of all our competitors. Routes, maps, styles of play. Same as I do online. If we stick with the plan, we have as good a chance as anyone else."

Olivia smiled and pointed at the ceiling. "From your lips to God's ears."

❖

Their first game was at eight the next morning. The crowds making their way to the convention center surprised Sam. She'd watched plenty of tournaments online, but it was completely different being here. Once they had cleared security, the space opened into different areas for gameplay testing, open play, the amateur tournament, and the pro arena.

"Whoa, this is lit." Jarek's head swiveled as they walked through the rows and rows of gaming stations. "I've never seen so many gaming stations in one place before."

Sam agreed. When she was in school for her massage therapist license, she'd gone to the gaming room at her community college. There had been thirty or forty stations in a single, windowless room, and she had found that crowded. This was insanity. There must have been a hundred stations for game testing, not counting the tournament zones.

In the distance, she could see the circular pro arena with its giant overhead lights and the enormous monitors for the audience to watch the competition. *What must it feel like to play there?*

"So where are we supposed to be?" asked Olivia from behind Sam.

"There." Jarek pointed at a roped-off section ahead of them. The gaming stations were mostly empty, and a line had formed at the entrance.

An attendant was checking badges and collecting everyone's phones. A woman took them and placed them in holding containers. The officials had given them specific rules: no streaming and no messaging with outsiders during play.

Jarek elbowed Sam and gestured with his chin behind her. The Seoul Daggers *Siege* team was approaching. Already ranked number one in the pro tournament, they held their heads high and their backs straight. Even their team jackets were pressed and clean. Ahn Ji-ho, the Reaper, with his unsmiling, beautiful face, led the group. He looked like a member of BTS, not a professional gamer. She knew he was like a rock star in Korea. How Augustan Gaming had lured him from playing *PUBG*, she had no idea, but so far, he'd made the transition seamlessly. He noticed her watching and gave an almost imperceptible nod.

Jarek turned and was staring in the opposite direction with a dazed expression. What was he looking at now? A woman with shoulder-length blond hair, wearing a soft silk blouse and a tight pencil skirt was making her way through the crowds. If they'd been in a movie, the background music would have sounded the arrival of someone important.

Olivia snapped her fingers in front of Sam's face. "Earth to Sam. *Vamos*, dreamy. We have some games to win."

Sam was slow to bring her attention back to the entrance line for the amateur corral. Genuine beauty was hard to turn away from. An angry player stormed past her and shouldered her. She stumbled backward and ran into someone.

The moment she heard the clatter of the tablet on the floor, she knew she'd collided with the woman in the heels. She leaned down to retrieve the device, cringing at the thought of how this was the way she was going to meet a real-life Aphrodite. She stood to find steel gray eyes assessing her. There was an air of command about her. She had responsibility for something.

"Sorry," Sam mumbled.

"That's all right," the woman took the tablet from her and smiled. "Not much room to move today."

"Yeah." *Genius comment, O'Brian.* She looked like an idiot and a klutz.

The woman's eyes dropped to Sam's badge. "Enjoy the tournament, Sam. Good luck."

She walked through the crowd nimbly with a sixth sense, like New Yorkers on a crowded sidewalk, and Sam couldn't keep her eyes off her. Sam might have held her breath for a moment. She could still see the woman's long blond hair as she moved through the sea of gamers, leaving a trail of turned heads in her wake. How did she possibly handle all that attention?

Through security and settled into her seat with the competition facing them on a separate row of computers, Sam went through her pre-checks. Her keyboard and mouse were acting normally. Her configuration settings were the way she liked. The tournament staff had requested the settings a few weeks prior, so everything looked the way she wanted it. The ambient light in the arena was much brighter than her gaming room at home, but there wasn't anything she could do about that.

Olivia turned to Jarek. "Hey, Jarek. I've been meaning to ask you something. Why do you play a female character in pink camo?"

"I've always played female characters. In the real world, when people see me coming, they cross the street. The police slow down to see what I'm up to. Women won't get in elevators with me. But I'm a big softie. I'm telling you true. Ask Sam."

Sam nodded. He was the sweetest person she had ever known.

"So I like to pick characters that get attention and seem less threatening."

The exact opposite of how Sam picked her avatars. She chose the most generic male character she could find, usually the default, and rarely used stickers or customizations because she didn't want to stand out. She just wanted to play. Because she loved the competition, the strategy, the challenge of the games. Maybe she should have stuck with single-player games, but they didn't have the chaos of the human mind or the comradery of a clan.

But chaotic wasn't the same as unpredictable, and every player had their ticks, quirks, favorite styles of play, and favorite map positions. She'd already watched hours of streams for all of their potential opponents, looking for predictable elements. She'd debriefed the team last night on the four teams they had to play today to make it to the next round. Jarek and Olivia had tried to stay awake while she ran the video back and forth in slow motion for them on her laptop, highlighting potential map lanes and heat maps of gameplay.

She put her headset on to block out some of the surrounding chatter. Without her phone and her home computer, she couldn't listen to her music playlist for inspiration. So far, the entire experience unnerved her. Her team played a warm-up game on a map of their choosing against bots, but bot competitors, no matter how high their settings, never played like humans. A player on the opposing team stood staring at her over her computer monitor. She removed her headset.

"Two girls?" he said to his companions and laughed. He pointed at her. "I thought that bitch was a dude."

She huddled in on herself a little, ready to get the game started. Stay calm, she thought. They were trying to get her emotionally riled up.

Olivia jumped to her feet and said something rapidly in Spanish.

"Watch your language," said the college-aged volunteer monitor tasked with overseeing their gameplay for cheating.

Olivia stared at the attendant in disbelief. "I told him to enjoy his weekend because he won't make it past this round. What part of that was foul language? The Spanish part? Aren't you going to reprimand him for his *language*?"

"This is why girls shouldn't play. Too thin-skinned," taunted the player on the other team.

"Please keep it clean. Both of you." The observer's voice cracked.

Sam put a hand on Olivia and pulled her to her seat. "Let's get on with it."

Everyone had signed the competition guidelines, and the other team had already broken the rules. Was the observer's admonishment considered a verbal warning? It seemed like the application of the rules was a joke. At least the live stream wouldn't have the opponents in-game audio available. Who knew what they would say to each other?

Jarek's legs bounced up and down. Nerves. If they could get this first game over with, settle in, and loosen up, things might go better. Sam pulled on the neckline of her new team shirt. The tournament supplier had given them all a jersey with their team's name. She'd gotten a size larger than the sizing chart since she hated tight clothing, but she wished they'd had a hoodie version. She could cover her head and block some of the surrounding stimulation. It was warm in here, and it smelled like sweaty, unwashed guys. The smell might be the worst, almost taking her out of her pregame meditation.

"Ready, everyone?" asked an official with a bit of a gut and a receding hairline.

The countdown began for the first game. Their opponents had won first choice during a random selection. They'd picked Destination on the Monastery map. Sam heard a woman's voice as she settled her headset over her ears. Her thoughts returned to the woman with the heels and the blond hair. What must it be like to walk around this place looking like her? How much confidence did she need to be on display for thousands of mostly young men? Sam's thoughts weren't purely innocent, either. She was probably no better than the guys.

The game started. She was already confused and had to switch gears. How had she allowed her mind to wander so far from the game? Her team played exactly the strategy they had discussed the night before, but as she moved to her designated coverage lane, a sniper took her out. Her team played on while she waited.

"You, okay?" Jarek asked in the headset.

"Fine," she replied. "Get the win."

This game mode choice was single elimination style, no respawning. All she could do now was wait. She had made a rookie mistake, and she had let other thoughts muddy her mind.

They lost game one.

The opposing team members leaped to their feet, giving high fives to one another and redirecting their energy from the win to whoops and yells. The player who had taunted Sam at the beginning of the session stood and glared at her over the monitor with smug satisfaction.

She wouldn't make the same mistake in game two.

Jarek was next to fall to the pressure. He had moved too quickly, trying to compensate for the previous loss and had been lured into crossfire. They lost again.

Game five was their choice for map and game style. Sam chose the gameplay called protection. Each team would get four chances to hold a position against the attacking team. This was what they were best at. They had to win this game, or they would lose their first match, five games to zero.

Then, they found their rhythm and dominated every map. Elation filled Sam when they'd won their fifth game in a row. They'd done it. They'd won their first match. Only three more matches today, and they would survive until tomorrow. Their opponents were less enthusiastic now that they had been beaten by a team with two girls. The most humiliating thing was when the captain of the other team shook Jarek's hand and ignored her and Olivia. She was the captain, not Jarek. But she didn't let it matter. The win was a win.

She should have been thinking about the next match; instead, she scanned the convention floor looking for the woman she'd seen earlier.

Time for a vibe check, O'Brian.

If the woman was gay, she had to have a girlfriend. Didn't everyone who looked like that? Besides, she was out of Sam's league. Time to think about something other than sexy calves. She imagined massaging them. Whoa, this was getting out of hand. Games. She needed to focus on the games.

CHAPTER THREE

L auren was ready to get out of her heels. Her feet were killing her. She'd been on the gaming floor for fourteen hours. They'd locked up the exhibit hall, and the last of the professional competitions had ended. Now she was ready to make a quick exit to her hotel room and have a warm bath. She followed a stream of gaming attendees with enormous backpacks that she knew were full of laptops, headsets, phones, batteries, snacks, and a change of clothes. Gamers who hadn't bothered to spend the money on a room slumbered in chairs and on the convention hall floors. If only they'd remember deodorant or cologne.

"Lauren?" She heard her name cut through the background hum of conversations. "Sweetie, darling." With her dark hair, pouty lips, and immaculate style, Yesenia Avila looked like a model from a Milan or Paris runway. She trotted excitedly toward her on her four-inch bloodred heels, leaned in, and kissed her on either cheek. "I don't know about you, but I'm ready for a drink." They walked across the sky bridge connecting to the convention hotel.

Yesenia was exactly what Lauren hoped she could be eventually. Always put together. Taken seriously by all the men around her. Able to make changes at Augustan Gaming that appeared to stick. Not to mention every external communication released from her office was ironclad, the only ambiguities intentional. Lauren couldn't help but follow her around like a puppy at conventions, hoping to join her team someday soon.

When Yesenia saw the hotel bar, she exclaimed, "Oh, cantina," and jogged toward the entrance. Not an easy feat in those shoes.

Lauren smiled and followed as Yesenia ordered for them both. "How are things at Augustan?" Lauren asked.

"Good. They'd be better if my boss would bring you on to our team, but we cut staff this quarter to make our financials look better. There will be more opportunities. Do you still like working for the Barrage?"

"That's a loaded question. I'm fine. Busy. The guys are so young. And the team house makes it worse. When they aren't in strategy meetings and practice games, it's like a frat house. We tell them to shower, eat their vegetables, see a dentist. PR and parenting weren't what I expected, and I thought when Will hired me away from Guarantech, I wouldn't have to stand on a convention floor all day. He said they needed to improve their image. I didn't think he meant literally. I'm on the exhibit floor as much now as then."

"You have a tough job." Yesenia leaned closer as if to keep others from overhearing. "We're getting pushback at Augustan from our institutional investors. We're willing to drop the franchise if necessary. They don't like Will's antics."

Drop them? That was a new wrinkle. How would that look on her resume? Losing sponsors was one thing, but losing a franchise was another. "You mean strippers at the team house or the swatting incident?" Embarrassment filled her by merely speaking about the outlandish behaviors of the Barrage team members aloud.

"Both."

"Will sacked the player as soon as he got the call from your CEO. Now that the *Siege Encounter* team is short a player, the manager is considering taking a *Call of Duty* player and slotting him in, but that comes with its own set of problems."

"Better to lose a tournament than a franchise."

Lauren nodded slowly. "Facts." Thoughts swirled about how to tackle this issue with Will. So far, he wasn't exactly receptive to her suggestions for overcoming the bad press.

"If you have any influence, tell him to not replace the guy with another similar one."

Lauren swept her hand around the bar. Several of the guys in the room looked at porn on a laptop, and a few others played some version of musical chairs with alcohol. "Easier said than done." At the end of the wide arc of her arm, she saw a guy alone at the end of the bar in tech wear: baggy black cargo pants with straps dangling from the pockets and a dark hoodie. The guy had pulled up the hood, so all she could see was the bare outline of his cheek and a sharp chin. He reminded her of a character in one of her anime shows. Perhaps a brooding superhero waiting to show himself at the right moment.

Yesenia sipped her drink. "Have you gotten a peek at Ahn Ji-ho on the Korean team yet?"

"I haven't had much time to do anything but run errands for Will."

"Oh darling, he is beautiful. Flawless skin."

"Isn't that a bit of a stereotype?" Lauren tried to keep her attention on Yesenia while still glancing at the figure at the end of the bar...such a smooth, muscular forearm.

"I wasn't being disparaging. Korea is the capital of plastic surgery and skin care. I'd love to know their beauty secrets." She placed a hand on her flawless cheek.

"Says the woman who looks like an airbrushed cover of *Vogue*."

"Speak for yourself, darling."

"Are we done with the mutual admiration society?"

"Okay. Let's talk Seth. I saw he's managing a *Call of Duty* team now."

Lauren felt the groan even if she didn't make the noise out loud. "Let's not."

"I thought you two were going to get married and make babies." She waved her hand in a sort of dismissive way, as if she had never believed that would happen.

"Apparently, the rules of dating didn't apply when he was on the road."

Yesenia made a scrunched face. "No chance at reconciliation?"

Lauren shook her head. "I've got more respect for myself. I came back once before. Fool me once and whatnot."

"I'm sorry to hear that. You deserve better." She swept a hand up and down. "Look at you. Beautiful, put together, competent. He should have kept his penis in his pants."

Lauren nearly spit out her drink. She laughed. "Yes, he should have." They clinked their glasses together.

As they talked more, Lauren glanced at the person in the hoodie. He had long fingers like a piano player. She tried to shake the curiosity. She'd already been there, done that. Gamers were nothing but overgrown adolescents, and sometimes actual adolescents, but thank God, those couldn't come in a bar at this hour. "How're things with the Czech engineer?"

"Bohdan," Yesenia said dreamily. "Fabulous."

"I don't know how you do it. Four thousand miles apart. Different countries. Different languages."

"Don't worry. The language of love is universal."

Lauren rolled her eyes. "Cringe."

Yesenia waved over the bartender and took care of both of their bills.

"You don't have to do that."

"I didn't. Augustan Gaming did." Yesenia gave a hint of a conspiratorial smile and waved the credit card. "We talked business. It's okay." She patted her arm and gave her a kiss on the cheek. "Same place, same time tomorrow?"

"Sure." Lauren smiled and returned to her glass of single malt. Her father had turned her on to scotch. He had taken her to her first tasting at twenty-one and explained the nuances of flavors that made a good scotch. She'd thought it was an old person's drink, but she loved her father, and had gone along to humor him. The variety of flavors had surprised her, ranging from peppery to sweet. The one thing in common that they all had was that first sip burn. Once she took that first sip, everything was superb.

She twirled the glass and watched the dark golden liquid cling to the sides. Slower to fall than water, as if it wanted to stay spread across the surface. Now she appreciated that her father had given her one of the best lessons in her life. One thing about scotch was she drank it at room temperature, meaning she could nurse a glass for hours if she wanted. No one pressured her to "have another." Scotch was the perfect drink for a light drinker like herself.

Her eyelids were feeling heavy. Time to end her night. A table of three men all stood at the same time. Two of them waved at the third and left the bar while the last one moved in her direction. She steeled herself, taking the last swig of her drink, ready to deflect his advances because she was certain he was coming to talk to her.

"Hey there, you here for the tournament?" His proximity made her uneasy.

She glanced at her lanyard. Too late to say no. "Yep."

"Iconic. Me too." He grinned too broadly, spoke too loudly, and nodded repeatedly. "I play *Encounter*. Are you familiar with it?"

"What team are you with?" She tried to sound friendly but indifferent, hoping he'd get the hint that she wasn't interested in him in the least.

"Um, I'm not playing in the tournament this time, but I'll be in the next one." He pointed at her empty glass. "How about I get you another, and I can tell you about how gaming works?"

He didn't even ask if she wanted another or if she already knew about gaming. She desperately wanted to call his bluff, doubting he could qualify for a tournament. That would make him think twice about hitting on women with a lie, but she had on her team badge. Her job was to make everyone like the Baltimore Barrage. It wouldn't do for her to insult some social gamer who had a Twitch stream or a YouTube channel with a million followers.

"Thank you for the offer, but I don't need another. As a matter of fact, I was about to leave."

He placed one arm on her chair and the other on the bar, making it impossible for her to get past without being more assertive. What a dick move. Anyplace else and she'd tell him to step back. She tried to get the bartender's attention and saw the person in the black hoodie approaching. He pulled down his hood.

No. *She* pulled down *her* hood.

The woman from the gaming floor. The one who'd knocked her tablet out of her hand. Lauren's stomach fluttered as she approached. Something about the intensity in her stride. She knew she was coming to assist, and she liked it.

The woman's androgynous appearance made her exceedingly handsome. That was why Lauren remembered her. Her warm hazel eyes stayed on Lauren until she was within an arm's length. She made a nearly imperceptible glance at Lauren's badge.

"Hey, Lauren. Sam O'Brian. We met earlier." She turned to the guy and said, "Excuse me," and moved his arm from the bar. "I'm so sorry, I didn't see you sitting here. I've been meaning to ask you a few things about tomorrow's competition. Do you have a few minutes? Can we talk in the lobby where it's quieter?"

"Absolutely." She nodded at the guy, who looked annoyed, but he stepped back so she could stand. "Have a nice evening."

As they walked, Sam stayed a step behind her like a bodyguard. Lauren stopped near the concierge desk in case the man from the bar had followed them, but he was nowhere to be seen. She let out a sigh. "Thank you, Sam. I'm not sure if you actually want to discuss something with me, but it will have to wait until tomorrow. I'm exhausted."

Sam pointed a thumb over her shoulder. "I saw that douchebag boxing you in, and I figured you could use a hand."

In her heels, she and Sam were the same height, but if she took off her shoes, she would be at least two inches shorter. Uh-oh. She shouldn't have had that scotch. Now she was already thinking about kissing a stranger.

"Okay. Well, I'll see you around." Sam turned to leave.

Lauren realized she had been standing in some sort of daze. "Wait."

Sam turned back.

"What team are you with? I remember seeing you earlier. On the tournament floor."

"You've never heard of us. We're an amateur team."

"Did you win today?"

"We did."

"Congratulations."

Sam smiled. She had a pretty smile. "Thanks."

Lauren watched her walk away. Something in the way she sauntered through the lobby kept Lauren's attention, a relaxed gait with a quiet confidence. She thought about how she might look to Sam. Well-dressed, her posture rigid, and her hair neatly fixed. Nothing about her said comfortable or relaxed.

Once back in her room, it wasn't until Lauren was halfway through taking off her makeup that something clicked. She moved to the bedroom and found her phone. She texted Frank: *Wasn't Sam O'Brian an amateur you had on your list?*

Frank: *Yes. Why? Did you track him down?*

Lauren: *I did. And he's a she. I think we just scored a marketing coup.*

Frank: *Good luck selling this to Will. I'll let you spin it. That's your job.*

What luck! A woman gamer in the top amateur ranks. All she could hope was that one of the other teams hadn't signed her yet. But if Will's hesitancy to hire a woman was rampant in the industry, something told her Sam would still be available. Now she needed to find out if Sam was going to be a problem or not. She'd completely forgotten about brushing her teeth as she pulled out her laptop. She needed to do a little research. If Sam O'Brian had an OnlyFans site or something, she was going to be a no go. At least for the team.

An image popped into her head about what Sam O'Brian might look like in a sexy pose. It seemed counter to what Sam had brought to the bar tonight. Lauren brushed it aside as quickly as it came in. What was in that scotch?

Chapter Four

Sam's keyboard clattered like those Riverdance dancers that her grandma O'Brian made her watch at New Year's. Everything was working. By the end of the game, they were leading the match. One more game and they were going to the finals. One more. How was this even possible? They'd won a few online tournaments, but this was so different. A crowd gathered around the section of the floor where they were playing. It wasn't the pro stage with all its marquee video screens, special lighting, and circle of seating, but it was still more than sitting in her basement computer room at home.

Olivia and Jarek huddled around and stared expectantly at her. This was her strength. Choosing the next map. She'd watched hours of gameplay last night, hoping to learn something about their opponents, but her mind had wandered more than once to Lauren.

Last night, she'd seen Lauren heading into the hotel bar with another, just as fabulous woman in heels that would have broken Sam's ankle, and even though she rarely drank, she'd slipped in behind them and sat at the far end of the bar. Their ability to draw so much attention but seemingly ignore it fascinated her. Half the men in the bar had sat up straighter the minute they'd walked in. When that asshat had blocked Lauren from leaving, Sam had jumped into action without thinking.

"Earth to Sam." Olivia raised her eyebrows. "What are we doing?"

She needed to stop. "Let's do Monastery." She glanced at their opponents. "They're really aggressive. It's a good map to sit back and let them come to us. Especially the areas with multiple levels. We stay underneath for the close-range stuff. I guarantee you, they will go for at least two long shooters here and here. That means we'll be taking on only one of them at any one time. By the time the other two change their tactics, we'll be so far ahead on points, it won't matter."

Jarek nodded. "I'm glad you like to do the research because I had a good night's sleep last night, and I'm going to need a nap after this."

"The statistics say this is how they play eighty percent of the time." She pointed at the match scores. "We can lose three games before we are in a must-win situation. Chance is on our side."

Olivia ended the conversation by interrupting in a loud voice, "Which means, let's do this."

And do it they did. The win was quicker than Sam had hoped. She gave Jarek a high five afterward.

"Ms. O'Brian?" said a woman's voice. Lauren, with the amazingly immaculate hair and those amazing calves.

Olivia made fun of her: "*Ms. O'Brian.*"

"I'm sorry," Lauren said. "I shouldn't have assumed. Do you have a preferred way for me to address you?"

"Sam is fine," she said awkwardly. Lauren brought a lot of attention with her. The kind that made Sam feel uncomfortable. All those guys looking at her like she was theirs to take.

"Do you have a minute to talk?"

"We really need to start planning for the final tomorrow."

Jarek and Olivia moved in closer. "I need a nap," said Jarek. "What about you?" He elbowed Olivia.

"Huh? Oh yeah." She yawned and stretched. "I'm beat. We can meet up in the room in an hour." She blew Sam a kiss and took Jarek's arm, leading him away. Jarek's head stayed on a swivel as he passed Lauren.

Sam hoped she hadn't noticed. "Apparently, my teammates have abandoned me, so I'm all yours." Wow, that was not what she'd meant to say. "I mean, what's up?"

"Have you ever thought about playing professionally?"

"Is that a joke?"

"No joke. Have you ever wanted to play professionally?"

Sam had to let the words sink in. She'd spent her entire childhood dreaming of being a pro player, but every time she'd gone to join a local team—her high school team, her community college team—she'd been told there weren't any slots. She'd never even gotten a tryout. And there was one obvious reason. No one wanted to play with a girl. "I'd be lying if I said I hadn't thought about it."

Lauren pointed toward the food court. "Let's get a coffee and talk."

Sam followed, even though she didn't want a coffee. Lauren could have said, let's go buy some Imodium, and she would have fallen in beside her. As they moved through the play floor, Sam was amazed at the speed with which Lauren could walk in those heels. How did she do it? The only time Sam had worn heels was when she was a bridesmaid in a cousin's wedding. She'd sworn never again after that fiasco. Not only had she looked ridiculous, but she'd had blisters for a week. Lauren was tough.

"I wanted to thank you again for last night."

Sam gave a sheepish smile. "Yeah. No. That was nothing."

Lauren stopped and took her shoulder. "You saw someone in need, and you helped. It wasn't nothing."

Sam rubbed the back of her neck and looked at her sneakers. Except for the fact that she'd followed Lauren into the bar. She wasn't going to bring that up right now.

"I work for the Baltimore Barrage, and you've caught the eye of our CEO."

"How does he even know who I am?"

"Your stats are being updated online after every match. Lots of people know who you are. You're in the number three position in the amateur rankings for the tournament."

Sam kept stats on her performance, but her spreadsheets were for tracking her own growth and personal development, to prove to herself that she could play just as well as everyone else. She'd never thought someone might see her rank and want her to go pro. The idea was exciting, and yet at the same time, she couldn't believe Lauren was really talking about her.

They continued past the test play area. So many young gamers playing for their first time. That was her not long ago, aching to play on the best equipment and test herself against others.

"As a matter of fact, you're number twenty-four in the *Siege Encounter* all-time rankings when looking at a per match average. Especially standoff."

Sam tried to pay attention, but Lauren's tone of voice kept distracting her. Warm, sweet, and soothing.

"We lost because of you," exclaimed an older teen boy dressed in a Johns Hopkins sweatshirt. He was yelling at a girl, maybe sixteen, in the seat next to him in a standard three-versus-three setup. "You can't just sit back and snipe. Don't you know how to play? Fucking camper." A few of the guys around him nodded.

The girl stood. Her expression said everything. Being called out had humiliated her. Sam knew the feeling well. "Sorry, I need to do something," she told Lauren. She leaned on the empty gaming station. "Want to try your luck with me?" she asked the guy.

He looked at her and laughed. "Sure."

Sam turned to the girl who had been playing with him. "Want to be on my team?"

She didn't look Sam in the eye. "You heard him. I'm not any good."

"I heard a blowhard blame you for his poor play." Sam waved her to the three competitor seats across from the boy and his new teammates. "Let's just have fun."

"Okay. Cool. Yeah."

One of them taunted, "You're going down," and the others responded with more juvenile snickers.

"Anybody else want to play with us? We need a third," Sam asked to the crowd behind them. When most declined, she wasn't surprised. Boys didn't like losing, and they must have thought she was going to lose.

"I'll play." A boy about twelve hopped into the open seat.

"Omar, get out of that chair before I drag you out. They don't want you playing with them," said a woman who must have been his mother.

"Please, please. I'm good at *Fortnite*. I can do this."

The mother gave Sam an apologetic look.

"I'm totally fine with Omar playing with us." Sam leaned close to him. "I don't like bloody graphics. Do you mind if I change your game settings so it doesn't make me puke?"

"I don't mind blood," he replied and puffed out his chest. "But if it makes you sick, I'm okay with turning it off."

Sam set his station to be as kid friendly as she could. Despite the game being rated seventeen plus, kids played all the time. He said he'd never played on a computer keyboard, so she connected a console controller for him. She also muted the lobby audio so he wouldn't be able to hear any inappropriate language.

She turned to the girl. "Okay. So…"

"Quinn."

"Quinn. What style of gameplay do you like?"

"Sniping."

"Run and gun sniping or cover fire?"

"I like to hold a spot and pick them off."

"What about you, Omar?"

"I'm gonna go at them hard. I'm fast."

The leader of the other team yelled at Sam. "You ready yet?"

"Okay. Let's do this."

❖

Lauren stood next to Omar's mom, watching the game on the monitors. She'd watched Seth play enough to know what was happening. Usually, gameplay made her nauseous, but Seth had insisted she rewatch his tournament wins. She'd gotten good at not focusing on the screen and pretending. But in this case, she was truly interested.

Sam hadn't tried to make the kids play a certain way or tell them what to do. She'd asked what they wanted, and she was letting them play their own games. She was moving around the outside of the map in a wide arc, picking off the competitors, protecting the girl from being caught from behind, and letting the boy have fun, even though he was mostly running into the middle of the map and getting eliminated.

The nice thing was, it didn't matter. Sam didn't score anywhere near the points she was capable of. She was leagues more talented than her opponents, but that wasn't why she was playing. Lauren knew she was teaching the teenager on the opposing team a lesson about girl gamers and helping Quinn realize there was nothing wrong with camping, all while letting Omar have a good time.

Lauren wanted to inform Omar's mom that her son was playing with a future professional, but technically, she and Sam hadn't even started discussing it yet.

Sam and her team beat the others handily. A chorus of "GG" and "good game" ended the encounter. The older teenage boy seemed to be impressed and asked Sam a few strategic questions. Even he knew she was skilled.

When they walked away, Lauren was more certain that Sam was the right player for the Barrage. She wasn't as sure that the Barrage was the right team for Sam. She was genuinely a good person and obviously empathetic to the plight of less advantaged players. The Barrage was the type of team that might leave her emotionally defeated, and Lauren wasn't certain she wanted to see that happen. She shook it off. This was a job, and Sam was an adult. She'd make the right decision.

Chapter Five

S am held on to the cold door handle to her room but didn't open it. How was it possible that she might actually go pro? She repeated the conversation with Lauren over and over again, trying to parse out any possible misunderstanding. But every time, she came to the same conclusion. The Barrage was offering her the chance of a lifetime.

Her thumb hovered over her phone app. She wasn't ready to push the button quite yet. Once she entered the room, she'd have to explain what had just happened to Olivia and Jarek. Would they be happy for her, or would they be hurt? She'd always wanted to play full time, but would it be worth it? She opened the door.

Olivia sat cross-legged on the end of their bed talking to Jarek, who slouched in the chair by the window. "What did she want?" she asked.

"She was a snack," said Jarek.

Olivia got up and flicked him in the ear. "Is that all you think about?"

"Pretty much all any guy thinks about."

Sam flopped on the bed and stared at the ceiling. She thought of how pretty Lauren's eyes were. "I hate to admit it, but Jarek is right. She's something."

Olivia sat by Sam. "Spill the tea. Was this business or *pleasure*?"

"Liv."

"I saw the way you looked at her. This may be our first time together offline, but you're an easy read."

"I'm not dead."

"So?"

"It was business."

Olivia sat up straight. "What? What did she want?"

Sam's throat felt tight as she worked up the courage to tell them. "She said the Barrage are interested in signing me."

"Signing?" Olivia said the word slowly. "You mean go pro?"

Sam nodded.

"OM Fucking G," Olivia said, then a long string of Spanish. She screamed, ran to Jarek, and started jumping up and down. "Sam's going pro."

He frowned. "Yeah, I heard her."

Olivia looked at her expectantly. "Tell us what happened."

She told them everything. It wasn't easy to admit that she was scared and excited at the same time.

"What about us?" Jarek motioned between himself and Olivia. Sam could see it on his face that he was feeling abandoned. She knew that feeling well.

"Are you kidding me?" Olivia put a hand on Jarek's shoulder. "One of us is going to the pros. Be happy."

Their differing reactions made her uncomfortable. "I haven't said yes."

Olivia pointed a red fingernail at her. "You better. Otherwise, I'm never going to talk to you again."

"Well, I said I wouldn't do anything until we finish this tournament." She grabbed her laptop and opened it. "I have some thoughts on tomorrow's final."

Jarek made a face. "I wish I'd stayed asleep."

This was exactly what she'd been afraid of. Jarek was her best—and one of her only—friends in Havre de Grace. He had been a soft-spoken giant of a kid at eight who had been teased mercilessly for his size, and she had been a withdrawn transplant from the south. They had gravitated to one another easily, and this had grown into a friendship once they'd determined they both enjoyed gaming. Whether or not he knew it, he had made her arrival in Maryland less stressful.

She would need his support going pro. He had every right to be hurt. The Barrage had picked her and not him. Even if she believed they both played well enough, someone at the Barrage thought she was better. Or maybe Lauren wanted her because she was a woman. She hoped that wasn't the case. She didn't want to be a token female player. She wanted to be a top player, male or female. Either way, she didn't want to go it alone again.

The next day, the amateur finals were at ten in the morning. Sam was a little off her game. Last night, instead of visualizing her gameplay, she'd replayed her conversation with Lauren a couple dozen times. Going professional? Was it even a possibility? Would they really offer her the position? What about her dad? What about her clients? Would they be understanding if she took some time away to chase her dream? What had all those hours and hours of gaming been for if not to bring her to this moment?

And what of Lauren? Sam had to admit, it would be difficult to be around her and not find her attractive. She was in charge of communications for more than just the *Siege Encounter* team, so maybe they wouldn't have to spend a lot of time together. But really, she'd like to spend time around her, if only to watch her over a computer monitor.

As she walked toward the central dais where the pros would go head-to-head later in the afternoon, she passed the Seoul team doing live shots and quick interviews. All of them stood erect, shoulders back, almost at military rest. The absolute opposite of most of the other teams. Ahn Ji-ho wore a pair of sunglasses, making it impossible to see his eyes. He smiled at the cameraman and waved at the crowds in the circle around the stage.

"Who wears sunglasses inside?" asked Sam.

"He's flexing for the crowd," replied Jarek.

Olivia bumped her shoulder. "Want me to go tell him that?"

Sam smiled. "Sure. Go on."

Olivia walked toward him. Sam grabbed her sleeve. "I'm kidding."

The teammate to Ahn Ji-ho's right, a bit more of a geeky teenager, narrowed his eyes and leaned in as Sam passed, saying something in Korean. She frowned and kept moving. She didn't know what he had said, but she didn't like the sound of it.

"What did he say?" Jarek could barely contain his excitement, and why not? One of the top players in the world had spoken to her. "He might have been inviting you for a drink or something."

She shook her head and shrugged. "I don't know, but I don't think it was anything nice."

"Jeez, what use is it being part Korean if you can't speak it?"

The familiar feeling of being judged for not being Korean enough rushed through her. "I'm Irish, too, Jarek. Why don't you learn Korean?"

He raised his hands in defense. "Okay. Okay. Chill."

"Why'd he think you'd know Korean?" asked Olivia. "Honestly, you look really white to me."

How did he know? People guessed she was all manner of ethnicities and nationalities. Was she "insert generic Asian here"? Was she Armenian? One time, a guy had asked if she was a Laplander. She had to google that one. And no matter what they saw in her, she heard "other" in her head.

"It's in your bio," said Jarek.

She was confused. "What bio?"

"On the tournament website. They put bios up for all of us since we're in the finals."

"How did I not know this?"

"Because all you do is analyze gameplay?" he replied.

Truth. She spent an excessive amount of time playing and watching games. But she liked it. Gaming allowed her to ignore the parts of life that she didn't enjoy as much. Now here she was in a competition she'd never imagined she'd be participating in.

Sam took her seat for the match. Stage lights flooded the space. The competition equipment was the best money could buy. They'd even given her the choice of headsets—on-ear, in-ear and over-ear. They had open and closed back styles. She chose the over-ear closed, something that would block the sounds around her. Keep her focused.

She reached up on her shoulders to raise her hood but found none. Augustan Gaming had provided them with jerseys with large company logos across the chest and back. She liked her hoodie. All around her, she could see people taking photos and videos. Going pro meant she'd lose her anonymity and her privacy. Imagining herself onstage looking as cool and confident as Ahn Ji-ho and the others seemed nearly impossible. She'd have to be satisfied with her headphones to quiet her thoughts for now.

A guy with a steady cam on his chest and a surprisingly small camera on the arm stuck the lens in her face. Her first instinct was to put her hand over it. Couldn't he take pictures over her shoulder or something? He moved around to shoot each of the others. This final was being live streamed all around the world. That seemed impossible. Why would some guy or girl in Columbia or Italy—or Korea—want to watch her play *Siege Encounter*?

The actual final was a blur. They won the first game and lost the second. Won the third and fourth, lost the fifth and sixth, lost the seventh and won the eighth. It came down to one last game.

Sam looked around at the crowd. So much shouting. They obviously had their favorites, and it wasn't her team. Except for a couple of kids in a small group.

"Sam. Sam!" Omar stood at the barricade around the stage, yelling at the top of his lungs. He waved frantically to get her attention. She waved back. He bounced up and down and said something to another boy with him. A security guard made him head back to his seat.

Sam could make out Omar's mom and another man, probably his dad. Next to them was Quinn and what must have been her parents and a younger sibling. Sam guessed she wasn't so unknown anymore.

"Your first fans," said Olivia. "And they don't even know you're about to be a pro."

Maybe it wouldn't be so bad if her fans were more like Omar and Quinn. "I haven't signed anything yet. Besides, I may wash out in a week."

"Not happening," said Jarek on her other side. "You're going to do it. For all of us, Sam."

That was the first encouragement he'd given her since last night. He was talking to her, and that was relieving. Hopefully, he'd feel the same way when she started showing up on social media in her Barrage gear.

"We need to all show out for this last game. Okay?" She slumped and added lightly, "Way embarrassing to finish my amateur career with a loss."

One more game and they would be the champions. Unfortunately, thoughts of going pro and thoughts of Lauren had distracted her, and she hadn't done nearly the research she normally did. She let Jarek pick the map and Olivia choose the way they would play it. It was a relief not to be the only one responsible for making choices. They were a team, and they would win or lose as a team.

As soon as the game started, she moved as quickly as she could to her position at the bottom of the staircase on the left. She popped her head above the stairs and drew fire from the other team. They had two players in the same location. "I've got two on the long upper corridor." She tossed a smoke grenade to keep them occupied and thinking she was coming out.

"The other one is in the central courtyard," said Olivia.

"No one on the right," said Jarek. "I'm going to try to take them from behind."

"Jarek, stay put. Stay calm," said Olivia.

He didn't listen. One of the two competitors on the top corridor had moved to cover the left flank and took out Jarek as he moved across the open space. First points to the opponents. But this was a respawn game, so Jarek was back in a moment.

"My bad," he said.

"Stick with the plan," said Olivia.

Soon, they were all playing as Olivia had asked. Sam glanced at the points on her screen. They were ahead. But before long, the other team was ahead. Then, they moved ahead again. Back and forth, a close game. Closer than she had hoped. Someone popped her at the top of the stairs at a distance. She never enjoyed going out that way. She was a short-range combat type, catching them with a shotgun at a bend in a hallway. Though these tournaments required them all to play with the same weapons and no attachments, they still had their favorite styles of play.

Now she saw her team was ahead by ten points, then twenty, then fifty, and unexpectedly, they won. She ripped off her headset and threw it in the air. Olivia screamed in Spanish and hugged Jarek, who was literally blushing with his face pressed against her chest. Sam couldn't believe it. They'd won the inaugural amateur tournament for *Siege Encounter*. They were the best of the amateurs, at least for today.

A member of the other team shoved his keyboard onto the floor, but he and the team's captain congratulated them. Only the player wearing his ball cap backward muttered, "C U next Tuesday," as he walked past her and Olivia.

Seriously, grow up, she thought.

"He'd better be glad my mother's not here. She'd tear him a new—"

Sam nudged her with her elbow and spoke softly between gritted teeth. "Cameras. Live stream."

Olivia pulled her into a hug. "And that's why I love you. Always keeping your cool." Olivia ran to where the usher held their gear and retrieved their phones. She handed them out and held up her own. "Selfie time."

Olivia held the phone above them in a way to get the gaming stations behind them. The three of them crammed into the frame and smiled.

Sam's phone began vibrating. Her public social accounts and her *Siege* account messaging system were filling with vitriol. Most of it was sexual. Some was crass. Some threatening. Olivia was staring at her phone as well. Her expression told Sam that she was getting the same thing.

The dark side of women in gaming had thrown a shadow over the day. She scrolled through the messages, each one angrier and more disgusting than the last. They'd won the biggest tournament of their lives, but she should have known no one would let them enjoy the win for long. She glanced at where Quinn was waving from the audience. Sam hoped that, someday soon, the Quinns of the world wouldn't have to take this kind of abuse. Unfortunately, that day wasn't today.

Chapter Six

L auren watched the scenery go by through the Amtrak window. She could have driven up to Havre de Grace from Baltimore, but I-95 was a mess at this time of day on a Friday. The interstate turned into a bumper-to-bumper racetrack later in the afternoon before turning into a parking lot.

Outside the train window, the journey showed the underbelly of Maryland. Industrial parks separated by a few moments over the Gunpowder River, more greenery, more industrial distribution centers. But thirty minutes on the train was a restful way to make the journey up to Havre de Grace, as long as she didn't miss the train back.

She hadn't been asked to track down a player before. Her job was marketing communications, but she had gladly taken the task. She'd looked for Sam after the final on Sunday, but Sam had disappeared as soon as the competition had ended. Lauren had tried to call her but got an out of service message. She'd also tried the email address on the tournament application form. She'd gotten a baffling auto reply with the words, "Fuck you." Not what she had expected from the woman she'd met and spoken with, who had seemed polite and protective. So here she was on the train making an in-person visit to see if she could bring Sam onboard.

The northbound Aberdeen station was nothing more than a covered platform and a dozen parking spots. She walked to the edge of the parking lot and looked across the sea of SUVs. She did not miss commuting. Living within walking distance of the office was the best part of her job.

A small Toyota pulled into a parking spot in front of her. The woman driver waved. Lauren checked the license plate against the app and opened the door.

"Pearl?"

"Lauren?" the driver asked. She had a broad smile and a vintage cab driver's hat seated on her curly red hair. Stuck to the dashboard was a Chihuahua statue with a bouncing head. The car was clean and a new model, but it smelled vaguely of baby powder.

"How was your train ride?"

"Fabulous. I love not having to drive I-95."

Pearl took them through a small neighborhood and onto the Pulaski Highway toward Havre de Grace. She was a careful driver, giving plenty of distance to the cars in front of her and not rushing to get to their destination.

"Pearl. Will you be available later this evening? I need to make it back to the station by 7:35, or I'll have to wait for the late train."

"I pick my daughter up at daycare after this, so I don't normally drive after 4 p.m. If you can handle a six-month-old in the back seat with you, I can work something out."

Lauren thought of her niece, Bunny. She was eight now and adorable. "I have no issues with sharing the ride." Pearl gave her a number she could text if she needed a ride later.

The destination turned out to be a single-story home covered in white siding with a detached garage. There were no trees or bushes of any kind and nothing decorative. No welcome mat, or wind chimes, or color of any sort. Only a lone white van in the driveway.

"Can you wait a moment until I figure out if I'm at the right address?"

"Say hi to Mr. O'Brian for me." Of course Pearl would know who lived in the house. Havre de Grace wasn't that big.

Lauren knocked.

The man who opened the door was tall, graying at the temples, and not Sam. He held the door open only enough that she could see him but not the rest of the house. "What do you want?" He seemed suspicious of her, but he appraised her the same way most men did, with a languid look up and down.

"Hi, I'm Lauren Johanssen. I'm looking for Sam O'Brian."

"What has she done?" he asked.

"I'm with the Baltimore Barrage." When he showed no recognition, she added, "We're a professional computer gaming team."

"Professional computer gaming?" He opened the door a little wider. "I didn't even know there was such a thing."

"Are you Sam's father?"

"Yes." He didn't offer his first name.

"I'm trying to reach her to discuss a position on our team. She hasn't been answering my texts or calls."

"Burner number."

"I'm sorry, what?"

"She uses a burner phone number. Unless you're trying to schedule a massage, she doesn't want to talk to you."

"A massage?"

"That's what she does for a living. I told her to get a degree in medicine or something. She's smart, but she didn't listen to me. Used my GI bill for a glorified spa license." He opened the door wider and stepped aside. "She should be home soon if you want to come in."

Lauren was uneasy about his demeanor. Perhaps his wariness and his unkempt appearance, but the house beyond him looked tidy. She turned and waved at Pearl, who waved back and drove away. Now she had no choice but to accept his invitation.

"Pearl said to say hello."

"Pearl? Oh, that kid has been trouble since she was a teenager." He closed the door behind her. "Would you like a beer?"

"No, thank you."

He walked away without inviting her to sit, so she meandered to the curio cabinet in the corner. Inside were little figurines of angels in different poses, an Irish leprechaun with a pot of gold, several green plastic army figures, and what looked like a lobby card for the original Star Wars movie. On the wall next to it hung an ornate crucifix with Jesus's head covered in the crown of thorns, blood dripping from his hands, feet, and side.

She examined a picture of Sam's father in an army dress uniform. Next to it hung a shadow box full of medals, ribbons, patches, and a nametag with O'Brian. Sam's father returned from the kitchen, beer in hand.

"Are you still in the Army?" she asked.

He looked at the shadow box. "Nope. Discharged five years ago."

She pointed. "What do all these ribbons represent?"

He lifted his chin and stepped closer to the wall. "Overseas Service Ribbon, Afghanistan Campaign Medal, Purple Heart, Bronze Star, jump wings, and a lot of specialties. They gave me this one just for learning how to shoot a rifle."

She examined him more closely. "You were in Afghanistan?"

"I did eight tours."

She couldn't control the surprise in her voice. "Eight?"

He pointed to the next photo on the wall. The man in the uniform looked a lot like him, but the uniform was an older style. "Family business. My dad served from Vietnam through the Cold War. My grandfather served in World War II and Korea, and my great-grandfather served in World War I, but he was a Marine."

"Did Sam serve?"

He made a sour expression. "She doesn't have the stomach for it."

Time to change the subject. "She's a great gamer. One of the best women players we've ever seen. That's why I'm here."

"If you say so."

As if conjured by their discussion, the front door opened, and Sam stepped inside. She placed a folding table and a duffle bag on the floor before shutting the door. She appeared surprised. "Um, Lauren, right? What are you doing here?"

"I came to talk to you about becoming a member of the Baltimore Barrage."

"You were serious about that?"

"I tried calling you several times."

Sam looked sheepish in response. "Can you give me a minute to put away my gear?" She trotted off, leaving Lauren with her dad.

"Is she really that good?" he asked.

"She is."

He took a sip of his beer. "I'll leave you to it."

After he'd left the room, she noticed another photo on the opposite wall. As she drew near, she could see it was of a little girl dressed in a frilly white dress with a gold cross around her neck. She had a white bow in her dark hair. She was certain it was Sam, perhaps at seven or eight.

"First communion."

Lauren jumped. Sam stood next to her, examining the photo.

"Irish Catholic." Sam pointed at the Irish flag hanging on a peg by the door.

"Ah." Lauren looked around. "I don't see any pictures of your mother. Was she military as well?"

"She's dead." Sam said it the way someone said they had pancakes for breakfast. No emotion.

"Oh." Her natural desire to comfort others fought with her sense that Sam didn't seem to need her platitudes. "I apologize for surprising you like this. I tried to find you after the tournament, but one of your teammates, Olivia, said you went home right away."

Sam didn't look at her. "I needed to decompress. Long weekend and all that. Things I needed to do here."

Lauren followed her eyeline to the small kitchen she could see through the arched doorway. Mr. O'Brian sat quietly, drinking his beer. No radio. No TV. No internet devices. As a matter of fact, she didn't see a TV or computer in the house. Was Sam implying she had to care for her dad, or was it something else? "I haven't been up this way in a few years. Is Bomboy's still open?"

Sam's face lit up. "The best fudge in Maryland? Hell, yeah, it's open."

Lauren couldn't help but return the smile. "I take it you're a fan. I didn't bring my car. I took an Uber from the train station. Is it close enough to walk there?"

"We're only a few blocks." Sam glanced at Lauren's feet.

Lauren looked as well. She'd worn flats today, and Sam had shown concern about if she could walk that far in heels. Sam opened the door and gestured for Lauren to go first. It was a lovely day.

"Your father said you work as a masseuse."

"Massage therapist."

"Sorry, massage therapist."

"It's okay," said Sam. "Most people don't know the difference. I work in medical environments with patients who are in pain. Sometimes, I do a full massage, but a lot of times, I just rub their hands or their feet or their head. Especially when they have mobility issues."

"That sounds rewarding. Helping people feel better."

"I'm no nurse. They're the actual heroes, but I try to do my bit to make people comfortable."

"Well, that makes it a little harder to lure you away. Professional gaming is only entertainment, but I'm here to convince you to sign with the Barrage and play *Siege Encounter* professionally. I tried to reach you several times. I have to say, your email auto reply is *creative*."

Sam smirked. "Don't you mean surly?"

Lauren smiled. "I didn't want to insult you right away."

"That's all right. I can be abrupt. Comes with living in an Army family. Direct. Purposeful. Profane." She said the last word like a TV announcer, in a deep booming voice.

Lauren realized she was still smiling, and so was Sam. "I'll keep that in mind. In my job, that would get me fired…quickly."

"Good thing you aren't here to recruit me as your assistant."

They turned onto the main strip along the Susquehanna River. It still looked the same as she remembered it. A few more condos than her last visit.

"Speaking of here. Have you always lived in Havre de Grace?"

"I've lived in Harford County since I was eight. Before that, I lived in North Carolina."

"I thought Army brats moved all over the place?"

"Hey now." Sam pointed at herself. "Not a brat. Well, maybe a little." She slipped her hands in her pockets. She grew more serious. "I lived with my grandparents during most of Dad's active service."

Lauren didn't push the subject. She could see the darkness that had crept across Sam's face when she spoke of it, but she was curious.

Sam pointed. "Bomboy's."

"Oh my God, I can't wait. It's been years."

Sam pulled the door open at Bomboy's and let her go through first. Lauren could get used to all this door opening. Was someone going to revoke her feminist card if she liked it when another woman opened her door? The smell of chocolate hung heavily in the air. She followed Sam to the counter and, after staring at the blocks of freshly made fudge, she ordered herself a single slice.

Sam leaned closer. "You're going to want more than that. Trust me."

Lauren shivered. Maybe it was the way she'd said it or maybe it was how close she'd been. She watched Sam place an order before she asked the girl behind the counter for a second slice.

Purchases complete, Sam opened the door for her once again. Lauren thanked her. She wondered if Sam did it all the time or if it was because Lauren was here offering her a job. Seth might have done it when they first dated. It all seemed so long ago, she couldn't really remember.

Sam pointed down the street. "You up for a few more blocks? We can walk down to the park."

Lauren checked the time. She still had an hour before she needed to head to the station. "Sure."

"You said you've been here in the past. Are you from Baltimore originally?" asked Sam.

"Towson. I moved away after college. When the Barrage offered me a job, I was happy to be coming home."

Sam exclaimed, "My grandma loves the Peppermill restaurant."

"In Lutherville?"

"Yeah. My cousins and I take my grandparents there every few months. I swear, they know everyone in the place."

"My parents moved over to Chestertown on the eastern shore a few years ago, so I don't hang out in Towson anymore."

"That's a haul."

"My mother called me a few days ago and complained that I haven't been to see them since I moved back to Baltimore."

Sam got serious as she said, "You should go."

Lauren remembered that Sam's mother was dead. "You're right. I should." As much as her mother could annoy her, she was alive and well and living not that far from here. She couldn't imagine what it must have been like for Sam to lose her mother. "How old were you when your mother died?"

Sam frowned. "I was almost nine."

The same age as her niece, Bunny. She tried to imagine how Bunny would feel if she lost her mother now. How would she have felt at that age? She couldn't even conceive of it. "Can I ask what happened?"

"She was ill." Sam shifted uncomfortably on the bench. "Look, I don't really like talking about it."

She had the urge to reach out and run her hand along Sam's shoulder. To comfort her. Instead, she changed the subject. "So how long have you been gaming?"

"Since I could reach a keyboard."

"Have you ever wanted to be a professional?"

"Yes and no. I dreamed about it, but I never thought it would happen."

"Why not?"

Sam looked at her as if she'd asked the stupidest question ever. "Not a lot of professional gamers are women."

"That's true, but I'd like to change that if I can. I've convinced the Barrage that you're what we need for the *Siege Encounter* team."

Sam looked pensive rather than excited. "Why me?"

That seemed like an unusual question. She imagined most of the guys she'd known, Seth included, would have assumed they were the best player. As a matter of fact, they would have assumed they were the best player even if they weren't. "You were the best amateur player at the tournament. Shouldn't that be reason enough?"

They'd reached the park. Sam led her to a bench nearby. Lauren took a deep breath and looked at the clear blue sky. The waters of the Susquehanna flowed into the Chesapeake Bay, widening out in front of her. Several sailboats glided through the water in the distance. She needed to go see her parents. Go out on the boat with her father for a few hours.

She opened her little white box of fudge and took a bite. She couldn't hold back the groan of delight.

Sam gave her a self-satisfied smile. "I told you."

"I'd forgotten how good this is." She took another bite, and an embarrassing noise of contentment came from her lips. As soon as the fudge melted on her tongue, a flood of memories filled her mind. Back when her grandmother had been mobile and not limited to the grounds of the assisted living facility. She practically inhaled the first slice. She closed the box. "Okay. Enough of that. I'll save the rest for later."

"Won't last that long." Sam popped a piece of her fudge into her mouth. "I say it won't make it back to Baltimore." She carefully opened the little piece of paper that wrapped her second slice and broke off another piece. Lauren watched her place it in her mouth. Why was food so sensual?

She shook the thought and focused on the task at hand. She pulled a thick stack of papers from her tote. "I printed out the contract proposal for you." When Sam didn't take them from her, Lauren laid the contract on the bench between them. "You'll want to have a lawyer review this, but it is an official offer to play for the Baltimore Barrage *Siege Encounter* team."

Sam licked some fudge from her fingers. "Can you give me the short version?"

"Fifty-thousand dollar guaranteed salary for the first year. Your share of any tournament winnings. Full health insurance."

"I can make that doing what I do now if I work full-time. You're asking me to take a chance on faith that I might get winnings. That's like a company that offers a chance of a bonus at the end of the year. No guarantee."

Sam would not be a pushover, which impressed Lauren. It would serve her well because Will liked to push everyone. "The company also covers living expenses. Everyone lives at the team house. In our case, it's a team building with several teams housed on different floors."

"So I would have to live in Baltimore?" Sam crumpled the empty fudge paper and dropped it in her box.

Lauren could see the hesitation in her expression. "If it's the money that is a concern, I'm sure the team would cover any moving expenses."

"I don't have much to move," Sam said it with a bit of melancholy in her voice.

"All the players live in the team building. Your day is structured to provide strategy sessions, gaming practices, and then your choice of downtime or pickup games at night."

Sam gave her a questioning look. "The Barrage has a reputation online as a boy's club."

Darn it. Sam was aware of the bad press. "Well, they hired me to change that. Are you concerned or worried about your safety? If so, I can talk to the owner. The Barrage has never had a woman player on any of their teams before, so things will have to be adjusted."

"No. I can take care of myself." Still, she looked concerned.

"Is there some other reason you wouldn't want to live in Baltimore?"

Sam shrugged. "I do a lot here."

"But…"

"But I've wanted to play games for as long as I can remember. Olivia, my teammate, said if I didn't do this, she'd never speak to me again."

She needed to try a different tack. "I saw how you were with those kids at the tournament. You were inspiring and kind. I'm sure they will never forget you. If you play for the Barrage, you'd be reaching thousands more kids and be an inspiration for them as well. You would be proof that girls can do anything."

Sam stood and threw her empty box away. She stood with her back to Lauren for a few moments, then came and sat again. "After the win on Sunday, my teammates and I got spammed hard on our gaming accounts with all kinds of horrific shit. I've dealt with it a long time, but it never feels good. Guys threatened to harm me if they saw me at another tournament. What kind of sick person says that?"

Lauren was aware of the toxicity and ferocity facing women players. Everyone at the company received online garbage but probably not to the level Sam would be facing. She leaned in and locked eyes with Sam. "Kids who want to be just like you far outnumber the internet trolls. We can't let the keyboard bullies win. Besides, we both know one guy in his apartment can string together a bot army and publish thousands of posts in an hour."

"I'm impressed you know so much about it."

Lauren raised an eyebrow. "Because I'm a woman?"

"Touché."

"I'm a gamer, too."

Sam's eyebrows rose. "What games?"

"*World of Warcraft* mostly."

Sam nodded slowly as if considering the new information. "Is that how you ended up with the Barrage?"

"No, I started out as a pharmaceutical rep at Guarantech. I couldn't have done either job without knowing three times as much as the men around me." She sat a little taller. "You know what sucks for me working in a mostly male environment? I have to approach every conversation with, 'maybe if we do,' and 'maybe I'm wrong, but.' Otherwise, I'm a pushy bitch, and they tune me out."

Sam looked surprised by her candor.

"You deserve to play as a pro, and you deserve to win the prize money. I know the base pay sucks for someone like you, who has a career already. Most of the guys have been in the business since they were teenagers. Heck, most of them still are teenagers. But I have a feeling about you. You'll help the team win. I know it."

Sam seemed to search her face as if looking for a lie. Lauren wasn't lying. She meant every word. Sam leaned forward, resting her forearms on her knees. "I don't know what percentage of people who message me hate me for real, but it's enough that even if a few dozen do, including other players, it doesn't help my self-esteem."

Lauren laid a hand on her shoulder. "I'll be here for you. You won't be alone in this." She withdrew her hand and patted the stack of papers. "Take this home and read through it. Talk it over with your father." She laid her business card on top of the stack. "Here's my card. Put my info in your phone and reach out to me if you have questions." She looked at the time. "I need to call my ride if I'm going to catch my train."

After a brief hesitation, Sam said, "I could drive you back to Baltimore."

Sam's offer surprised her since it would be two hours round trip. Although being together in the car would give Lauren more time to get to know her. Something about Sam made her want to get to know her. "I appreciate the offer, but I'm sure you have better things to do."

Lauren texted Pearl for her ride. She watched the golden sunlight glitter on the waves, calling to her like a familiar song.

"You like the water?" asked Sam.

Lauren smiled. "I do. Being on the water is the most relaxing thing I can imagine."

"More than a massage?"

Sam's expression seemed innocent enough, but Lauren's mind couldn't help but wander to thoughts of Sam giving her a massage. "Sailing is like meditation for me." They sat quietly for a few more minutes until Pearl arrived at the park.

Lauren reached out her hand before entering the car. Sam's hand felt good in hers. It fit. "I hope you consider the offer." She reluctantly let go. Sam beat her to opening the car door. She slid into the back seat next to Pearl's daughter, who gave Lauren a cute baby smile from her car seat and then returned to gumming a stuffed bunny.

Sam leaned in the open car door. "Hey, Pearl."

"Hey, Sam. How's your dad?"

"Good thanks. Your daughter is getting big."

"I know. Crazy, isn't it? Wasn't long ago we were tearing it up together. Gonna be about twenty years before I can do that again." She laughed.

"Be safe." Sam didn't slam the door. She shut it carefully and waved as they drove away.

"I didn't know you were here to see Sam," said Pearl. "She's a character. Smartest girl in school but never wanted to do anything but play computer games. How was Mr. O'Brian? She's been taking care of him since he retired from the Army. Must be tough."

"Why is that?"

"He came back messed up. PTSD. Real bad. Like run-around-the-yard-yelling bad. Used to get drunk and want to fight people. She's a good egg, but that's a lot to deal with."

Through the back window, she got a last glimpse of Sam standing motionless on the sidewalk. A father with PTSD. Her mother gone when she was too young. "Yes. It must be."

Chapter Seven

S am watched the car drive away. She gripped the contract in her arms like it might all blow away with a strong breeze off the bay. This was what she'd always wanted. To be a professional gamer. But she'd never thought it would happen. She walked to the grocery store, did some shopping, and headed home. She needed to get food prepared for the week so her dad would have something to eat. He hated cooking for himself. If she wasn't here to do it, would he be okay?

At the house, she found her dad seated at the kitchen table and her grandmother O'Brian making a large pot of what smelled like her famous potato soup. She placed the groceries on the table and kissed her dad on the top of his head. "Hi, Grandma. I didn't see your car."

"Your grandfather drove down to look at that shop with the wooden duck decoys. As if he's ever going to go hunting again."

Sam began unloading the canned goods into the pantry. The contract Lauren had given her sat on the entry table in the living room. There were a lot of pages. It was intimidating to think about. Having her grandparents here wasn't a bad thing. They'd need to know if she decided to sign it. She couldn't leave her father here alone without getting their input.

Her grandmother addressed her dad. "You used to like to duck hunt before..." She trailed off.

Before he had watched his squad leader step on a mine and evaporate? Before he'd gotten thrown clear and found out later that two of his buddies had died as well? Before he'd spent night after night on the far edges of civilization, standing watches while the enemy lobbed mortars and RPGs at them? He sat and stared at nothing most of the time. In his own world, if he wasn't waking from nightmares during thunderstorms and yelling at the top of his lungs to take cover.

Her grandmother ladled out three bowls of soup and set them on the table. She didn't ask if Sam was hungry, and no one said no in this family. Sam pulled out a chair and sat obediently and bowed her head.

Her grandmother said grace. "Bless us, O Lord, and these thy gifts which we are about to receive from thy bounty through Christ, Our Lord. Amen."

Sam made the sign of the cross and said in unison with her dad, "Father, Son, and Holy Spirit."

Guilt washed over her. She and her dad rarely said grace anymore. They'd given up that tradition a long time ago. As a matter of fact, she hadn't been to church since Christmas Eve Mass the last time her grandparents had insisted she come. They didn't push her father to take part, but they insisted she stay in good graces with the church.

They knew she was gay. When she mentioned that the church didn't want her, her grandfather said something about loving the sinner and hating the sin. The answer was not helpful. Being a lesbian was not a sin. She wasn't hurting anyone else. She tried to be good and caring. Wasn't she here right now, taking care of her dad? Guilt flooded in as she thought of the contract she'd left on the table inside the front door.

The soup was delicious. For a few minutes, the only sound was the clinking of spoons against their bowls.

"Your father tells me a woman was here offering you a job in Baltimore."

Sam nodded, not looking up from her dish.

"What kind of job is it?"

"Professional gamer," replied Sam.

Her grandmother sounded surprised. "Is this some kind of joke you two are having on me?"

"Nope. It's a real thing. I'd get paid to play computer games." Her grandmother sat back against her chair. "Well, I'll be. I never thought I'd hear that. You've always liked computers. Even when you were a little girl. I remember dropping you off at the library and picking you up when they closed. You'd be on that computer the entire time."

Her father stood and placed his empty bowl in the sink. "I'm going to take a nap."

"I'll wake you when your father's back," her grandmother said as he walked away. She started washing the dishes.

"I can do that." Sam took over for her.

Her grandmother smiled and dried her hands on a dish towel. "I'll start putting the soup in the freezer."

They worked in silence for a while.

"Are you serious about this job?"

Sam looked toward the empty living room. "I don't know, Grandma. I don't think I can leave Dad here alone."

"I can take care of his meals while you're in Baltimore." She spoke softly. "I've been thinking of coming over more often anyway."

She had a simultaneous sense of relief and guilt. "You should enjoy your retirement. Not take care of us."

"We've decided not to move to Florida."

That was a surprise. They'd been planning for it for years. "Why?"

"Everyone we want to see is here. Your dad, all your aunts and uncles, you grandkids. Why move to Florida and hang out with a bunch of old people?" She placed several Tupperware containers on the counter. "We're looking at some property near the beach in Delaware, but for now, we'll be staying in Bel Air."

"It doesn't feel right to make you come down all the time."

Her grandmother turned and put her hands on her hips. "Sam. You've been taking care of your dad long enough."

Wasn't she supposed to take care of him when he so obviously couldn't take care of himself? "You've always said the most important thing in life was giving before receiving. You should be doing less, not more."

Her grandmother's hand was warm and soft against her cheek. "I'm his mother. I'm sixty-nine, not ninety. Let me help for a while. You need to be out there in the world meeting people. Finding yourself someone who'll take care of you someday. Baltimore sounds like the perfect place. You'll be close by if we need you, but you're far enough away you can start living your life without worrying about your dad."

Sam smirked. "Are you saying Havre de Grace is not the center of the world?"

"When you were little, you'd make your grandpa take you all the time to watch the Amtrak pass over the Susquehanna. Don't you want to be on that train? Going places and seeing things? This is your chance. Don't miss it. Before you know it, you're too old to enjoy it."

"Thanks, I think." She walked to her dad's room and knocked.

"Come in."

She'd known he wouldn't be asleep. He hid in his room a lot, and he never napped.

"Dad, what would you think if I moved to Baltimore for a few weeks?"

He sat on his bed looking out the window with his back to her. "Is this about the job offer?" He turned his head so she could see his profile. "She was pretty. The woman who came looking for you. She said you were one of the best gamers she's ever seen."

"She said that?" Maybe Lauren had been trying to make her dad proud of her. Seemed like something she'd do. "If you don't want me to, I get it. I don't want to leave you here alone."

"You do you. I'll still be here when you need a place to sleep."

"Are you sure?"

"You're not a kid anymore, Sam. You need to make up your own mind. Doesn't matter what I think."

Not a resounding approval, but it was as close to one as she would get. She came around the bed and kissed his forehead. "Thanks, Pops."

She stepped into the hall and closed the door behind her. She texted Lauren: *If the offer is still good, I'm in.*

The reply started with a string of celebratory emojis: *I'll have our lawyer send you an online version of the contract that you can digitally sign. Welcome to the Barrage!*

Though she wouldn't admit it out loud, Lauren's enthusiasm and encouragement helped her feel better about the decision. With someone like Lauren in her corner, she might handle what was to come. She wasn't stupid enough to think the worst trolling was behind her. She had a hunch that it was merely the beginning. But it wouldn't be so bad if she had someone like Lauren to look at while she took the abuse.

CHAPTER EIGHT

To Lauren, the sixth floor of the Barrage headquarters smelled vaguely like unwashed teenage boys from her high school days. The smell triggered a dozen memories she'd rather not have thought about.

"How old is she?" asked Alec Nguyen, the team manager.

"Twenty-five," replied Lauren.

"She's too old." He talked over his shoulder as he walked.

Lauren followed behind. "Dylan's twenty-six," she pointed out.

"He's been a pro for almost ten years. She's too old to compete at this level without having been a professional. She'll drag down the team."

"How was she supposed to get any experience?" she said with irritation in her voice. "Most girl gamers drop out before they're old enough to get a contract, long before they even have a chance. This industry is…" She paused to find a word that Alec wouldn't disregard. "Unfriendly to young women."

"You said it, I didn't."

"*Siege Encounter* is a brand-new game. She's been playing as long as anyone else on the team."

Alec grunted.

She added for effect, "Augustan Gaming is breathing down Will's neck about this franchise. We lose them, and there will be a domino effect with the other sponsors and leagues."

Alec leaned down and picked up a dirty pair of boxers. He threw them at a young man lounging in an egg-shaped chair. The guy threw them off himself and yanked his headset off. "Hey."

"I'm not your mother. Pick up your shit," said Alec.

"Those aren't mine."

"I don't care who's they are. You want game time? Keep this area clean."

She followed him through the living room and out onto a sizeable balcony. He leaned against the railing and lit a cigarette. He took a deep drag before he continued. "Where am I supposed to put her? All we have are dorm rooms. If I give her one all for herself, I'll have no leverage on these guys. We have a hard enough time keeping the underage players from sneaking girls and beer into the building at night."

"I'll look into renting her a separate apartment nearby. Whatever the solution, you'll have to make it work. My job is to make sure that any messaging coming from here goes through me. We can't have stories of the guys wandering around naked and calling her babe." She paused. "Or worse."

"Oh, they can be much worse," said Alec.

"That's what I'm afraid of."

Alec leaned both forearms on the railing and looked at the street below. "Will is onboard with all this?"

"Augustan is forcing his hand."

"Well, if she sucks, she'll be gone, or I will. I'm not ruining my reputation because the team can't win." He pointed at her. "You mention that to Will."

Lauren got the message loud and clear. "Let me know what you need to make this work."

He threw his still lit cigarette over the balcony and shook his head.

Back down on the first floor, she followed Will around as he moved from place to place. It was impossible to overlook the fact that she had been following men around all day. He stopped and played Ping-Pong with an intern. She tried to get his attention.

"Alec says no to finding a room for Sam upstairs. We'll need to find her an apartment nearby."

"Not happening." He slapped the ball back at the college kid across from him. He would not give the kid a break. Once a competitor, always a competitor.

"What do you want him to do, then? Put her in the dorm room with the others?"

"She looks like she can handle it." He slammed a kill shot and gave a yell of excitement.

Lauren held her tongue. It was stupid comments like those that made her wish she could tell him the truth, but she'd learned the hard way that men like Will had no interest in being told they were wrong. She knew she'd get farther with honey than by pointing out what an asinine thing he said. "Will, we need a solution. Sam will be here in two days."

"She can stay with you." He gestured casually with his paddle. Dismissively.

"Excuse me?" Surely, he was joking.

"Put her up for a few weeks. Take some per diem to cover the expense. Work it out with Nate."

"I'm not sure that's the best idea. Maybe I'm wrong, but I think a short-term rental would be as financially feasible." She wanted to swallow those words, but she knew he hated being wrong, and she had to couch her reply in terms less threatening to him. "I don't even have a guest bed."

He held up the game and turned to her. "Come on, Lauren. I need you to be a team player. You said Alec thinks she's going to wash out in a couple of weeks. Just put her up until then. Okay? Great." He went back to serving.

He had put her in her place in front of the intern. No wonder her coworkers questioned her judgment every time she asked them to do something. She turned on her heel and made for the door. Fine. If Will was going to make her do this, she'd take off early to get her home office ready for an unexpected guest...on the company credit card.

It wasn't until she was halfway to her apartment that she realized Sam would be living with her for an undetermined amount of time. Sam, who made her take notice every time she saw her. This might be a complicated summer.

❖

Sam found the apartment complex easily. Lauren's apartment building was brand-new, with lots of glass. The Canton neighborhood, though close to Fell's Point and the Inner Harbor, was like a suburb. Wide clean streets, lots of parking, and plenty of typical stores. If it wasn't for the renovated brewery buildings and the tighter street grid, it could have been anywhere from Bel Air to White Marsh.

She used the call box.

"Hey. Glad you made it okay. I'm going to buzz you in. Take the elevator to the fourth floor, then turn right." How was it Lauren's voice sounded so sexy through that tinny box?

After Sam found her way through the swanky entryway and up the elevator to the apartment, she stared at the door for a few moments. This was it. Her new life started now. She took a deep breath and knocked.

The door opened. Lauren stood there in casual clothes, looking like she had been preparing to do yoga or go jogging with her hair in a neat, high ponytail. Even out of her tidy business wear, she looked commanding and incredibly sexy. She smiled and beckoned to her. "Come in."

Sam carried her clothes in a large duffle strapped to her back. Everything else—her gaming laptop, headphones, controllers, VR headset—were all in the hard-sided rolling suitcase. Exactly the opposite of most people, but she didn't much pay attention to clothes. She had several sets of sweats and cargo pants, a bunch of similarly colored T-shirts and two hoodies. She wore the same pair of Adidas every day.

As she stood in the narrow hallway, the apartment seemed smaller than she had expected.

"Let me show you your room so you can put your stuff away." Lauren opened the door to the right and stepped away, letting Sam take her cumbersome load inside. The room had no closet and no windows. That would work. She didn't have much clothing, and she didn't like competing light sources on her screens, anyway. The room contained a bookshelf, a modern desk with no drawers, what looked like a good desk chair, and a loft bed hovering six feet over the desk.

Lauren had slipped in behind her. "Technically, this is a study, so there wasn't any room for a bed." She pointed at the loft bed. "I bought that yesterday at IKEA. I hope it's comfortable. The instructions said it's safe for up to two hundred fifty pounds."

Sam unslung her duffle and dropped it to the floor. "No bringing home a date, then?"

Lauren looked like a deer in the headlights.

Sam quickly tried to reassure her. "I'm kidding."

"Gosh, I hadn't thought about that." Her cheeks held a soft flush. "I haven't had a roommate since college, other than my boyfriend, Seth."

"Does Seth live here too?" That would be uncomfortable.

"Oh no. He never lived here. We lived in Atlanta. We broke up last year."

"Sorry?" Sam asked it as a question, since she was never sure if people were unhappy or happy about their breakups. She'd had none to speak of since the longest she'd dated anyone was about three months.

"Nope," Lauren said emphatically. "Not sorry." She motioned to the hallway. "Want the rest of the tour?"

"Especially the bathroom." She shrugged. "Long ride down."

"It's right here, next door on the right. I'll be in the living room."

Sam closed the door behind her. She looked around. This place resembled a Martha Stewart catalog. All the towels matched. There was a small cabinet with fake flowers and a dish of rolled wash cloths. She opened the door to find multiple rolls of toilet paper. On the counter under the mirror were neat rows of bottles. She leaned down. Several moisturizers with unusual names in curved bottles, an electric toothbrush with multiple types of toothpastes, rinses, and floss sat in neat rows. Like in a hotel, the hairdryer was mounted on the wall.

She was afraid to look under the counter, but her curiosity was piqued. She found the most complex looking set of cases sitting on tiered shelves. Each one holding either makeup or toiletries. She reached in and took out a little plastic bag, a hotel shower cap. Her father and she had shared a bathroom in the house, and between them, they maybe had a few dozen items. Here, a dozen shampoos and conditioners adorned the shower alone. This neatness worried her. She wasn't a tidy person and never had been.

When she returned to the hallway, Lauren waited at the far end of the apartment, silhouetted against the sunset in the distance. Sam sauntered up behind her. The view from this side of the building was a panorama of red brick buildings, but the sunset was throwing a pretty red glow across the sky.

Lauren gasped and grabbed Sam's arm to steady herself. "You scared me."

"I'll try to be louder next time."

"Not your fault. I'm easily startled. I'll get used to having you around."

She let go, and Sam missed the feeling.

"Living room. Kitchen." Lauren pointed at the wall of kitchen appliances in the open floor plan. A small counter with stools separated the kitchen area from the living room. The order of everything was overwhelming. Nothing was out of place. All of it was impersonal. Even the artwork was generic. Although it matched the couch and wall colors, it revealed nothing about who Lauren was.

She pointed at the door opposite the bathroom. "That's my bedroom." Sam noticed she didn't offer to show her. Maybe that was where she secretly put all her clutter. Maybe the room was filled to the brim with boxes, clothes, and photos. She smiled thinking about it.

"What?" Lauren smiled, seemingly noticing.

"Nothing. I'm just happy to be here. That's all." She'd keep her suspicions to herself.

"I tried to make a little space in the refrigerator for you." She paused. "That's a joke. I eat a lot of takeout. If you're anything like my gamer ex, I assume you do too?"

Should Sam tell her she could cook now or later? She'd keep that to herself for a little while. "Sometimes."

"Do not, under any circumstance, go to the pizza place across the street. That is Italian cardboard."

"Good to know."

Lauren looked at her fitness watch. "I have a call with Will in a few minutes. I'll leave you to it." She stopped and pulled something from a small bowl on a tiny hall table. She returned and placed a key fob in her hand. The keyring was Pikachu. Perhaps Lauren wasn't completely square. "Don't want you getting locked out."

"Thanks."

As Lauren headed to her bedroom, Sam tried to get a glimpse through the door, but the door closed too quickly. Definitely a secret bedroom hoarder.

She unpacked her toiletries but left her clothes folded in her hardcase luggage once she'd emptied it of computer equipment. She'd use it as a temporary closet. Then, she took a walk around the neighborhood to get her bearings and see what was around. No number of online maps and reviews could beat seeing a place herself: watching the people on the street, the smells, the activity, or lack of it. This wasn't Havre de Grace. Something about the vibrancy of the neighborhood was appealing, even though she hid in her hoodie, watching, not participating.

Once darkness dropped, she returned to the apartment building. She stopped in the weight room. The guy on the treadmill eyed her warily, as if she'd come in off the street and didn't belong. He was right; she didn't belong here. She was merely a girl from Harford County whose entire house could fit in this exercise room.

When she swiped the fob at the apartment door, she was tempted to knock and warn Lauren that she was back. What if she was showering or walking around in something skimpy? She reprimanded herself for even thinking about it. Lauren was hot in a straight woman way. Sam had no interest in being someone's first. Lauren would have zero interest in her anyway. Most women stopped texting as soon as she mentioned her *hobby*, which was now her occupation. Occupation. That sounded insane. She was a professional gamer.

When she didn't see Lauren anywhere, she assumed she was in her room. She'd be hiding too if she had an unknown guest in her house. She flipped on the overhead light in the office and opened her gaming laptop. While it booted, she examined the bookshelf that contained a predictable list of marketing books with titles about building self-confidence, communications techniques, and getting what you want in life.

Lower on the shelves were Leigh Bardugo's Grishaverse books, the *Divergent* novels, and a lot of Sarah Maas books. Tucked between them was a single photo of a group of people on a sailboat. It was hard to tell the size of the boat from the picture. The older woman in the photo must have been Lauren's mother. They looked nearly identical. Sam had finally found something personal in this impersonal apartment, and now she felt like she was treading unwanted in Lauren's space. She slipped it back where she'd found it.

What surprised her the most were the unexpected contents on the bottom shelf: a dozen paperbacks with titles like *Endless Love*, *The Duchess's Gardener*, *Dream Lover*, and *Perfect Trust*. Romances. The entire shelf was full of them. Several shoved sideways on top of the others because there was no more room.

Great. A romantic as well as being beautiful and successful. She tilted the first novel toward her. A photo of a man's naked torso filled the cover. Surprisingly, the second one, *Like They Do in the Movies*, had an illustrated cover of two women facing one another. She flipped it over and read the description on the back. Whoa, not a straight romance. Okay. Was Lauren a fan of all romance, or was it possible she was on part of the spectrum of LGBTQ+? That stirred her mind in an entirely different way. She shoved the books back in their place and sat at her computer.

By the time she'd fished out a pack of oyster crackers from her backpack and opened them, Jarek, Olivia, and Ashton had arrived on her screen. Three boxes of video heads stared back at her.

"How's it going as a pro, *chica*?" asked Olivia.

She answered with a mouthful of crackers. "I don't know yet. All I did was move."

"What's the apartment like?" asked Jarek.

She picked up her laptop and swung it in an arc to show the room behind her. "I'm staying in Lauren's office for now."

Ashton, who'd been a backup player for them for a long time and had taken Sam's place on the team, jumped in. "Shouldn't you have your own room? What kind of company is this?"

"Lauren, the hot one from the tournament?" asked Jarek.

"Hey. She's the head of marketing and communications." His comment embarrassed her, as if Lauren could hear them talking. She checked. The door was closed, and she was on her headset, so Lauren would only hear one side of the conversation if she walked by. "This is only temporary until I make it through the probationary period."

"How long is that?" asked Jarek.

"Three months."

"Why are you on probation?" asked Ashton. "Did you do something wrong already?"

A memory of her childhood in North Carolina meant she heard, "Ah, bless your heart," in her head.

"That's what they call a trial period," replied Olivia. "If she doesn't show her stuff by then, they can cancel her contract."

"Guess you better play well, or you'll be back playing with us." Jarek attempted to sound lighthearted, but she could hear the pain in his voice.

Sam crumpled her empty cracker package and set it aside. "You guys told me to go pro. Are we going to discuss my job or play?"

"I think we were admiring your new roommate and dissing your bedroom," said Ashton. "Do you have a picture of her?"

She glanced at the bottom bookshelf at the edge of the photograph. "No." She wished they'd focus less on Lauren and more on gaming. Now, if she could only follow her own advice.

"Can you even play a non-ranked game now? Like, is there anything in your contract that keeps you from playing with us?" asked Jarek.

She had read through the contract, but it was pages and pages of legalese, some of it so boring, she might have dozed a few times. She didn't remember reading anything that said she couldn't play pickup games with her friends. "I'll play on my alt-account. My main account was reported for illegal play and a dozen other rules infractions after our win. I'm finally out of review jail, but I don't want anyone knowing I'm online."

"Yeah, the trolls hit all of us, but the news that you were going pro probably drew more attention to your account," said Olivia.

"The sexual content is the worst part." Sam replayed several in her mind, wishing she had never read them.

"Sexual? No one sent me anything like that," said Jarek.

"Because you're a dude," said Olivia. "Isn't as fun to threaten you with sexual violence."

Ashton's expression changed from disbelief to anger in a flash. "Send me the message threads, and I'll track these guys down for you."

Retaliation wouldn't be worth it. Neither would reporting them to the system admins or the police. No one cared. Overworked and overwhelmed, the people responsible for overseeing the systems struggled with the abundance of online garbage, and the automated machine learning responses mistakenly flagged breast cancer survivors instead of pornographers. The only solution would be fines. Big ones. Because money would allow for hiring people to investigate, but that wasn't going to happen.

"Come on, let's play. My schedule is going to be tight after this. I want to have tonight feel as normal as possible."

"It's going to be okay, Sam. You're going to be great," said Olivia.

Great. What did that even mean? That she'd be able to keep up with her teammates who'd been pros for a decade? That she'd win a lot of games for the Barrage? Or did it mean she would do something she loved and make a living at it? Whatever it meant, she hoped Olivia was right. And part of her hoped she'd stick around long enough to get to know Lauren a little better. Maybe.

CHAPTER NINE

Lauren smiled at the barista behind the counter of the coffee shop.

"Latte or a café au lait today?" the barista asked with familiarity.

"Café au lait. And a black coffee."

The barista marked a small sheet of paper and stuck it on the counter for the two workers making the drinks. She leaned in and smiled. "A guest?" The tone of her voice implied an overnight visitor.

Lauren smiled and shook her head. "A new roommate."

The barista laughed. "You're taking all the fun out of this game. One of these days, I'm going to be right."

Lauren tapped her credit card on the screen in front of her. "I promise, if anyone special arrives, I'll mark the occasion with an unusual drink order. That will give you the clue."

The barista rubbed her hands together. "You're on. I look forward to it."

Back at the apartment, Lauren found Sam standing at the window in the living room, her hands in the pockets of a pair of black joggers. She wore a matching lightweight black hoodie with the hood down. Lauren was beginning to see a pattern in her fashion style.

"Coffee?" Lauren placed the cup on the counter. "I wasn't sure how you take it, so it's black."

Without turning toward her, Sam said, "Sounds great." She turned and approached the counter. "Sugar somewhere?"

"Oh." Lauren reached into her tote and retrieved a few packets. "Here."

"Thanks." Sam rubbed her eyes and yawned.

"Let me guess," said Lauren. "Late night gaming?" She tried not to sound accusatory. Seth used to stay up all hours playing, and he was so loud that he kept her awake much of the time. She was relieved that she hadn't heard a thing last night.

Sam pulled out a barstool and took a sip of coffee. "Yeah. This is great. Thanks."

"Is the room okay? Do you need anything?"

Sam shrugged. "I'm good. New place. You know how it is. I'll get used to it."

"If you need anything, let me know." She grabbed her keys and the tote that doubled as her purse. "Ready to start your new life?"

Sam ran her hand through her short shaggy hair. The movement was incredibly sexy, like watching a sportswear advertisement. Trying to shake the thought, Lauren dug in her purse as if looking for something. "Ready as I'll ever be."

Being six blocks from work had its advantages. Less time commuting being the most important one, enjoying the outdoors for a few minutes was another. They walked together in silence. Lauren glanced at Sam. She seemed relaxed, looking around at the buildings.

What Lauren heard was her heels on the rough concrete, birds singing, and the occasional car. She liked it. Soon enough, her whole day would be filled with conversation.

Was Sam nervous or anxious about the day ahead? Should she reassure her? No, she was overthinking it. Sam appeared fine. She was relaxed. Nothing about her posture was tense. She looked like she'd been making this walk her whole life.

"Ready?" Lauren asked as they stood in front of the doors of an old brewery building.

Sam nodded.

❖

When Sam walked in, there was a girl at the front desk wearing heavy makeup who looked so young, it was hard to believe she was out of high school. The length of her fake nails caused her to type at a slow, careful pace. Then, it was on to find the middle-aged woman office manager tucked in a tiny windowless room, who explained the health insurance benefits and gave her access to an online portal where she could sign up for participation in the 401K after the probationary period.

Afterward, Lauren escorted her to a slightly balding man in his late thirties. "Will. Sam O'Brian is here," she said.

He turned with a big cheesy grin, like he was trying to win Sam over in a game of dodgeball. His teeth were blindingly bright, a few too many whitening strips. His slacks were a bit rumpled, and he had fancy sneakers, one of those brands that partnered with an exclusive artist. She only knew that because Jarek loved collaborations. "Samantha, great to meet you."

She grimaced. She didn't like to be called Samantha. Sure, it was on all the legal documents, but she had told Lauren that she wanted to be known as Sam. Only her grandmother Shaw in North Carolina had ever called her Samantha, and that was not a pleasant memory.

"Settling in?" he asked as he grabbed her hand a bit too firmly and shook it vigorously. "Lauren treating you okay? I know she lives in those fancy apartments over on Toone."

"Yep. All good."

"Sandy get you all settled with the paperwork?"

She nodded.

"Great." He called out to a younger guy with a face full of acne and sporting a bang perm that was four inches long, "Peter, take Samantha up to her team's floor, would you?"

The kid led the way. Sam glanced over her shoulder at Lauren. They locked eyes for a moment. Sympathetic was how she'd have described Lauren's expression. That didn't make her feel great.

She left Lauren in Will's office and followed the kid back to the main entryway. "I'm Peter."

"Sam."

He stopped at the elevator.

"Where are the stairs?" she asked.

"Um." He looked around as if he'd never seen them. "Oh. Over there." He pointed at a red exit sign hanging from the ceiling.

"Which floor?"

"Four."

"I'll meet you up there."

"I'll come with you."

She took the stairs two at a time, leaving poor Peter huffing and trying to catch up. If she had the choice between elevator and stairs, she always took the stairs for the exercise. Her maximum was thirty floors because of the time it took, not because she couldn't do it. And she could haul butt down. In a fire emergency, she'd leave poor Peter behind.

She wouldn't really leave him behind. She wasn't that callous. In a real emergency, she'd probably be the one who got left behind. With her luck, she'd still be looking for a house cat that didn't exist as the firefighters arrived.

All the tech Sam expected from a professional operation filled the *Siege Encounter* team floor. She was impressed.

Peter led her to an oblong conference table. "Alec, the newbie is here." He gave her a nod and headed away.

Her new team manager reached out a hand. "Alec Nguyen."

"Sam O'Brian."

"Glad to have you on board, Sam." He cleaned the whiteboard with an eraser. "Ever played with a college team or anything?"

She shoved her hands in her pockets. "Nope. Tried but they didn't want me."

"Well, I'll try to get you up to speed quickly. Have a seat while we wait for the others."

She sat and rubbed her hands, a habit she had when she felt uncomfortable. Alec had hit on the one fear she had coming into this situation. She had no previous experience with a team other than amateur online play. Jarek and she were already friends when they'd created their team. Olivia had reached out to Sam years ago when they were still teenagers playing *Call of Duty*. She'd never played with people she hadn't personally gotten along with. The thought of starting over made her nervous.

"I do double duty as the team manager and coach, so we'll spend a lot of time together. I ordered the equipment you requested. You'll be using station three from now on." He pointed to a row of computers nearby, each with dual monitors. Above them hung larger monitors that she assumed were for Alec to observe the team play. "Once you get acclimated, if you need anything else, let me know, and I'll take care of ordering it. I can't promise you'll get everything you want, but I'll try."

The chair alone looked like it cost more than all her equipment put together. "I'm sure it will be great." Maybe this wouldn't be so bad.

A young guy slammed his backpack on the table across from her. Even though he couldn't be more than eighteen, he wore a mustache that reminded Sam of pictures of her grandpa O'Brian from the late nineteen seventies. "Alec is lying. I've been asking him to get a new PS5 controller for the game room. Nada."

"Not a priority, Perry," said Alec. "This is Sam."

"Saw your win at the convention center," Perry said.

Did that mean he liked it or didn't care for her gameplay? She gripped her hands tighter in her pockets.

"Ah, the newb is here," said another teammate who sat next to Perry. He scowled as he sat heavily in his chair, rocking it backward. He spread his legs wide and adjusted himself several times. Sam hoped he did this without thinking about it. If he did it on her account, her reaction would disappoint him.

Alec made the introduction. "This is Dylan. He's the team captain this season. During competition, he'll be making all the play calls when in live play."

"Understood," she said.

A guy in a pair of wrinkled khakis, Converse tennis shoes, and a Baltimore Ravens jersey, his hair in a short, dirty ponytail, rushed into the room and sat at the only open seat left at the table. "Sorry I'm late."

Alec introduced him. "Luke, this is Samantha O'Brian. Luke's our backup player."

"Hey." Luke looked away from her and down at his backpack. She got it. No one wanted to be bumped by the newbie.

"Backup might change," said Dylan as he looked directly at her. Perhaps he was pissing on her leg like a dog marking his territory. Nothing new about that. Guys had been doing that to her since she'd started playing online, trying to get in her head and psych her out. She did a good enough job of that herself.

Alec asked her a few questions about how long she had been playing *Siege Encounter*. Did she play anything else? What was her favorite load-out when playing? More technical questions. She knew it was mostly to suss out if she was a good player or just a temporary seat warmer that checked the box about gender diversity.

Later in the afternoon, the guys talked about their plan for the scrimmage. She stayed quiet, listening, trying to determine who was who in the room and what would be the most important thing she could add. Already, she could see that Dylan thought he was smarter than everyone, and maybe he was. She didn't know. Luke deferred to him about everything, including what they were going to order for lunch.

A few times, she found her thoughts drifting to what Olivia or Jarek might say in this situation. She was certain Olivia would have already given them what for in Spanish a few times. She smiled at the thought.

"You think something is funny about that?" asked Dylan.

She'd obviously missed something. She shook her head. "Nope."

"What's your thoughts on it?"

She adjusted in her seat uncomfortably. She hated making a bad impression in the first hour. "Sorry, I got distracted."

Dylan flailed his arms as if she had missed the biggest thing ever. "Great." He looked at Alec. "You got us a newb who's ADHD."

"Dylan," said Luke quietly, "I've got ADHD."

Sam was getting the impression that insensitive was the prime descriptor for Dylan.

He waved off the comment. "I'm not talking about you."

Perry crumpled an empty bag of Utz. "Can we move on?"

Alec looked at his watch. "I've set up a scrimmage with a college team. Starts in fifteen." He looked at Sam. "This will be a great opportunity for you to get a sense for things without it counting toward our ranked points. Go ahead and get set up."

The equipment was good. The keyboard was exactly like her own, but the key action was stiff. She checked all the settings for the game and changed the lighting levels for the monitors. This was the opportunity to prove her stuff.

"Get me a Red Bull," Dylan said to Luke, who hovered behind him and sprinted to get the drink for him.

Sam couldn't help herself. "Is that part of the role as backup? Getting drinks?"

"What?" Dylan frowned as Luke put the can on the table in front of him. "The backup does whatever is necessary to help the team. Isn't that right, Luke?"

He nodded. "Do you need one, too?" he asked her.

"No, thanks." She wasn't going to make Luke get her a soft drink. She could do that herself. So could Dylan if he wasn't trying to lord his role as team captain over everyone. She missed playing with Jarek and Olivia already.

The first game was a disaster. Her strength was researching opponents, understanding their strengths and weaknesses, and playing accordingly. Being thrown against a talented team with no information, with little cohesion with her teammates, and a bit of second-guessing her role, meant she played like shit. Probably the worst game she had played in a couple of years.

"Don't worry," said Perry. "Happens to all of us when we first start."

She appreciated his support.

"Yeah, but you were what, fifteen when you went pro?" said Dylan. "Hope you've got more than that when it counts."

Sam could feel the heat on her cheeks. This was her chance to prove she could be a professional. She had to do better.

Games two and three, she played incrementally better, but nothing she would want to use as a demo reel of her best performances. They played two matches, and they won both, but Sam was feeling depressed about her gameplay. This was not how she had imagined things going. She'd walked over with Lauren this morning feeling nervous but excited to be here. Now she wondered if she was supposed to be here. Had this been a mistake, after all?

Alec clapped to get their attention. "Okay. Take a break and meet back in an hour for the postmortem."

Sam swung around in her chair and watched the others walk away, laughing, familiar with each other. She was the outsider again, and no matter how hard she tried, her memories of being the different kid flooded her.

Luke turned back and approached her. "Did anyone show you the gym or the cafeteria?"

It was a kind gesture. He wasn't anything like Dylan, and he didn't seem to have the confidence of Perry, but she thought they could get along in time. "I only know how to get down to the main office," she replied.

"Everything is on the second floor."

"Thanks."

He smiled and nodded before rushing to catch up to the others.

She was impressed that they had a gym until she witnessed most of the guys executing their exercises with improper form. There were several guys she hadn't met yet, probably with the other game teams like *League of Legends* and *Call of Duty*. Seemed like they were trying to impress her or trying to intimidate her. A few more years of this and they'd be hiring her to help relieve all their joint pain.

The cafeteria was full of vending machines, no actual prepared food. The office manager had given her a card for accessing the building and another one for food and drinks. They gave her a per diem. Made sense. These guys could eat the company bankrupt, she imagined.

She took a seat in the corner and watched the door. Each time someone entered, she looked up, hoping it might be Lauren. Though they barely knew each other, Sam was at ease around her. And she could use that kind of comfort right now.

Back on the team floor, Sam found herself the only one taking notes during Alec's debrief on the scrimmage. She even asked him for some video links to old matches she could watch to get up to speed. He promised he'd send them to her. Then, he took a call and stepped away.

"Anybody know where Zach ended up?" asked Perry through a mouthful of chips.

Dylan glanced at her before answering. "Some second level team picked him up right away."

"I don't know why they had to fire him," continued Perry. "She had on pasties. Not like she was completely naked."

Dylan laughed. "Some people don't have a sense of humor."

Sam wasn't getting involved in this conversation. If they didn't know the difference between hiring a stripper at a private home and one at a workplace, she wasn't going to give them that lecture. Not on her first day, at least. Instead, she left them and found a private corner where she could call her dad.

"O'Brian," he said. He didn't have a cell phone, so he answered the landline with his name, never sure who was on the other end. She felt sorry for telemarketers who called him. Most of the time, he hung up on them within the first three words.

"Hi, Pops."

"What's wrong?" he asked.

"Nothing's wrong. I wanted to check on you. Let you know I got here okay."

"I wasn't worried."

He was never worried about her unless she was spending too much time on a computer. Strange set of priorities. "I'm at the office now, getting to know my teammates."

He didn't respond.

"Everything going okay there?" she asked.

"Nothing new here."

"Did you eat? I put some meals in the freezer for you. You can heat one up in the microwave for two minutes on high." She never bothered to tell him how to use the reheat settings. It was easier to have him overcook his food than struggle with explaining the nuances of the microwave. When he didn't respond, she knew he wasn't going to ask her anything about her day. "Well, I've got to get back to work. Call me if you need anything."

He gave her his standard pep talk: "Give 'em hell."

"Roger that."

She slid the call button off and stared at the screen. Before her mother died, he had been sweet, fun, and playful. After her death, his stateside visits had become shorter. It was almost as if he wanted to stay in Afghanistan, away from her. Even when he was stationed at Fort Benning, now Fort Moore, in Georgia, she had had to stay with her grandparents in Maryland. Everyone said it was better for her to have stability, but she had wanted to be with him. He was all she had left of her mother. He had memories of her, and every now and then, he'd share them unexpectedly. Just not today.

A Nerf football hit her in the head, bringing her out of her gloom. "Sorry," yelled Perry from the other end of the room. She picked it up and tossed it back.

Day one was feeling extremely long. She was looking forward to returning to her closet-size bedroom at Lauren's apartment. Or maybe it was Lauren she was looking forward to.

CHAPTER TEN

By nightfall, Sam was brain-dead. New people. New competition. New teammates. New strategies. A lot of thinking and a lot of sitting. She missed her clients. Working with her hands helped balance her tendency to be in her head for hours on end.

She juggled two bags of groceries from the neighborhood store as she opened the apartment door. Lauren sat on the sofa, legs crossed, her computer in her lap. Even in casual wear, she looked immaculate. Nothing out of place. Sam put the bags on the counter between the living room and the kitchen.

"Hey, roomie. How was your day?" asked Lauren.

"Long." She pulled the eggs from the bags first. "I'm going to make myself an omelet for dinner. Would you like one?"

Lauren looked up, surprised. "That sounds fantastic. I'm starving. I didn't have a chance to eat anything yet."

Sam moved around, putting the groceries away. She opened the refrigerator. A bottle of orange juice, a couple of single servings of yogurt, and a potentially dangerous block of cheddar cheese stared at her. "I take it you don't cook much."

"I haven't even turned on the oven since I moved in. I usually order in," came Lauren's reply.

Sam added the items she'd bought and closed the door. "Lucky for you, I cook all the time for my dad, so I'm experienced at meals for two. Consider it a thank-you for letting me stay here for a few weeks."

"I'm the lucky one. You're cooking for me." Lauren returned to typing while Sam moved around the kitchen.

She found a frying pan that looked like it was brand-new. Not a single scratch on the nonstick coating. With a little opening and closing of cabinets, she'd found everything she needed, but she should have looked for spices before she'd gone to the store. There wasn't a single bottle of red pepper flakes or anything else with any heat in it.

"Do you have a sensitive stomach?" she asked.

Lauren looked up. "I'm not sure what you're asking. Do you mean, do I vomit on roller coasters or at horror movies?"

Sam laughed. "Sorry, I meant, is there anything you can't eat? Like spicy food, mushrooms, peanuts."

Lauren made a face and blushed. "Not sure why I went straight to vomiting. I'm sorry. No, I don't have any food sensitivities. Thanks for asking."

"Then you'll be great to cook for." Sam cracked the eggs in a bowl. She turned away after saying that. A wave of guilt swept over her for having a moment where she wanted to cook for Lauren while leaving her dad alone at home for so long for the first time.

"Was your mom a good cook?"

Sam stiffened. "I don't remember." The words came out flat. She moved to cut the green pepper.

Lauren's voice was soft and full of warmth. "I'm so sorry. How old were you when she died?"

"Eight." She hacked at the pepper with more force than she intended.

"Wow. I can't even imagine what you must have gone through. That is so young."

"I don't want to talk about it." What she meant was, I can't talk about it. If I do, I will lose my shit and cry in my food. She didn't like feeling weak and vulnerable.

Lauren said nothing else. After a few moments of silence, Sam heard her typing once again. She hadn't meant to be so abrupt. This wasn't the first or the last time she'd be thought of as abrupt and unfeeling. At least, that was what her last girlfriend had told her. What did Lauren think? Sam didn't know her yet, but if her past experience was anything to go by, Lauren would feel the same as every other woman she'd interacted with.

She plated the omelets and put them on the counter because there wasn't a dining table, not even a small one. She assumed Lauren must eat at the bar. "Order up."

Lauren moved her laptop and came to retrieve the plate. "I'm going to eat on the couch. Join me?"

Sam settled next to her on what seemed more like a love seat than a sofa. Her knee hung dangerously close to touching Lauren's.

"This is so good," Lauren said, her mouth full. "You will not want to do this often, or I might kidnap you and keep you here."

That didn't sound terrible. The warm glow of the city at night filled the windows. She liked it here. The compactness of the apartment was comforting. Being in a small space felt familiar, but unlike her dad's home with its scuffed paint, holes in the walls, and filthy carpet, this place's every finish was perfect. A little like Lauren herself.

"Like I said, think of it as a thank-you," said Sam.

"With your schedule, I'm sure we'll rarely see each other. I'm surprised you're home so early."

Sam tried to figure out that statement. Did it mean she didn't want to see her? Or did it mean that they would never have a chance to aggravate each other? "Alec took pity on me."

"How'd it go with the guys?"

Sam shrugged. "Fine. I didn't play my best."

Lauren waved her fork. "I'm certain you'll do great. Anything done well takes time, right?"

"I guess." Sam looked up at the television. An animation on the screen was paused. Cherry trees painted in light pink and white blossoms filled the screen, and loose petals floated across the sky, frozen in place. "What are you watching?"

"A show about a girl whose family forces her to marry a man who is supposed to be a bad guy, but he's protective and good to her. He helps her come out of her shell and become powerful. There's a supernatural element to it as well. Now that I think about it, it's sort of a Japanese *Beauty and the Beast*, *Cinderella* mashup." She seemed to have an aha moment.

"You're into romance, aren't you?" asked Sam.

"Why do you say that?"

Sam pointed at the TV. "And the books in the office."

Lauren covered her face with her hand. "Oh God. I forgot about those."

"No judgment. I'll admit, I snooped."

"It's fine. Snoop away. I do love romance novels and romantic anime and romcoms. I even like silly Hallmark movies where they don't even have the first kiss until the very end."

"Tell me the truth, which do you like better? Hallmark movies or those books in the office?" Sam grinned. She was pretty sure she knew the answer. She'd thumbed through a few pages to know the content was spicier than any Hallmark movie.

Lauren turned a pleasant shade of pink. "I plead the fifth."

When they'd both finished eating, Lauren took the dishes to the kitchen. When she returned, she pressed play on the anime and put her computer in her lap.

Sam should have gone to her room. Studied some games. Reviewed her session notes from today. But she didn't move. Watching the slow-moving animation relaxed her. She didn't bother to read the subtitles. She didn't need to know what was being said.

Lauren bashed on the keys of her computer. "Ugh. This laptop is driving me crazy."

"What's it doing?" Sam asked.

"Nothing. That's the problem. Seems to freeze in the middle of things. Then, it will start working again. I've been meaning to take it in to one of those fix-it shops, but I don't have the time."

"Is it a work computer?"

"No. I use a tablet at work. Easier to carry around. This brick is mine, but I do like to do research for work on it. Craft press releases. That sort of thing."

"If you want me to, I could look at it. See if I can do anything to make it run faster." She couldn't help herself. Technology she could fix, even when she couldn't fix anything else.

"Would you?" Lauren seemed genuinely excited. Then, she seemed to change her mind. "I can't make you do that. I need to suck it up and take it into the men in black ties."

Now it was a challenge. "I love tinkering with computers. If we were real roomies, I'd do it for you." Weren't they real roomies? They were temporary roomies. Not the same thing.

"That would be so great, but you have to let me compensate you."

"Pay me?" She wasn't going to take money from Lauren. "Let me look at it tonight. If I think it's something that might take some work or need a part, we can talk about it. Okay?"

"Sounds good. I don't think I have anything too personal on it. Nothing I'm embarrassed about."

"You sure? No slash on here where you're shipping your favorite anime characters?"

Lauren looked at her with a blank expression. "I have no idea what you asked me."

"Fanfic. Stories about two characters you want to see be together. Like Loki and Thor."

"Loki and Thor together. Like, sexually?"

Sam nodded.

"That's a bit mind-blowing."

"Let's talk about fanfic another night. First, I'll see what I can do about the lag."

"I appreciate that. Let me finish this application, and it's all yours."

"What are you applying for?"

Lauren made a face, one that seemed to coincide with a moment of either embarrassment or hesitation. She dropped her voice as if someone might hear them. "You can't tell anyone at work."

Sam stuck out her pinky. Lauren looked at it. "Pinky swear."

Lauren linked their pinkies. "I'm applying to Augustan Gaming. There's a woman who works there who is amazing at her job, and I would love to work with her. Learn from the best, right?"

"Augustan's headquarters is in Toronto, isn't it?"

Lauren nodded. "Yeah. I'd have to move to Canada. My parents would not like that, but I've always wanted to work with my friend, Yesenia. And you know as well as I do, Augustan makes some of the biggest titles in the world. Games that make billions. They have offices everywhere, and that would mean an opportunity to travel outside the US." If there was such a thing as stars in one's eyes, that was the way she looked as she spoke.

"Well, get typing. That application won't write itself."

Everything about today had been stressful, and Lauren was her only friend so far. But if she was going to leave for Toronto at the first chance she got, then it wouldn't do for Sam to get too close to her.

Keep your head down, O'Brian.

CHAPTER ELEVEN

L auren took a sip of coffee, only to find it had gone cold. Her focus had been on the press release announcing Sam's hiring. She'd wanted to talk about how groundbreaking her playing for the Barrage was, but Will had asked her to rewrite it several times, focusing more on the upcoming tournament prep and less on Sam herself. *Sorry, Samantha.* He'd been adamant that they should use her full name in all the press.

Speak of the devil, Will grabbed a chair, flipped it around, and sat, letting his arms hang over the back. "I need to know how it's going with Guarantech. Any movement on their sponsorship?"

There were moments when she thought he might have only hired her for her connections. "I've reached out. They are interested in talking, but it isn't going to do any good pushing them."

He unwrapped a piece of gum and popped it in his mouth. "I don't get it. If I could get them to call me back, I'm sure I could convince them to back us."

She knew the promotions manager at Guarantech well. They'd both started out as sales reps. She was no pushover, and she would never answer Will's cold calls. His plans always consisted of taking company reps out, plying them with drinks, promising them results he couldn't deliver, and getting them to sign a contract then and there. If he wanted a deal with Guarantech, he needed to do it her way, not his.

"If anything changes, you'll be the first to know."

He pushed up from the chair. "Good." He stepped away, then turned back. He snapped his fingers. "I need you to sit in on a meeting for me this afternoon. Three o'clock. Sandy knows the details."

She called after him as he moved away, "I can't. I have a photo shoot with Sam this afternoon."

"Send Bob."

She narrowed her eyes. "Can't do that."

"Call in to the meeting from wherever you are," he said as he walked away.

Typical Will. Sometimes, she wondered how a man who had so little ability to plan had ever become the owner of an esports group. Her phone chimed. As if a perfect moment for a soothing balm, she received a notice that her paycheck had been deposited into her bank account. The compensation she received made the work bearable. For now.

She stuffed her tablet and phone into her tote and took the elevator to the fourth floor to find Sam. The team was in the middle of a scrimmage. She stood against the wall and watched, hoping to find the right moment to pull Sam from the match.

"*Aah*," said Perry. He smashed his keys in rapid succession. "No. No. *No.*" He threw his hands in the air.

"Left. Left. He's on the left, damn it," said Dylan.

Next to the two of them, Sam appeared relatively calm. She said nothing and played her game. Lauren watched the score on the screen above them. They were losing. Not by much, but the timer was ticking down on the game.

"You dick." Dylan was obviously yelling at an opponent, though they couldn't hear him. The timer ran out, the game was over, and they'd lost. "For fuck's sake. They're a second division team." He turned toward Sam. "Next time, when I tell you to do something, you do it."

Sam replied calmly, "I did."

"Well, you didn't do it fast enough. We need everyone showing out next weekend in Indy."

"Alec, I need to borrow Sam for the afternoon."

Sam turned in her chair when she heard her name. Lauren smiled at her. It was reflexive.

"Luke, you're up," said Alec.

Luke looked excited. He'd been sitting on his hands, but now he signed on while Sam signed off from her computer.

Lauren overheard Dylan say, "Now we'll take this," as she and Sam walked away. She wondered how it made Sam feel to have Dylan berating her. He was one of those guys who liked to pick on those he saw as weaker than him, but Sam didn't seem weaker at all.

"Where are we going?" asked Sam.

"You have a date with a camera."

"Hmm, okay."

Lauren drove to the photography studio in a reclaimed industrial warehouse along the harbor. The walls were exposed brick, the ceilings two stories high, and the windows ten feet tall, with multiple panes of opaque glass. Diffused light filled the space. Perfect for a photo studio. Sam looked pathetic while the makeup artist worked on her. The look she gave Lauren was like a dog going to the vet. A, "how could you do this to me," expression.

So far, she had been the perfect houseguest. Lauren had quickly found out that she was a skilled cook. Soups, stews, and plated meals started showing up in her refrigerator. Delicious smells filled the apartment. Since Sam's day started later than Lauren's, she must have been cooking in the mornings when Lauren was already at the office. And she'd fixed Lauren's computer, leaving it on the coffee table with a cute little sticky note, as if the computer had written it.

As she watched the photography team transform Sam, she saw a mirror of her experience. The Barrage was making her the team's arm candy, and she knew Sam hated every moment. But there was nothing she could do. Any complaint and Will would tell her to get it done for the good of the company. She wanted to make everyone happy, but this was difficult.

Lauren had no idea how to make the photo shoot more palatable. She couldn't imagine getting up in the morning and not putting on foundation and mascara. Her grandmother had told her to never leave the house without blush and lipstick at a minimum. How many times had Seth said he liked her better with more makeup? Sometimes, she wanted to keep it minimal and more natural, but he'd wanted it heavy, like a photo filter version of herself. He'd liked her as arm candy, and she had caved to his desires.

The photographer's assistant asked Lauren to stand on the spot under the lights for a moment so he could make sure the lighting was in the right location. Under the glare of the main lights, Lauren thought about how many times she'd spoken on streaming video about new drug formulations that might or might not have been effective and how many questions she'd had to deflect about Will's past and the team's indiscretions. Would her entire career be nothing but making apologies for men's bad behavior? Behavior that seemed to get worse with each passing year?

The photographer, Sylvia, came to the front edge of the backdrop carrying a surprisingly large digital camera. Lauren assumed the technology would have made them smaller, but it seemed the pros still liked real glass optics. "Is our new star ready?" Sylvia asked.

Sam stopped where the assistant led her. She looked stiff and uncomfortable. Lauren empathized.

Sylvia must have sensed it, too. She placed a hand on Sam's shoulder. "Never done a shoot before?" Sam shook her head. "What kind of music do you like?"

"Boy Genius."

"Good choice."

The assistant seemed to know what to do without being asked. He used his phone, and momentarily, music filled the space.

"You like King Princess?"

"Yeah, of course." Sam seemed to give Sylvia a knowing smile, and Lauren felt like an outsider.

"Take a couple of deep breaths before we get started." Sylvia patted the camera. "I'm going to take a few test shots, and you can see what I'm getting. If you're overwhelmed, let me know, and we'll take a break. Okay?"

Sam tucked her chin and looked up with her eyes. "That's some nice tech."

Sylvia showed her the features and discussed the lens length, ISO, and aperture she was going to use. Some more discussion of lighting, color temperature, and angles. Sam's questions seemed much more than polite chitchat. She seemed genuinely interested, and it was obvious she understood photography.

"You a photographer?"

Sam shrugged. "I like to get textures for virtual builds. I need to set different lighting sources in my 3D environments so they look natural."

"Wow. That's cool. Is that a hobby?" Sylvia started taking shots from different spots on the floor.

Sam nodded.

Lauren tried to follow the conversation. 3D environments and virtual builds sounded like more than a hobby.

"So you like computers, I take it?"

"I love computers. I've been gaming since I was little. Anything with a puzzle, a goal, a strategy, a way to better my score."

"Remind me not to challenge you to a game. I think I'd probably lose. But that might not be so bad."

Sam's eye glinted in response.

Was Sylvia flirting with her? They continued their banter for a few minutes. Sam was visibly relaxing. She was also putting out a serious charm offensive vibe. It was working. Sylvia stopped and put her head close to Sam's, showing the pictures she'd taken.

Lauren's stomach tightened. There was definitely some kind of attraction going on between the two of them. "Can I see what you've got so far?" she called. She heard the pettiness in her voice. "I'm on a deadline for these shots."

Sylvia touched Sam's shoulder. "Take a break for a minute. Want a Coke or something?"

The assistant appeared at Sam's side and asked what she wanted. Sylvia walked back to where Lauren stood and showed her the shots on the back of the camera. They were amazing.

"The camera loves her," said Sylvia. "You're going to have a hard time picking what you want."

She wasn't kidding. Sam was the poster girl for not needing filters and touch-ups. Lauren paused on the one that captured the moment Sylvia had flirted with Sam. There was mischief in Sam's eyes. She might have been guarded and reserved when she was gaming, but that moment caught something Lauren couldn't describe. What if Seth had looked at her like that? Had he ever looked at her like that? He'd given her plenty of looks. The same ones every man who'd ever found her attractive had given her. Straight-up nice tits ogle.

They hadn't spoken openly about it, but she suspected Sam was gay. In different circumstances, Lauren might have explored her feelings and confirmed Sam's sexuality, but their current situation made it clear that it was not her concern. She was here to make sure they had suitable photos to share with the media and to promote her at the next tournament.

"You're doing a great job, Sylvia." She tried to recover from her earlier shortness. "Can you get a standard crossarm, low-angled shot where she looks confident? Cocky, even."

"I'll give it a try, but she's a bit more Kristen Stewart than Djokovic."

Kristen Stewart. That was exactly what she was showing in those eyes. Sultry and reserved. Like she didn't care about any of this. And yet, there was a discomfort she seemed to wear like a halo.

Lauren glanced at her phone. Three o'clock. She called in to the meeting for Will and spent the next few minutes listening to a new vendor drone on about how much better the features of his accounting software was than their current software. Now she understood why Will had passed this task on to her. She half listened while she watched the photo shoot.

Sam tugged at her jersey as if it was ill-fitting although it had been tailored for her. When she crossed her arms, it looked more like she was defending herself from the world rather than an arrogant call to arms. All the other team members Lauren had brought for their photos had leaned into the macho stances as if born for it. They'd been the ones to flirt with the women makeup artists and Sylvia, not the other way around.

Lauren abruptly ended her call, tired of listening to the vendor's inane and exaggerated claims, and strode to the makeup chair and retrieved Sam's sweatshirt. She stepped under the lights and approached. Sam raised an eyebrow at the interruption. Lauren handed her the sweatshirt. "Humor me. Put this on, and let's get a couple of shots. Okay?"

Sam shrugged as if she didn't care either way and pulled it over her jersey.

"Get a few shots with her turned away, just a glimpse of her cheek and jaw. Darken the lighting so she's a bit silhouetted against a lighter backdrop."

Sylvia nodded. "I like the way you think."

That had been the first glimpse of Sam that had intrigued her. The moment she'd seen her sitting at the far end of the bar. Her rescuer when she had needed one. That would be the shot that best represented her. An enigma. The team's secret weapon.

When they were done, Lauren thanked everyone and promised ice cream at her next visit. She dropped Sam back at the office.

Sam stood at the open car door. "Not coming in?"

Lauren shook her head. "I have a dinner scheduled." Sam's expression seemed to sadden. "A vendor dinner," she quickly added. "Don't worry, I doubt the food will be as good as yours."

Dinner ran long. Lauren had to listen to the sales guy talk about his kids and his new deck and his vacation to Mexico. Nothing she cared about, but she'd put on the same expression she'd perfected on the exhibit floors at conventions. As if nothing in the world was more interesting than the use of composite decking for the long-term beauty of his house. He mansplained composite decking to her, even though she had told him that the marina near her parents' house had recently used composite decking for the docks.

He no doubt never even knew that she was barely listening. She faced him, kept eye contact, and nodded in all the right places. All the while, she wanted to go home. Especially now that she had someone at home to talk to. She wondered how Sam had done in the scrimmage. She was a skillful player; Lauren was certain of it. But this was a team sport, and if she didn't gel with the team, she'd be gone.

At home, she threw her key chain in the dish by the front door and headed to the kitchen for a glass of water.

Sam had come out of her room and sat on a stool. "Hey."

"Hey." Lauren placed her water on the counter between them and leaned forward on the bar. "How was your day?"

"Okay."

"Does that mean you did well?"

Sam shrugged. "We beat them, but Dylan doesn't seem to trust me yet. Alec didn't give me much feedback, so I'm not sure how I'm doing."

Lauren moved around the counter and over to the sofa. She took off her heels and rubbed her foot. "I'm sure it will work out. Everyone wants to win, right?"

Sam strolled over to her. "Want me to work on that?"

"What?"

Sam pointed at her foot. "Massage therapist. Remember?"

Lauren shook her head. "Gosh, no. I can't ask you to do that. I'm just tired. My feet ache after a long day."

Sam kneeled near her. "Yeah, because heels are terrible on your feet. You should see some of the ladies' feet I work on. Fifty years of heels and lots of podiatrist visits."

Lauren frowned. "You need to work on your sales pitch."

Sam took her foot in her hands and massaged it.

She leaned her head back and closed her eyes. The kneading felt blissfully soothing. "Oh my God, that feels so amazing."

"Thanks." Sam gave her that little charming smile she'd seen several times now.

Lauren had never been one to get a massage. The idea of a stranger touching her did nothing for her. Every time Seth had offered to give her a back rub, it had been a prelude to having sex. Because why else would he even bother to touch her? But this was supremely wonderful and unexpectedly relaxing. "Want to get married?" she murmured as a joke. She leaned her head forward when Sam switched to her other foot. "You can cook and give massages. Why are you not already taken?"

Sam shrugged. "I guess you have to have a life to find someone to marry."

Lauren thought back to when she and Seth had been together. She had broken up with Chloe and had thrown herself into her work. She was motivated and traveling all the time. Seth had seemed like the perfect partner. He was always on the road or as busy as she was. Now, as she watched Sam work so diligently on her feet, she wondered whether she had ever been in a relationship at all. She gestured for Sam to stop. "Thank you. That was unbelievable. You are amazing."

"I can keep working. Your muscles are still cramped. I could work on your calves to loosen them as well."

That thought struck her right between her legs. She could not have Sam working on her calves. "You've had a long day, too." She patted the sofa next to her. "Sit. Relax."

Sam did as she asked. "The photo shoot wasn't as bad as I thought it would be."

"We got some great shots."

"Sylvia had an amazing setup. That camera was dope."

"I overheard you saying something about shooting textures for something online?"

"Oh yeah. I build custom environments for different virtual worlds."

"Virtual worlds?"

"You know. Modding home spaces in virtual environments. People love to customize their lobbies or homes in different games. When you turn on your headset, you want to be in an amazing red canyon or a fantasy cavern or a high-rise apartment that looks like a billionaire owns it. I've been doing a side hustle since I was fourteen. Those were computer-based ones, not VR. I don't do many of them now, what with gaming and my actual job, but I still like to build them for myself and my friends."

"When are you going to show me some of these virtual homes? Sounds amazing."

"Anytime you'd like."

"I've never experienced virtual reality."

"Really?" Sam seemed surprised. "But you've gamed. I thought you'd have some background in all of it."

"I used to date a professional gamer who thought VR headsets were silly. He called them the Wii 2.0." She lowered her voice, imitating a guy speaking. "Real gamers use a keyboard and mouse."

"Was the Seth you said was your ex Seth Madden?"

Hearing his full name made the entire relationship seem so long ago. She would have been Lauren Madden if things had gone to plan. "Yup."

"He's a great player."

"Was. He's a team manager now."

"Can I ask what happened between you two?"

"Several other women."

"Big yikes. That's shitty."

"Yes, it was," Lauren agreed. "Which is why I said I'd never date another gamer. Too much temptation. Too many late nights. He left me to do everything, and I mean everything. Laundry. Banking. Taxes. Rent payments. Car servicing. You name it, I did it."

"Not every gamer is like that," said Sam.

Lauren glanced at her. No. Some of them made delicious dinners and gave foot massages. She shook the thought from her mind. "You've met your team. Alec asks me to make their dental appointments and schedule haircuts for them. Nope. Not going to happen again ever. Not in a million years."

She heard the words leave her lips, but she didn't really believe what she was saying. Sam wasn't like any other gamer. Maybe because she was a woman but mostly because of who she was. Kind, sensitive, comfortable. She could take care of herself and others. She didn't need Lauren to do it for her, and that was very attractive. Very.

CHAPTER TWELVE

Lauren had difficulty getting to sleep. She replayed the discussion with Sam about not wanting to date gamers. Why had she been so adamant about it? It was almost as if she was warning herself not to be attracted to Sam—for several reasons—not the least of which being that they worked together, and dating could get messy. That assumed Sam was interested in her the way she was interested in Sam.

She blew out a frustrated breath, turned on the lamp, donned her glasses, and grabbed the paperback from her nightstand. The cover showcased the half-naked torso of a musclebound man. No face. Done that way so she could imagine the perfect man. Funny, she couldn't imagine any guy at the moment. Nothing about the story held her attention, and it wasn't making her sleepy, which had been her hope. Thoughts of Sam crept in at every chance.

Thirsty, she slipped from the covers and padded to the door. In the hall, she found herself face-to-face with Sam. Not only that. Sam was dressed in nothing but a T-shirt and a pair of tight boy shorts. She was slim, with narrow hips. With the light falling from the open bedroom door, Lauren noticed her defined legs and arms. Her bangs fell over one eye. She carried herself with a casual confidence and a teasing sensuality, like the famous photo of James Dean leaning against the wall in his black leather jacket.

A familiar squeeze of desire hit Lauren squarely between her legs. Warning bells went off in her head. She pointed to the kitchen.

Sam pointed at the bathroom door. As she moved away, Sam said, "Nice glasses."

"Thanks." She was embarrassed. No one saw her in her glasses anymore. She'd had contacts since high school. Seth had hated her with her glasses on. He was always taking them off before he'd kiss her. He said she looked too much like a university professor to be sexy. And yet, it was the only thing Sam had seemed to notice.

She waited in the kitchen until she heard the office door shut before she returned to her bedroom. She didn't want Sam to feel awkward about their encounter. Or maybe she didn't want to feel awkward about being horny. Now the image of Sam in her underwear was stuck in her mind.

She put her glasses carefully atop her book and turned out the light. She tossed and turned. The want was still there, and she knew she wouldn't get back to sleep if she didn't take care of it. She wasn't worried about Sam hearing her, as she had never been vocal. She was always self-conscious about letting go. Her lack of vocalization meant that Seth usually assumed she was finished at the same time as him. In reality, she had to complete the act herself after he was asleep.

How long had it been since she'd been with someone? She slipped her hands between her legs and rubbed herself. Slowly at first, visualizing her version of the cover model on top of her, pressing where she needed it most. But that wasn't what she wanted at all, and her mind substituted Sam hovering over her with her hair falling across her face. She imagined Sam looking at her with the same casual sensuality from the first time they'd met at the bar and then in the hall. Sam, with her boyish androgyny and cool confidence.

Lauren let out a gasp as the orgasm hit her. Afraid more uncomfortable sounds would escape without her permission, she slapped her free hand over her mouth. Seriously, what the hell? And now her mind was racing to catch up with her satiated body.

Or not satiated. She lowered her hand and found that she was ready to go again.

And while she rubbed, thoughts bubbled through her mind. What would it feel like to be pressed against Sam? What did her muscles feel like? What did her lips feel like? She came again with even more force but kept herself quiet.

She lay still, breathing heavily. That had been unexpected and powerful.

Only problem. How was she going to look Sam in the eye at work tomorrow?

The string of fairy lights Sam had hung cast a purple glow over the room. She sat at the desk, her head in her hands. She'd fought to keep her jaw from dropping when she'd encountered Lauren in the hall. Standing in the light from the bedroom in her camisole, her nipples throwing shadows against the silky fabric. There was a gap between the hem and her bikini-cut underwear, and peeking out from underneath the waistband, Sam had seen the hint of a tattoo. Lauren, with all her sophistication and composure, did not strike her as the body art type. She couldn't see the full design, but the dark lines were tantalizing enough that Sam could imagine running a finger along the edge of the underwear and pulling the fabric away from the skin.

And the glasses. Shit. She'd looked super smart.

Thank God she had said, "nice glasses" instead of, "nice nipples." That would have been awkward. But Lauren looked sexy in those glasses, and Sam had a thing for the smart nerd look. She was certain her heartbeat had been loud enough to wake the neighbors. She'd slunk back to her room as fast as she could but not before she'd taken a glimpse of Lauren's bedroom, disappointed to find it was as devoid of personal stuff as the rest of the apartment.

She grabbed her hoodie from the back of the chair, placed it over her face, and muffled a groan of frustration. Why was she stuck with a roommate who was hot and straight? It wasn't fair. And it made no sense.

She had never allowed anything, especially women, to take her focus away from gaming. Sure, she noticed good-looking women, but she was always less interested in them than they were in her. They always came on to her, usually walking away as soon as she mentioned gaming and computers.

That left a handful who had dated her for more than one night. Really, only one had made it longer than three months, and Sam had pushed her away as soon as she'd said the L word. Love was terrifying. The word, that like a car crash, could take everything from her in a moment. Rather than get her heart broken, she preferred to end a relationship before it ever started. Let the girl find someone who could love her back and save Sam from constantly waiting for the end to come.

Gaming, on the other hand, was something she could control. She could win if she played well enough. If she focused. If she kept love far from her mind.

She thought back to rubbing Lauren's feet. Massaging people had been her job for five years, five days a week. All body shapes and types. Never had she thought about anything but doing the best job. And then she'd touched Lauren's feet, and her heart had jumped into her throat. Her pulse had beaten so strongly, she'd been afraid Lauren could feel it through her fingers.

This was going to be a long three months.

The clock on the computer said two a.m. when she signed on. She missed her friends. Jarek hadn't responded to either of the texts she'd sent telling him she'd be coming home on Sunday. He lived right around the corner from her dad, and she hoped they could grab a burger together.

Olivia was the only one still online to chat. Good thing she worked irregular hours at the restaurant.

"Hey, famous friend," said Olivia.

"Not yet."

"But soon," she said it like it was a given. "How's it going?"

"I did a photo shoot this week. It was weird. Makeup and shit." She didn't like being stared at by everyone in the room. Except when the photographer dropped a hint that she might be gay. But Lauren had looked like someone had stolen her puppy, and the moment had vanished. She didn't care about the photographer, but she hadn't gotten laid in a long time, and being noticed had felt nice.

"Oh my gosh. Did you see the photos? I need to see them. The guys will not believe you wore makeup."

"I didn't see them. I don't know if I want to." She had always been uncomfortable with her looks. As a kid, she'd stared in the mirror, turning her head and trying to see what made her different from the other kids. And no matter what she saw reflected back at her, she never felt like she was pretty enough.

"You're about to become famous, so you need to get used to it."

Famous? That seemed crazy. "With a bunch of folks like us, maybe, but not like Taylor Swift famous. She must have no life at all."

Olivia appeared to think about that. "Yeah. Still, I'd love to be in your shoes. And I'd be strutting my stuff." She turned her head, flipped her long hair, and made a little pout like she was a model.

Sam laughed.

"Now. Let's get serious. How's it going with the snack?"

Sam rolled her eyes. "She's straight."

"How do you know? Did she tell you she was straight?"

"No, but she said she dated Seth Madden."

Olivia sat up straighter. "Serio? He's a hottie."

"She said she doesn't date gamers because he went feral on her."

"What did he do?"

"Undeclared non-monogamy."

"He cheated on her?" Olivia broke into a string of Spanish that, combined with the deep frown on her face, sounded like scolding.

"Whoa, whoa." Sam raised her hands. "I have no idea what you're saying."

"I was letting him know he was an idiot." She side-eyed Sam like she was telling a secret. "With a few more adjectives."

Sam double-checked that her door was closed. She lowered her voice. "She's like the nicest person I've ever met. What was the dude thinking?"

"He wasn't thinking with his big brain." Olivia waved her pinky. "He was thinking with his little brain. Even so, she's hot. You should ask her out."

"Says the straight woman. I'm not into getting rejected. Especially not by my roommate for the next few months. Awkward." Sam grabbed her stress ball and squeezed it.

Olivia said in a singsong voice like a little kid teasing another, "You like her."

"Who wouldn't?"

"Somebody into bad boys."

"Besides them. Unfortunately, A, she's not gay, and B, she never wants to date another gamer again." There was also the fact that she wanted to move to Toronto and work for Augustan, but she had promised she wouldn't tell anyone about that. Better not to mention it to Olivia, either.

Olivia gave her a pointed look. "Ever heard of bisexuality?"

That got Sam's attention. She hadn't really thought about it, but there were moments that felt like Lauren could be into her. Like the way she'd gotten a little irritated at the photo shoot, almost as if she was jealous.

Olivia flicked her wrist. "And you are not just any gamer. You're the top girl gamer in the world right now."

"Of *Siege Encounter*. Not exactly *Dota2*."

"Technicality."

"The top player in *Dota2* might disagree. I'm pretty sure he made seven million dollars." Sam held up a finger. "Let's go back to point A again, Liv."

"Was that the not being gay point? According to the news, everyone is going queer."

"You aren't."

Olivia raised a fist in the air. "Solidarity, my lesbian sister. But I like my lovers muscle-bound, hairy, and a bit neanderthal."

Sam shivered at the thought. "To each their own."

Olivia raised her soft drink in a salute.

"Let's play for a few minutes. I need to clear my mind."

Olivia teased her again. "Because someone has a crush on their roommate."

Yeah. She was totally into Lauren, but she wouldn't let it distract her. She was here to prove women deserved to play with the guys. Grinding it out in a game with Olivia should have put her back in the right frame of mind, but the image of Lauren in her bikini underwear was hard to forget.

CHAPTER THIRTEEN

Will, Lauren, and a few others sat in the conference room. Lauren placed the printouts of Sam's photo shoot on the table.

Will scooped up a couple and stared at them. He shook his head. "No. No. No. These won't do."

Lauren was confused. "She looks great. I think Sylvia absolutely captured her energy."

Will threw the printout of Sam in her hoodie across the table. "This one doesn't even show the team logo...or the sponsors."

She stopped the photo before it slid to the floor. It was her favorite of them all. He was right. It wasn't the best branding. It didn't match the other team photos, but there was something about it she couldn't put her finger on that drew her in. Triggered her curiosity. Made her want to learn more about Sam.

He continued. "She needs more makeup, and we need to get her to grow her hair out. And for God's sake, get her a better wardrobe for interviews."

"She looks like a gamer," Lauren countered.

"She looks like a guy."

Lauren shook her head. Sam wasn't dressed in pink, and she didn't have long hair, but that didn't mean she looked like a guy. As a matter of fact, she was beautifully fit.

"Reschedule another shoot. Make sure the makeup artist understands we need her to look more feminine. And put a wig on her until her hair grows out."

"A wig? Seriously, Will? I think she looks great."

"Don't tell me you're playing for the other team?"

His comment startled her. "What?"

"Oh no, wait. You dated Seth? Are you bi?"

Her cheeks warmed. Her sexuality was none of his business, and she wouldn't bother to respond.

He pointed at one of the photos. "She isn't trans, is she?"

She took a few breaths to try not to say anything she'd regret. "It shouldn't matter one way or the other. She's an excellent player. She likes genderless clothing, and she looks good in them. The camera loves her."

"If I ran around wearing a skirt all day, people might think I was trans," said Will.

Nate, the older graying finance guy, added, "Don't tell that to Rowdy Roddy Piper."

Will frowned. "Who?"

"The wrestling great? Wore a kilt," said Nate.

"A kilt is different," said Will.

"Why? It's just a wraparound wool skirt in plaid," said Lauren.

Will curled his bicep. "It has a masculine heritage."

"You do know that women wear kilts, too," said Lauren.

"Enough with the weird clothing discussion." He pointed at the photos. "I can't have a fiasco like that beer company."

"Our audience is completely different," said Lauren. "Twenty-eight percent of under twenty-fives say they are queer or nonbinary or some other identity on the spectrum. Younger gamers are open to gender rebellion. They're into it."

"I don't know what gamers you're talking to, but most of the guys who play our games want women players to look the part."

"I'm talking about the audience for your product. If you want to expand the audience, you need to give them what they want, and Gen Z doesn't want binary conformity."

"We hired Samantha because you said we needed to soften our image. Be more inclusive."

"Her name is Sam." This was the sixth or seventh time she'd reminded him. By now, he was only doing it to piss her off. "She looks great in the team polo. She looks like the rest of the team."

"Get her to wear pink, for God's sake. And a skirt."

"You want me to tell her she needs to look more feminine?"

"If she wants to make money, yes." He gestured at her. "As a matter of fact, I think you should help her. You always look great. You know how to get men to notice you."

"Will," Nate said in a useless tone of warning. Will had no idea what he was saying was insensitive.

He turned to Nate. "Five thousand approved on the company card for clothing."

Lauren realized she was clenching her jaw. She tried to relax. This wasn't the first time she'd heard these things. She didn't dress this way to get a man's attention. She dressed this way to get ahead. She dressed this way for her job. Men like Will would never understand the difference. "I have a lot on my plate. Indy is coming up, and then I need to focus on the other leagues as well. I need to line up player interviews, approve the online video drops, send out the press releases—"

"I'll get Bob to take over some of your tasks."

"Bob?" He was a low-level grunt who hauled equipment for the team. "Will, he has no marketing training at all. These interviews can make or break your relationship with Augustan."

"He'll be fine. He's a fun guy. He can handle it." Will snapped his fingers. "As a matter of fact, give him your notes on the Guarantech deal."

She was certain her blood pressure spiked. "Guarantech held off on their sponsorship because of the bad press around the stripper incident. I've been working hard to get them back on board to sponsor the team. I called in a lot of favors for you because you asked me to." Sometimes she thought he'd only lured her away from Guarantech for her connections and how she looked in heels.

"Change Samantha's look by the time we get to Pittsburgh. Otherwise, she's gone, and I'll be disappointed in you."

Disappointed? Was that Will's way of threatening her job if this didn't work out the way he envisioned it? She collected the photos and tucked them back in the folder and barely listened to the rest of the meeting.

When the discussions ended, she pressed the elevator button three times in a row. Why was it taking so fucking long? Why was this her job to take care of? She liked Sam the way she was. She didn't want to change her for Will's sake. The clatter of her heels announced her arrival as she strode across the hardwood floors with determination. The *Siege* team was in their gaming stations in the middle of a match.

She gestured to Alec. "I'm borrowing Sam. I'll have her back for ranked play tonight."

Alec nodded and looked at his watch. "I need her back at eight thirty."

Lauren waited and watched the game unfold. Alec told Sam to pack up and go with Lauren. Sam's expression looked a bit concerned. Lauren didn't say anything to her as they got in the elevator. She was still angry, and she didn't want to take it out on Sam. It wasn't Sam's fault. None of this was her fault. She'd taken this marketing job knowing full well that Will had a reputation. She knew the company was having trouble. Still, she wanted this to be her steppingstone to Augustan. Prove she could handle whatever they threw at her. And she would.

She stormed through the front doors.

"You can move in those heels," said Sam.

She slowed. "Sorry, busy day."

"What's up? Am I getting fired?"

She turned and took hold of Sam's upper arm. Rock solid. She let go and tried to soften her voice. "No. No. Not at all. I have some things we need to go over before your next interview." Like how I'm supposed to change your appearance. This would not go well. "I'm starving. How about we talk over pizza?"

"Not the cardboard one you told me about, I hope?" Sam flashed a mischievous smile.

"Oh no, no, no." She shook her head vigorously. "That is not pizza. I've got a place. My treat."

"Free pizza? I'll take it."

A late afternoon crowd filled the restaurant. The walk-up order line was long, and after getting their slices, they stood around for a few minutes until two tall chairs in the front window freed up. The chairs were so close together, her knee touched Sam's when they settled in. Sam didn't move away. She didn't want her to move away.

"Not a lot of room," said Lauren.

"That's okay. Pizza is worth the inconvenience," replied Sam. She took a giant bite of her slice. "Wow. This is amazing."

"Told you." She took a bite of her slice, but all she could think about was the spot where her knee touched Sam's. She liked it.

"All right, rip the Band-Aid off," said Sam.

"What?"

"You've looked serious since you came to get me. Something is up. I'm ready for whatever it is."

Lauren relaxed. "Will looked at your photos, and he had some suggestions."

"What's the problem?"

Flustered, Lauren wondered how she could approach the actual issue without hurting Sam's feelings. "We need to do a reshoot."

Sam crossed her arms. "I thought you said they were great?"

"They are great. You look fantastic. Will wants us to soften them a little."

She could see Sam speculating. "Like what, exactly?"

"A little heavier makeup. Those lights can be harsh. Even the guys get makeup to cover the uneven qualities of their skin."

Sam touched her cheek. "Did I have a zit or something?"

Lauren laughed. Sam was so sweet. She put a hand on her forearm. Sam was surprisingly warm. Lauren wanted to brush her fingertips from her elbow to her wrist. Instead, she pulled her hand away. "Listen, don't worry too much about it. We'll shoot

with the same photographer. You two seemed to get along well."
She winced. Even she could hear the barb. Why had the flirting
bothered her?

Sam narrowed her eyes. Then, she shrugged and took a bite of
pizza. "Whatever. I guess I can't say no."

Lauren let her eat a little before she addressed the other issue.

"There's one other thing. You'll be spending the day with
me on Thursday. We're going to meet with a stylist. Do a little
shopping. All paid for by the Barrage."

"And this has to do with the photos?"

"It does. We're going to try a few things to soften your
appearance."

"How soft?"

She tried to lighten the mood. "Not as far as your communion
dress photo."

Sam lowered her slice.

"I understand you feel more comfortable in sportswear, but
we have to present a corporate image in interviews, and Will wants
us to get a few photos of you in outfits other than the team jersey."

Sam's expression fell. "You're putting me in skirts and shit?"

"Not necessarily." She hated making Sam feel uncomfortable
with herself. "I'm sure we can find some nice outfits that reflect the
look Will wants and still meet your approval."

"What exactly is *softening*? Tell me the real reason we're
doing this."

"That is the real reason." She would not tell her what Will
had actually said. There was no point. He was insensitive and said
things without thinking about others.

"Do I get any input in the color choices?"

Ultimately, no, but she needed Sam to feel like she had some
ownership of the process. "Absolutely." The word hurt her to say.
"We'll make it a nice day. Get some lunch beforehand or some ice
cream afterward."

"Ice cream for taking my soul. That doesn't sound like the
best deal."

Ouch.

Sam narrowed her eyes. "There's more, isn't there? I can see it on your face."

Damn, she hated that she was an easy read when something bothered her. "You'll be wearing a wig."

"A wig? Like an anime one? You are kinky, aren't you?" she said in a lighthearted manner. The glimmer in her eye gave Lauren a little thrill.

Lauren took a sip of water. She was glad she wasn't blushing. "We need to get you one you can wear until your hair grows out."

Sam shook her head. "Oh, hell, no."

"I know it may make you feel uncomfortable."

"Uncomfortable? How about not me?"

"I know this isn't ideal."

"You keep saying that *you know*, but do you really know?" She cast her gaze over her. "You're exactly what they want. Beautiful, sophisticated, feminine."

Hearing those words about herself made Lauren feel uncomfortable. How did Sam not know how sexually appealing she was? "Will wants you to portray a certain look."

"Do the guys have to do this? Have any of them had to wear a wig?"

"No."

Sam opened her mouth to continue arguing.

"But…but they adhere to rules about hair care and facial grooming."

"Is it a breach of contract if I refuse?"

"I'm not a lawyer, Sam."

Sam pushed her plate away. Lauren could see her working her jaw. Sam wanted to say something, but she was holding back. "Why is it I can't just play the game?"

Good question. "Because this is a business. And businesses need to make money. Will is the majority shareholder in the company. He thinks this will help generate ticket and merchandise sales and increase streaming revenue."

Sam gave her a piercing stare. "What do you think?"

That Sam looked fantastic in the photos. That her androgyny would be attractive to straight and queer women. Lauren was certain of it. If she oversaw the company, she wouldn't change a thing. But she didn't, so she had to make this work.

"The team needs you. You're a great player. There are no women players in the league at all. I know...sorry, I am aware that this is a big ask for you, but at least try it until you get through the probationary period. You'll be locked in by then and can start to push back."

"So you want me to stay?"

Did she want her to stay? Sam made her stomach flutter. She made her think about things she hadn't thought about in a long time, and thoughts of Sam had given Lauren the best orgasms she'd had in a while. And none of those things had to do with the team. "Yes. I do."

"Will this all be worth it? Changing everything about myself?"

If Lauren could get the team's image stabilized, bring on Guarantech as a sponsor, and help Sam become one of the most recognized women in gaming, that would be an accomplishment in her mind. But would that meet Sam's goals? "Omar, Quinn, and I will be rooting you on."

She could see the sadness flash in Sam's eyes. "You're like walking talking Catholic guilt right now."

"I'm not trying to make you feel guilty."

"Too late." Sam jumped off the stool. "I'll do it, but I won't like it. I'm going to walk back to the office."

Lauren wanted to reach out, but it was probably best to give her some space. This sucked. She hated every word she'd had to say. She didn't want to change anything about Sam, but they both had jobs to do, and hers was to repair the team's reputation. As soon as Sam proved her worth to the team, Lauren would make it up to her somehow.

CHAPTER FOURTEEN

S am was up early. Too early. This was a big day. She was
going to get her glam makeover. *Bleh.* She'd tossed and
turned all night thinking about how uncomfortable this whole
thing made her. She was a gamer, not a model or an actor. Why did
they want her to be something she wasn't?

She turned on her computer and looked at anything she could
read about her upcoming opponents in Indianapolis. Her Discord
login was automatic, so it wasn't long before she got a ping from
Callum, a player in Scotland who liked to fill in for her amateur
team from time to time.

Callum: *You're up late.*

Sam: *Early actually. Big day today.*

Callum: *Yeah? What they got you doing at the fancy pants
team?*

Sam: *Getting dressed.*

He sent back a string of confused emojis.

She smiled and typed back: *They want me to be more feminine.*

Callum: *What a load of bollocks. You all right with it?*

Sam: *No. Feels like a slap in the face. But it's my job.*

Callum: *Take it from me. Bank the money. Remember, no
matter how they dress you up and parade you around, you're still
the best woman player in the league.*

Sam: *I'm practically the* only *woman in the league.*

A shrug emoji appeared. *Then show them you're the best player. Bloke or woman or nonbinary.*

Sam: *Callum, I didn't know you even knew what that was.*

Callum: *I'm old, but I read. And my wife loves that show Heartstoppers. Lots of new information for me there. Speaking of work. I have a little stinking business to run. L8tr.*

Surprisingly, his texts made her feel better. He was right. She'd show them that they'd picked her for her gameplay, not her appearance. She'd beat their opponents. She'd make her...she'd almost thought mother. Who would she make proud? As nice as they were, her O'Brian grandparents had no clue what she was doing. Her dad probably still thought she was wasting her time playing on the computer. How about the man in South Korea who was her unnamed grandfather? Would he be proud?

She thought about what Lauren had said the other night. How she, Omar, and Quinn would support her. If she could hold on to that thought, she might make it through all this change.

The drive was short to the strip with the fancy clothing stores. Sam was certain she'd never been in a boutique in her life. In her head, she said the word several times, exaggerating it more and more each time for fun. She needed some fun. Shopping for clothes was her absolute least favorite thing to do behind cleaning bathrooms.

She took a quick selfie with the street of storefronts in the background, put a series of puking emojis on it, and sent it to Olivia, Ashton, and Jarek. Olivia responded with a pair of high heels and some lipstick. Ashton sent an animated congratulations GIF. But Jarek was suspiciously quiet. He'd been ghosting her since she'd signed the contract. She suspected he was still angry about it, but she wasn't sure why. Was he mad at her for leaving? Mad at the team for taking her out of all the members? Was he jealous? Did he miss her? She had no idea, and he wasn't giving her anything to analyze.

After parking, Lauren stepped out from the driver's side door and was greeted by a stylish woman with a tented hug. One of those hugs straight women did so their breasts didn't touch. Like they were worried that colliding breasts would be exciting. If anyone should have done the tented hug, it was lesbians. She would certainly do one if that stylist came anywhere near her and not because she was attractive.

Sam stepped from the car and came around to the sidewalk.

"Ah. This must be our experiment?" said the stylist.

"Sam." She stuck her hand out so there would be no confusion about tent hugs.

"Mimi." She had a weak grip and used only her fingertips. Mimi moved around Sam, assessing. She eyed her more intimately than a date but without an ounce of interest. Mimi was definitely not queer. "Nice bone structure. Lovely eye color. Great skin." She reached and took hold of the back of Sam's sweatshirt, tightening it so it strained against Sam's chest.

"Hey." Sam squirmed away.

"Athletic build."

Was that a euphemism for flat chested? She crossed her arms.

Mimi didn't seem to get the hint. She slipped an arm through Sam's and led her toward the shop with a large front window full of macramé dresses. Jesus Christ on a cracker. She hoped that was not what they were going to make her wear.

After the macramé dress shop had been a bust, they drove to a store with giant posters all over the front windows of women of every race wearing all types of wigs. Inside, two talkative older retail associates greeted them and got excited when Mimi said they were there to try a bunch of wigs. Sam sat in a chair in front of a mirror, and the parade of wigs began.

Lauren took photos with her tablet and typed furiously with someone about them. In public, she usually had a genuinely friendly expression, but while typing, her expression waffled from aggravated to exasperated. Whoever was on the other end of those texts was irritating her.

The first few wigs were a little longer than her current hair but fuller, covering the shaved sides. The invisible approver nixed those quickly, and more elaborate wigs appeared. Once the wig that made her look like Marie Antoinette went on her head, Sam made a ridiculous face and said, "Let them eat cake." Lauren laughed. Mimi rolled her eyes and went back into the wig stacks with one of the employees.

Sam snapped her fingers and shouted to no one in particular, "Where's Louis?" Then, with a straight face, she added, "I feel as if I'm about to lose my head."

"Stop," Lauren said between giggles. "I need you to be serious for at least one photo."

Making Lauren smile pleased her.

She tried on a few more wigs until the unseen text advisor made the final choice.

Mimi leaned close to Lauren and asked, "Does he have a Katniss Everdeen fetish?"

Sam didn't hate the choice of a long braid, but she wasn't happy to have to change the way she looked. They were right; it did make her look a little like Katniss Everdeen. Probably even more so when she wore the team jersey. With that purchase settled, they went to the next set of boutiques.

By the fourth store and the thirtieth outfit, she was beyond irritated. When she lost some of her amusement, she threw the latest skirt over the door into the common area beyond. She didn't care if it seemed petty. She was getting tired.

"I take it you didn't like that one," she heard Mimi say. "I'll give you a minute. Would you like a soft drink? Or perhaps you'd prefer a glass of wine? I know I would," she muttered.

Sam didn't answer. She pulled on her cargo pants and sat on the wooden bench. There was a soft knock.

"Can I come in?" Lauren's voice had a melodic quality even muffled by the door.

"Yeah, I'm decent."

Lauren entered, closed the door, and leaned against it. "I know this is a lot of change for you."

"There you go with all that knowing," she murmured.

"You've been a good sport, and you looked fantastic in everything. It's going to be hard to choose from all the fabulous looks." Her fingers grazed the crepey fabric of a pink top on a hanger as she spoke. "Are there any that you'd feel most comfortable wearing?"

Sam shrugged. Some of them were fine. The plainer ones. But the colors were awful. Black or charcoal gray was all she wanted. She stood and approached and leaned against the mirror beside Lauren. "I have a question for you."

Lauren turned to her. The room felt smaller. Sam had wanted to be assertive with her question, but she melted a little as she looked at Lauren. She wanted to...what? Kiss her? She looked at the awful pink shirt instead.

"Why is it, as the only girl on the team, I need to look more feminine? Prettier? The guys don't have to look more manly. Or be fit. Or even be clean. Have you smelled Tyler on the *Legends* team?" She waved her hand under her nose. "He smells like a week-old egg salad sandwich."

"I know it may seem that way, but everyone gets a stylist for interviews."

Sam stared her down. "They all wear a team polo." She hadn't gotten this far without being the queen of research. "I looked up every interview and pregame online show I could find. They're slobs. Wrinkled shirts. Sweaty. Hair unwashed."

Lauren seemed to be thinking about how to respond. Sam knew she was good at her job. Never offensive. Never angry. Never even frustrated. It must have taken a lot of energy to stay that put together. Sam held her gaze and moved closer. She couldn't seem to help herself. She could smell something that Lauren wore, a perfume or a hair product. Light and clean, not overwhelming.

When there was almost no distance between them, Sam stopped. Lauren's expression changed. She swallowed. Her brows furrowed slightly, but she stayed put. Sam looked at her, really looked. Her eyebrows. Her lips. The slight curve of her nose, almost imperceptible but there, making her imperfect but still flawless. Whatever was happening, she needed to get ahold of herself.

"Why can't we buy a cashmere hoodie and call it a day?" Sam whispered.

Lauren let out a breath and stuttered slightly. "Let me see what I can do." She grabbed the handle of the door and backed through. "I can't promise anything."

Sam called after her more loudly, "I'm sure Mimi can find one."

She sat back down on the bench. Her imagination was playing a movie in her head. In her mind, she had pushed Lauren against the door, run a hand across her cheek, and leaned in to kiss her. She knew it was a bad idea. They worked and lived together. Version two of the movie ended with Lauren giving her a nice firm push away. Ah, come on, that wasn't fair. Now her dreams needed consent.

Mimi knocked and stuck her head in the dressing room. "I have an idea."

This was starting out concerning.

"We need a little relaxation. I think all of us could use a break. How about we get a sandwich and go to the vintage store nearby and have a little fun? I think we'll find a few items that may fit your vibe better there."

Sam's stomach growled in response. A sandwich might help her get through the rest of the day without hating them all at the end. This was probably Lauren's idea. She was becoming the queen of food bribery. Oh great. Now she had a vision of Lauren feeding her a sandwich. She let out a groan.

Lunch had been a deserved respite from the constant barrage of Will's opinions on everything from colors to styles to the wig choice. He had told Lauren she should oversee dressing Sam, but when she had informed him she was taking Sam to meet a stylist, Will had insisted she send him photos of everything under consideration.

As they sat on the porch of the little restaurant, she watched Mimi and Sam verbally joust about the best Instagram photo filters and whether online ads should be accompanied by notifications that said when photos had been retouched.

"If the color has been corrected to hold a certain overall color palette, then I'm not seeing the real item. If I order it based on the Insta post, and it's emerald green instead of chartreuse, I'm out time and money until I get my refund. I may even have to pay a restocking fee. They need to clearly state that the product photos have been messed with." Sam tapped her finger on the table as emphasis.

Something in the way Sam made her point by leaning forward made Lauren's heart skip a beat. She replayed the moment in the dressing room when Sam had leaned toward her and whispered. Her body responded even now with a shiver.

Mimi sipped her drink and responded with a wave and a, "Honey, if we had to do that, there wouldn't be a photo in the world that wasn't covered in caveats."

Lauren smiled. She was certain Sam had never bought anything in chartreuse, but at least she and Mimi were getting along.

"I'm not saying every photo," Sam said. "I like artistic license. I even like some generative AI stuff. But not when the goal of the photo is to get me to literally click here and buy now. Have you ever seen those ads where the product is this big and a dog or something is in the photo with it and is obviously the wrong size? Like, is that even a real product photo?"

They walked down to the vintage shop. A wooden sign hung above the door with a logo of a goat eating a pair of pants. Underneath, it said, Diamond in the Gruff. The store was another building that had been a house at one point and was now three floors of vintage clothing, hats, jewelry, and shoes.

Mimi was on a mission. She went to gather items while Sam strolled along, thumbing a rack of leather jackets. Lauren followed, watching her. She wasn't the only one. Two college-age girls with septum rings, multiple ear piercings, strips of multicolor hair, and a lot of oversized vintage clothing caught sight of Sam and followed her with their eyes. When she passed, they giggled and whispered to each other. When Lauren passed, they were still watching Sam from a distance. They didn't even notice her. That was a strange feeling.

Lauren was used to all eyes being on her whether she wanted them or not. She noticed the rainbow patches and other signifiers of queer culture on the women's shoulder bags. If their reactions were anything to go by, Sam must have been lesbian catnip.

Being bisexual was sometimes a tough road for Lauren. College had been fun. She had dated men and women equally. Mostly, everyone had been in it for pleasure, hormones and lust in full bloom.

When she'd started working at Guarantech, she'd met Chloe, a free spirit and a feminist with a capital F. Always dressed in men's pants, looking and sounding a little like Katharine Hepburn. Her vintage car, long scarf, and driving gloves made it seem like she was born in the wrong era. And ultimately, she had not been interested in someone who was bi. When Seth had come along, unfazed by her past dating history, she thought she'd found the right partner.

Sam stopped and put on an ancient Easter bonnet. The brim had a bright pink bow wrapped around it. She turned to Lauren. "What do you think? Is it me?"

Lauren took it off her head and hung it back on its hook. "We both know that hat should be burned." She tossed her head toward the girls they'd passed. "You've got some groupies."

Sam looked over Lauren's shoulder. "Don't know them."

Lauren took a chance to infer that she knew Sam was queer. "They want to know you."

"Oh yeah?" Sam looked again. Lauren sensed she was teasing her. "Which one should I go ask out? The tall one or the one holding the *Hello Kitty* backpack?"

"Definitely *Hello Kitty* girl," Lauren replied, relieved that she'd been right. Sam was into women or at least open to it.

"Ah, you're biased. You want me to pick the one who likes anime like you."

"*Hello Kitty* is not actually anime. She was on products long before they made an anime with her in it. She was *kawaii* before *kawaii* was cool."

"*Kawaii?*"

"Literally Japanese for cute characters."

"You're into this stuff, aren't you?"

Lauren pulled a cowboy hat from the wall and placed it on Sam's head. "I might have had a thing for manga and anime as a teen."

Sam raised an eyebrow. No doubt she had seen the anime series list in her Netflix queue.

"Okay. I might still be a fan."

"Ladies, I have found the holy grail of vintage treasures." Mimi fought her way through the overflowing racks while carrying an armload of clothing. "This way. Amazing what a pleasant lunch and a glass of wine will do for inspiration."

Lauren swept her arm in front of her. "After you."

Sam looked nervous. It was an enormous pile of clothes.

This time, they did have fun. Sam stepped out from the dressing room in the first outfit. A mini top, a long patterned overshirt, and oversized trousers. She'd even found a pair of heavy black platform shoes that looked like Doc Martens on steroids.

"Ah, the aughts, my best decade," Mimi said wistfully.

Sam held on to the unbuttoned edges of the shirt. "What is on this shirt?"

Mimi leaned in closer. "Mushrooms, gnomes, and flowers."

Sam rolled her eyes. Mimi pushed her back into the dressing room. Lauren heard her say, "Try this, this, and this together." Then, she closed the curtain.

This time, Sam stepped out in black cargo pants, a white undershirt, and a black short-sleeved shirt with two thick vertical gray stripes down the front. Like a vintage bowling shirt. What Lauren saw were the corded muscles in Sam's forearms and the rounded bicep when she curled her arm. She wasn't big, but she was defined. And it was doing something to Lauren. Sam saw her looking and gave her a shy smile, one that said she'd caught her looking.

"Now this is your vibe, honey," Mimi said.

"Yes," Lauren agreed. She knew Will would never go for it, but she took pictures anyway and didn't bother sending them to him. She leaned against an old bookshelf that held jewelry and watched as Mimi paraded Sam out in more and more outrageous but somehow appropriate, outfits. Parachute pants from the eighties. Low-rise flared bell bottoms from the late nineties.

"You want me to try this on?" Sam held a black wraparound dress from the dressing room.

Mimi snatched it from her hands. "Heavens, no. That's not you." She stepped over to Lauren. Conspiratorially, she said, "Keep an eye on this for me. Original Diane Von Furstenberg from the seventies. What a find." She placed her hands together as if in prayer.

Lauren laid it on top of the bookshelf and promised to watch it for her. When she turned back to the dressing room, what she saw took her breath away. Sam was in black leather boots with several sets of buckles and vintage dark wash jeans with some looseness to them but not baggy. A ripped scoop-neck Rolling Stones concert T-shirt hung under a black leather racing jacket with a stand collar and several white stripes, one down the sleeve and one down the front.

She looked like she'd stepped off the set of a racing movie from the 1960s. And it was working for her. Lauren snapped a photo with her phone. She wanted to keep this one for herself.

"What do you think?" Sam asked.

Lauren couldn't articulate what she thought, which was that she wanted to run her hands down the front of that jacket. "You look amazing."

Sam cocked her head. "Any chance this is going to make the shopping list?"

Lauren shook her head. "I wish we could. It's so you, and it's amazing." She and Sam both saw the girls from earlier walking down the middle aisle. They were staring hard at Sam. Sam smiled at them, and they both fell into a fit of giggles and ducked through the clothes to the back of the store.

Mimi rested her chin on her hand and her elbow on her other hand and admired her selections. "This is your vibe, honey." Then, she helped her remove the jacket and hung it on the thick wooden hanger.

While Sam changed back into her clothes, Lauren handed Mimi the dress she'd been watching and her personal credit card. She grabbed the jacket and pressed it to her. She spoke in a whisper. "Do me a favor. Buy the jacket on my card. Make sure you give it to me when we leave. I don't want it accidentally mixed in with her other outfits."

Mimi raised an eyebrow. "Not like you to get personal."

"She deserves it. Anyone who has to wear the wig Will picked deserves it."

Mimi winked and strode away to the counter with a mix of personal and business outfits.

Sam exited the dressing room, now back in her clothes. She looked visibly relieved when Lauren said they were done for the day.

"I was afraid we'd be heading for lingerie next."

Lauren frowned. "You have a bra, right?"

Sam scratched her head and made a face. "Um, I have a sports bra."

"*A* sports bra?" Lauren asked incredulously. "Let me tell Mimi we need to make one more stop."

Sam came up behind her and touched her waist as she headed to the counter. Lauren wanted to stop and lean back into that embrace. She needed to get a grip. "Can't we not? Tell me what to buy, and I'll order it online," asked Sam.

Lauren glanced over her shoulder. She needed to keep her emotions in check. "Doesn't work that way. I promise, once we have the appropriate undergarments, you are free for the rest of the night."

"No offers of ice cream or something?"

Mimi met them at the door with several bags. When Lauren told her the next stop, Mimi rolled her eyes. "Oh, joy."

Lauren's mind went straight to seeing Sam in a bra, and now it was all she could think about. She blew out a deep breath. She'd duck out and make a few phone calls. Seeing Sam in that jacket was enough physical reactions for one day. Sam was a gamer. Her life was going to be one of late nights, surrounded by guys who lived a Peter Pan existence. That was not what she wanted for herself again. If only her body would remember that fact.

CHAPTER FIFTEEN

S am finished the one-on-one game against Luke. He was the only team member who wanted to warm up with her. Dylan always played against Perry. She was certain it was because he always beat Perry. That might be good for Perry, always pushing to do better against a more talented opponent. But it did nothing for Dylan except stroke his ego. She didn't understand why Alec didn't make them rotate and learn from each other.

Alec wasn't even here today. He was busy with administrative issues, leaving Dylan in charge of the upcoming scrimmage. Her mind was so busy with these other thoughts that she was surprised when she lost her match.

"GG," said Luke.

"Good game," she replied.

He leaned back in his gaming chair. "You seemed distracted."

"Not at all. You did great."

He shook his head. "I've been a pro for almost fifteen years. I know distracted when I play against it. You don't usually drop a map that way. Especially not that one. It's, like, your favorite."

He was right. It was her favorite map. Small, tight, lots of levels, and lots of corners. She was surprised he'd been paying her any attention. Dylan spent most of the time ignoring her. "I'm thinking about some strategies for the scrimmage today."

On the other side of Luke, Dylan pulled off his headset. "Not your job to worry about it. I've given you my thoughts on the approach."

She'd been waiting a few weeks trying to get to know everyone before she gave input, but being accepted as an equal with the guys had been more difficult than she'd imagined. They didn't do anything specifically to shut her out, but they didn't welcome any opportunities to allow her to take part in strategy at all. She shouldn't have said the *guys*. The culprit was Dylan. He seemed determined to keep her at an arm's length, a non-player character to his main character.

She took out her phone. "I did some analysis last night and examined our opposition's last three months of play, creating a few heat maps with their favorite lanes. I also determined their favorite maps and gameplay types." She dropped her files into the team chat. "If you take a look, I selected the maps they least like to play. Using an analysis of our own gameplay since I joined the team, I selected the ones I think we might challenge them on successfully."

Luke scrolled on his own phone, obviously looking at one of her documents. "Wow. You put a lot of work into this."

"My amateur team was successful with this approach. I thought maybe my analysis would be helpful here."

Dylan spun in his chair and looked at the ceiling. "Alec and I already discussed the plan for today. We don't need to do this kind of unnecessary extra work for a scrimmage."

Sam pushed the subject. "But you've chosen three maps that clearly give our opponents an advantage. If you look at the head-to-head comparison, you'll see what I was looking at."

"So? Do you want to get better or not? It shouldn't matter. You need to play better."

"I looked at our ranked play for the past few weeks, too. We're missing opportunities for points."

"And when you're the captain, you can discuss it with Alec," said Dylan, sounding as if that was the end of the discussion.

Of course, she wouldn't be captain of the team. She didn't have enough playtime or enough experience. "I want to help."

"Help by playing better," said Dylan.

She stood and took the time before the scrimmage to grab a Coke to collect herself. As she returned to the room, she could overhear the guys talking.

Luke said, "Give her a break, Dylan."

"Why?" Dylan replied. "No one ever gave me one."

"She put in a lot of work, and she's got a point about the maps. Look at this chart."

"I don't need to see the chart. I know what we need to do. We just need to execute."

"Why are you being so hard on her?"

"Have you looked online? We're a joke. No one thinks we're going to make it past the quarterfinals in Indianapolis. And you know why? Because we're the only team with a girl."

Sam hung her head.

"How long do you think she'll last?" asked Perry.

"Fifty says she washes out after Indy," replied Dylan. "Or sooner."

"I'll take Atlanta," said Perry.

"You're on."

Great. Her teammates didn't have any confidence in her. How was she supposed to have confidence in herself? She wasn't trying to be a problem. She wanted to win, and she'd learned that knowing as much as she could about her opponents, staying focused, and staying calm was the way she won. What was she doing here? Had she made a terrible mistake? She shouldn't have bought into Lauren's polished speech about inspiring young players.

She leaned against the wall. Now she had to walk into that room and pretend she hadn't heard any of what they'd said. In the past, she would have reached out to Jarek, but he was still ghosting her. She took her phone from her pocket and texted Olivia.

Olivia texted back. *Working. TTYL.*

She sucked it up and walked in and took her seat. Luke gave her a sympathetic glance. At least he hadn't bet on her end date.

❖

Lauren tried to stay focused on the meeting topics, but it felt like it didn't matter what she said; no one in the room seemed to listen. Nate was giving Will a lecture about the financial situation, and Will shut him out as well.

"You paid fifteen million for a franchise team in an unproven league. Your ownership stake is now at forty-one percent. You don't have room to take on more minority investors. If you do, you run the risk that one of the other owners will consolidate a takeover."

"I bought in to the *Siege Encounter* league because I could move some of the experienced players from the other franchises to this team. The ones who are about to age out of *Call of Duty* and *Counter-strike*. They know it's coming, so they took a salary cut. They'll work out fine until we build a younger group."

Nate shook his head. "I'll send you the latest financials. Take a look when you have a chance. I can't make money appear from nowhere, and we can't lose any more sponsors."

"That's why Lauren is going to get Guarantech on board," said Will. "Isn't that right?"

She raised her eyebrows in response. "I've been telling you. They are taking a wait and see approach. If the team can pull out a win in Indy, I think they'll be interested in talking. They're keen to sponsor a team with a woman player, and right now, we're the only group with one."

"Speaking of, I was impressed with the new photos of Samantha. What's your plan for those?"

"I'm sending out the press release and photos this week. Hopefully, we'll have a few interviews lined up for the Indy tournament."

"Did you change out the photo on the website?"

Lauren wanted to give him an eye roll, but she smiled instead. Of course she had done that, as well as writing about thirty blog posts about all their teams since then. "Yes."

"Great."

She spent the rest of the meeting thinking about why she was here. Was her mother right? Should she do something else? She'd enjoyed her trip to Las Vegas for E3. She'd talked to the few other women in the industry and saw what they were planning for the future. Still, the games aimed at girls were few, and none were particularly competitive or viable for an esports team like the Barrage.

Will walked about the conference room, gesturing and throwing thoughts around like glitter. His scattered approach to the organization meant that they all worked twice as hard to accomplish anything. Especially her. If she could get him on board with a few ideas she had that would build some good press. Sponsor a few tournaments for high schoolers. Give a couple of internships to women.

"Will, the tournament in Indy is during Pride month. I spoke to Helen over at Gateway Merchandising, and she said they can produce some on demand items we can link to from our website. There's a setup fee, but after that, no inventory costs. A few Pride items with Barrage branding would go a long way to reaching the younger audience."

"I'm not comfortable with anything that might create a backlash. It's just not a good time to do it."

"When exactly is a good time if not during Pride?"

"We'll talk about it later."

"Guarantech has Pride-themed merch on their site. So do all the big gaming companies. All the games have Pride-themed skins, including *Siege Encounter*."

"Fine. Get some stickers. Nothing too blatant."

Blatant? She had no idea what that meant. At least he'd agreed to something.

When she left for the day, she found Sam sitting outside the building on a small wall. She looked unhappy, her head hung low and her hands shoved in her pockets.

"Hey, whatcha doing?"

Sam looked up. "Trying to decide if I want to walk to the apartment to eat. We have late-night ranked play but not until nine."

Lauren had several errands to run, including an appointment for a manicure, and she should call her parents this evening, but she had the sudden urge to cancel it all. "I've got an idea. What if we go into downtown and walk around? Find a random place to eat?"

"You sure you have time?"

"Absolutely." Making time for Sam didn't seem like a burden at all. In fact, she looked forward to it.

Sam leaned against the door as they drove downtown. They had discussed how Baltimore needed a women's professional soccer team. Sam hadn't pictured Lauren as a sports fan, but it was cool that she liked soccer. Parked on the street near the art museums in the Mount Vernon neighborhood, Lauren suggested they walk up Charles Street until they found something they wanted to eat.

Sam noticed the sky darkening.

"Do you think it's going to rain?" Lauren asked.

Sam shrugged. "Want me to check my phone?"

"Let's keep going. I'm sure we can beat it." She picked up her pace a little. "Oh my God." She grabbed Sam's arm and pointed at a visitor taking a selfie at the monument on the square. "That woman looks like Piper Perabo."

"Who?"

"The actor. She was in *Coyote Ugly*."

"No idea what that is."

"Did you ever see *Imagine Me and You?*" Then, Lauren yelled loudly like a character from the movie.

Everyone on the street stared. Lauren laughed, her head near Sam's. Sam pulled her along to get them away from the others. She was laughing, too.

"My girlfriend Chloe adored that movie."

Sam's brain froze for a moment. Girlfriend? Did she mean girlfriend in the way straight women said it, or did she mean *girlfriend* girlfriend? She didn't have time to reflect on it as the ominous clouds dumped giant splatting raindrops and then a sheet of water on them. Lauren let out a little yelp, took Sam's hand, and jogged to the nearest doorway. Sam studied her features. Was there any chance she had meant a girlfriend the same way Sam would mean it? She wasn't going to ask and risk embarrassing herself or making Lauren uncomfortable.

Lauren tried to see through the frosted glass of the doors. "Must be a bar or something. Let's check it out."

Sam followed her through the double wooden doors into a long, deserted hallway to a large, mostly empty bar that looked like it hadn't changed since 1950. "Talk about a throwback," said Sam.

A female voice she didn't recognize sang a song that sounded like something from an old movie. Sad and sensual. A couple who looked like they should have been having an affair sat in the corner booth, and a middle-aged man in a rumpled suit sat at the bar.

"Look at these." Lauren drew her attention to a series of black-and-white photos on the wall. The people in them wore suits, cocktail dresses, and black ties. Dust lined the top of the frames. When she looked closer, she noticed that none of them looked like her, and the only black person in any of them was the waitstaff.

The windows high on the other side of the room lit up with a flash of lightning, and there was a loud rumble of thunder. Lauren turned, her hair stuck to her forehead. Sam wanted to brush it aside. Run her fingertips gently across her face. "Guess we should have a drink. Looks like we could be here awhile."

Sam pulled out a chair at the nearest table and gestured for Lauren to have a seat. "What do you want?"

"Scotch. Balvenie or Macallan are fine. Neat."

She repeated the names in her head so she wouldn't forget. She didn't know what either of them was, but the bartender did, thank goodness. When she returned, she placed the glass carefully in front of Lauren and slipped into the chair next to her. "One scotch. Neat."

"What did you get?"

"Shirley Temple." As she said it, the silliness of the choice embarrassed her. "I thought it would be more appropriate than a Coke." She removed the cherry and laid it on the drink napkin.

"Do you want that?" Lauren pointed at the cherry.

Sam handed it over and swallowed hard as she watched Lauren take it in her mouth. She looked away before Lauren could catch her staring.

"This place is like a time capsule," said Lauren. "I feel like we dropped into the 1950s. I think I might find my grandmother in one of those photos. She was a bit of a socialite in her day. She used to attend parties at the hotel next door."

The only place Sam's grandma O'Brian would've been was in the kitchen. Working-class Irish. "Is your grandmother still around?"

Lauren nodded. "My parents are older. They had me in their thirties, so my grandmother is eighty-eight. She's in an assisted living facility. She doesn't recognize any of us when we visit, but she seems to appreciate the attention."

"Alzheimer's?"

"No. Simple memory loss. The effects of aging and her long list of medication. Occasionally, she'll pull out a story from her youth. Most of the time, she's quiet but surprisingly happy."

"That must be reassuring." Sam's experience with elderly patients might scare her, so she kept that to herself.

Lauren took a sip. "What about you? Any grandparents?"

"My dad's parents live in Bel Air. Recently retired. Living it up. Planning to live out near the beach one day. After my mother died when I was eight, I lived with them. Everyone thought it was the best thing for me with dad going on so many deployments. My mother's mom lived in North Carolina."

"Is she still there?"

"She died last year."

"I'm so sorry."

"It's okay. We didn't talk much. She was ultra evangelical. Wasn't happy to have a lesbian granddaughter." There, she'd gotten that out of the way. Now Lauren knew for sure where she stood. "My O'Brian family is Catholic, so I can't say they love it either, but they try at least."

"That sounds so hard. Were you close to your North Carolina family at all?"

"Not really, no." Sam looked around the mostly empty bar. If she was going to talk about it, this was as good a place as any. "It's a long story." She took a swig of her drink. "You know I'm a quarter Korean, right?"

"I do. I also know you're Irish and Catholic and an amazing gamer."

"Were you curious about my background?"

"I'm more interested in how you treat me. Plenty of people think I got my job because of my appearance. If I did, it wasn't my fault. I can't control why someone hires me. I just hope that if I work hard, they'll see my success for what it is and not how short my skirt is."

Another lightning strike drew Sam's attention to the windows. "My mother's mom was an army nurse during the Vietnam era. She worked at base hospitals in Japan and Korea. That's where she got pregnant."

She watched Lauren for a reaction. Lauren only listened intently.

"I was eight when my mother died of a congenital heart condition while I was at school. She was always thin and frail. The worst part of my memories is that my North Carolina family treated her like she'd been adopted from Korea, even though she was born in the same hospital I was. She had the same blood running in her veins as theirs, but they seemed to act as though there was an otherness to her and me. She wasn't enough of something to be a Shaw. I'm not certain if it was because she was half-Korean or if it was because she was born out of wedlock, and I guess I'll never know."

Lauren reached out and squeezed her hand. She liked the way it felt.

"When Mom died, it took a week for my dad to be recalled from overseas. By then, I'd heard the whispers and the arguments through closed doors. It was settled by the time he arrived. My O'Brian grandparents came and moved me to Maryland, and Dad went back to Afghanistan. After that, it was 'never a good time' to visit, supposedly." A tear ran down her cheek, but she willed the others to stay put.

Lauren quietly allowed her to finish her story without interruption.

"I can't help but feel my grandmother was ashamed of getting pregnant in Korea, and I don't know why. Did she feel compelled to have my mother? Did she love my grandfather? Did she ever truly love my mother or me?"

Telling someone was a surprising relief. Carrying around the questions had felt like dragging a car that didn't run. She'd never spoken about it to her O'Brian grandparents because she didn't want to hurt their feelings, especially since they'd done so much for her. She was thankful when Lauren said nothing for a while. They sat in silence, sipping their drinks, Lauren's hand still in hers.

"So there you go. My story." Sam lightened her voice to sound more cheerful. Her eyes met Lauren's, and she could see the concern reflected in them.

"Thank you for telling me. If you ever want to talk more, I'm here for you."

Sam slipped her hand from Lauren's grasp. "Looks like the storm has let up. How about some food? I'm hungry."

Lauren stood and pushed her chair away. "Me too."

She felt grateful that Lauren had been the one to listen to her story. Lauren's warmth and quiet attentiveness had a calming effect on her. She found solace in the fact that Lauren listened without passing judgment, especially when talking about the time in her life when she had felt the most criticized. As she watched Lauren, the only nagging question left was, did Lauren mean girlfriend the same way Sam did? If so, things were going to be a lot more complicated because it was hard not to be attracted to someone like Lauren.

CHAPTER SIXTEEN

Indianapolis was the first tournament stop for the *Siege Encounter* team. Lauren stood off to the side of the main stage, watching the games on a monitor. She wasn't as interested in the match as in what the announcers had to say. Anytime a talking head went live, there was no telling what they might say about the Barrage. She needed to be prepared to counter any incorrect statements at the end of the tournament. Will paced back and forth behind the team.

Why he had to come to the tournament, she wasn't sure. The Barrage *Call of Duty* team was playing a league match in Baltimore against their biggest rival. Since they made a lot more money for the company, it seemed like he would want to be there. Instead, he was here, making her job more difficult. His well-known outbursts of both profanity and insensitivity were legendary. No telling what he would say.

And then, there was Sam.

Truth be told, Lauren had been distracted watching Sam instead of listening to the announcers. Ever since the evening they had been caught in the rain, she'd wanted to be closer to her. Standing near her in the kitchen. Looking for her during the lunch hour in the cafeteria. She knew what was going on, but she didn't know how to deal with it. The attraction was growing.

"Hello, darling." Yesenia approached and gave her a couple of air kisses.

During a lull between games, Lauren watched Sam reach to scratch her head. No. No. Don't touch the wig, she thought. Sam pulled her hand away just in time. What a relief. Women wore wigs all the time so that wasn't a big deal, but a wig askew in the middle of the final game. That would be a big deal.

"Augustan is going bankrupt," said Yesenia.

Lauren turned to her in shock. "Bankrupt? What?"

"Kidding. You were not paying attention. I needed to bring your focus back to me. You know everything is about me."

Lauren gave her a look. "I do not need your attempt at humor right now."

"What's wrong?"

"Nothing."

"Worried about the newbie?"

Lauren looked back at Sam. She was sitting stock still, like she was afraid to move for fear her wig would fall off. "Jesus, relax," she muttered.

"She does appear a little stiff. Whose idea was the wig?"

"Will chose it."

"What was wrong with her hair? I liked it. Very sci-fi chic."

"He thought she looked too much like a guy." Lauren couldn't help the exasperation in her voice.

Yesenia pursed her lips. "She has that quality someone like Tilda Swinton can carry off. Moments where she looks feminine and moments where she is masculine. And they are both attractive."

How was she going to broach this subject? Yesenia was a friend, but they collaborated for work, and she was Lauren's best shot at moving to Augustan someday in the future. If Lauren told her what was going on in her head, would that be too far over the line? She lowered her voice to a heavy whisper. "Have you ever found another woman attractive?"

"Of course." She began counting on her fingers as she spoke. "Cate Blanchett. Zendaya. Lupita Nyong'o."

"I meant in real life."

"We aren't playing celebrity crush? Oh, sweetie, if you think I'm attractive, I'm flattered, but Bodhan got here first."

Lauren knew she was teasing.

"My dentist, perhaps? She's quite beautiful."

"Your dentist? Ew."

"Why? Has a woman caught your eye? Don't tell Seth. It will hurt his manly ego. I'm intrigued, though. Do tell."

Now that Lauren had brought up the subject, she wanted to shove it back in the proverbial bottle. She glanced at Sam. She was in the midst of game three of the final match, and Lauren wasn't even paying any attention to the gameplay. "It was a hypothetical question."

"I see."

Lauren realized she'd given away the plot by looking right at Sam as they spoke. She looked around to make sure no one was listening. "Nothing has happened. And it won't."

"Why not? You're both adults."

"We work together. Christ, we live together."

Yesenia took out her phone.

"What are you doing?"

"I was checking the date to make sure it was still the twenty-first century." She put the phone in her purse. "No one cares, sweetie."

"Plenty of people care. And I care. I can't take my eyes off her. I'm supposed to be working."

Yesenia shrugged. "Drop a few subtle hints. Better yet, tell her you like her and see what she says."

"Are you insane? I'm not going to say, hey BTWs, since you've been living with me, I've gotten a crush on you."

"Why not? I'm assuming she's not your first girl crush." Yesenia gave her a knowing smile.

"No, she's not. I had a girlfriend before Seth."

"Sam's not a direct report, is she?"

"No."

"Is there anything in your contract regarding dating players?"

"Not that I remember."

"Do you think it would affect your productivity?"

She frowned. It was already affecting her work. She was standing here talking about Sam instead of doing her job.

"Ask her out to dinner. It's no different from asking one of the men hovering around us right now."

"Yes, but men are so easy to read. They're pretty much all the same. They admire my breasts, and they stand an inch taller and start sticking out their chests. I don't know if she is interested or not. I mean, a few times I thought she might be." The moment they'd unexpectedly seen each other in the apartment hallway came to mind. "But she's intensely private, so I'm not sure what she thinks."

Yesenia tapped a perfectly manicured nail on her temple. "I say ask her. What's the worst that could happen? She says no."

"Oh my God. I would die on the spot."

"A no would be that devastating?"

"Yes."

Yesenia looked shocked. "Have you never been turned down?"

"Not since I was fourteen. I had a terrible crush on Jim Bean."

"Jim Beam? Like the alcohol?"

"Jim Bean. Everyone called him Beanie."

"This is starting out interestingly. Do continue with Mr. Beanie."

"He was one of those guys who had gotten held back a few times, so he was much more mature-looking than the rest of the guys in our class. He was already sporting a spotty beard by the end of each school day. All the girls thought he was the hottest thing since Robert Pattinson."

Yesenia raised an eyebrow.

"*Twilight*?"

Yesenia made a little eye roll.

"Anyway. I was in calculus, and one of his friends told me he wanted to go out with me, but he was too shy to ask."

"Hold on." Yesenia raised her hand to make her pause. "You took calculus when you were fourteen?"

"Um, yeah. Didn't you?"

"Oh, sweetie. I was reading obscure Spanish literature, studying politics, exploring Barcelona as only teenagers can, and smoking cigarettes. Calculus did not even enter the equation."

Now it was Lauren's turn to roll her eyes at the terrible pun.

"So what happened with Mr. Beanie?"

"I got excited and went up to him when he was in a group with some of his friends, certain he was going to be glad I asked him out, being shy and all. Turned out, the guy in my class was pulling a prank on me. Beanie didn't even know who I was. Well, he did after that but not at the time. It was the worst feeling I ever had. I'd walk the halls, certain that everyone was staring at me and laughing. After that, I always let men take the lead."

"What about Seth?"

"He was practically drooling when we met. There was no confusion about it."

Yesenia leaned in closer. "I have a story for you now. If I hadn't made a move on Bohdan, he never would have asked me out." She waved a hand to emphasize her point. "Is a long-distance thing difficult? Yes. But when I'm with him, it is worth every extra effort. I'd do it again, too. What's that silly adage? You miss one hundred percent of the shots you don't take? But it's true. For me, happiness was worth taking the risk of rejection."

That sounded like Lauren's feelings about business.

Yesenia continued, "If you didn't know if Augustan would hire you, would you still apply?"

"Of course."

"Why?"

"Because I want it."

"And would you never try again if you didn't get it?"

"Of course not. So many factors go into hiring decisions. Budgets, retirements, lateral moves, favorite insiders."

Yesenia gave her a look that said, "Are you hearing what I'm not saying?"

"Oh." Lauren looked back at Sam. So intent and focused. Not like some of the other players who were yelling or jumping up and down when they got a kill or got killed. She stayed calm. And that external coolness, that James Dean in *Giant*, with his cowboy hat on and his boots up, was attractive. "I'm not sure it's a good idea."

Yesenia waved to another industry insider nearby. "I've got to go do my job." She surprised Lauren with a genuine hug. In her ear, she said, "Don't let this chance get away from you."

Lauren looked back at Sam on stage. Dylan and Perry were congratulating each other. They had won. Sam looked around, found her, and smiled. Lauren's stomach fluttered. She was definitely falling for her. Lauren got pulled into making a statement for one of the gaming news reporters and took her eyes off the stage.

Fifteen minutes later, someone stepped close, startling her. "Hey, roomie."

She was relieved that it was Sam but was also self-conscious, having discussed her feelings with Yesenia a few minutes ago. As they walked, she stole a brief glance at her. Sam walked with a lot of confidence tonight. She wondered if it was a protective swagger or real confidence. "You played great today."

"Thanks."

She thought about what Yesenia had said, but her throat tightened when she tried to come up with the words to ask Sam out.

"I've never been to Indy before," said Sam, breaking the silence. "I took a walk around the neighborhood. Did you know there's a canal a few blocks that way?" She pointed in a vague direction.

Lauren didn't. She was certain she'd spent every trip here at the convention center, the Westin, and a meal or two at Nada. She was always so busy, or she was trying to stay busy and not think about the fact something was missing in her life. Instead of asking Sam out, the dumbest words dripped from her lips: "I've got an interview lined up for you at 8:30 tomorrow, so don't sleep in. It's a podcast. No video. But please wear your team polo or jacket."

Sam saluted. "Yes, ma'am."

How could Lauren possibly follow telling her to get up on time with asking her out on a date? She couldn't. It would have to wait for a better time. She stepped into the elevator with an older couple who seemed confused by all the casually dressed young men filling the car. Sam waved at her.

"Aren't you coming?" Lauren asked.

Sam pointed. "Taking the stairs. Need the exercise."

Lauren stuck her hand in the closing doors and jumped out, apologizing to the others in the elevator. "Wait up." She followed Sam into the stairwell. What was she doing? She looked up. Ten floors. She could do it. What was the point of all that jogging if she couldn't walk up to her hotel room?

After two floors, Sam waited for her on the landing. "You trying to prove something?"

"Yes." She slipped off her heels and carried them. "That I'm kind of stupid. I'll remember not to wear these in a fire." On the third floor, she was huffing and puffing. Halfway between four and five, her heart pounded in her ears, and by six, her thighs were burning. "Why is this so much harder than running?"

"Activation of different muscles," Sam replied.

Lauren stopped and leaned over, trying to catch her breath. "How are you in such good shape? You're not even breathing hard."

"My old job required a lot of physical activity. I needed to be strong. Besides, I always take the stairs."

Lauren thought about it for a minute. It was true. She'd never been in an elevator with Sam at the apartment building or the office.

Sam bent to her eye level. "I could carry you and your shoes the rest of the way."

Lauren laughed through several deep breaths. Sam must have taken that as a challenge because she reached down and lifted her like she was carrying a bride over the threshold and began walking up to the next level.

Lauren grabbed Sam around the shoulders. "Put me down. You're going to hurt yourself." Her protest was half-hearted. When was the last time someone had carried her anywhere? When she had first dated Seth, when he'd been in a hurry to get to a bed or sofa in a moment of passion, and she was taking too long. She threw that thought out of her mind.

She did not want to think of Seth right now. Not when she could feel the muscles in Sam's back working as she carried her. She could feel how strong her arms were. All those baggy clothes Sam wore around the apartment hid her strength. Lauren's shirt had come untucked, and she could feel Sam's fingertips against her skin.

She laid her head against Sam's shoulder and listened to her breathing. Heavy and sure. She looked at the soft skin of her jaw where it met her ear. She wanted to reach out and run her finger down the side of her neck along the straining muscle. Underneath her collar. Down the front. To undo a button or two.

She raised her head. "Put me down."

"It's okay." Sam smiled. "I'm stronger than I look."

"Put me down," Lauren said more seriously.

Sam did as she asked when they reached the landing of the ninth floor. The concrete was cold. Lauren dropped her hands from Sam's shoulders, running them along her arms. Sam stared at her. Now she was breathing heavily. Was it exertion or desire? She knew which one it was for her, and she needed to get control of it.

Something had changed in the past few weeks. The dinners. The walks. Sam had even begun watching Lauren's favorite anime with her, though she rolled her eyes about the silly romances. She was like Lauren's dad. He said he hated the cat, but she'd find him asleep in his wingback chair with the cat on his lap.

The exit door opened. Lauren jumped away from Sam.

"Everything all right?" asked the hotel security guard.

Lauren ran a hand through her hair. "We had the bright idea of walking up the stairs." She dangled her heels and laughed nervously. "Not my best plan."

"Lots of folks do it. Have a good evening." The guard smiled and moved down the stairs to the floor below.

Lauren was mortified. Anyone who looked at her would know she was attracted to Sam. She pulled open the door and hurried down the hall.

"Lauren," Sam called.

"I'm taking the elevator. I'll see you tomorrow." She rushed to push the button, concerned Sam might follow her, but she didn't. When the elevator opened on the tenth floor, Lauren ducked into her room and closed the door, afraid to look behind her.

What was she thinking? Even if Sam wasn't her coworker or her roommate, she was a gamer. Her life was about to become late nights, travel, and weird online groupies. Seth had taught her a hard lesson about the gamer life. Twice he'd cheated on her. That she'd known of. How many others might there have been?

But Sam was hot, and every part of Lauren's body was telling her so. She stood with her back against the door, part of her hoping Sam would knock and ask to come in. She was certain she'd do it. She would slide the handle down and pull the door wide open. But she heard nothing. Of course not. Why would Sam follow her? She'd awkwardly demanded to be put down and had run away. Besides, was she even Sam's type?

When the knock happened, she threw open the door without hesitation. Only it wasn't Sam.

"Seth."

He pushed past her and came in without so much as a how are you.

Chapter Seventeen

Sam sat on the end of her bed. What the hell had happened? She thought they'd had a moment in the stairwell. But it must have only been in her mind. Why else would Lauren have run away? And by the time Sam had made it to their floor, Seth Madden was going into Lauren's room. Did they have a hookup planned? Surely, she hadn't called him in the elevator.

She must have scared Lauren when she'd picked her up and carried her, but she'd needed to do something with the extra energy around her. When Lauren had touched her arms and gazed into her eyes, Sam had wanted to kiss her. If the guard hadn't interrupted, she would have.

She flopped in the desk chair, lifted open her laptop, and slipped on her headphones. No surprise that her former teammates were on Discord. She messaged Olivia and switched to voice chat.

"All right, show-off. We watched your match tonight. Nice job."

"Thanks."

"What's up?"

"I think I did something wrong."

Olivia said something loud and in Spanish, obviously aggravated at the game she was playing in the background. "Ashton is not you," she complained. "Something at your company or at the tournament? You want me to bring the rest of the crew on for a postmortem? We're almost done with this game." Sam could hear the clacking of Olivia's keyboard as she was firing her weapon. "Son of bitch. That's like the fourth time this guy has killed me."

"I carried Lauren up the stairs," she admitted.

"Was she drunk?"

"No."

"Were you drunk?"

Sam didn't even bother to answer. Olivia knew better. Sam didn't let herself get out of control ever.

"Oh. No, no, no. Ashton scored more points than me? Hang on. Let me tell them I'm out for a game."

Sam waited while Olivia went silent. Her fingers itched to be playing with them, but she needed to rest before tomorrow's final.

Olivia returned. "I'm all ears. Did she fall or something?"

"Nope."

"I'm getting tired of twenty questions. Tell me what the damn problem is?"

She kind of wanted Olivia to guess rather than have to say it out loud. She was nervous thinking about it. "I think I almost kissed her."

"Almost as in you tried and failed? Or tried and had second thoughts?"

"Neither."

"You didn't try to kiss her, did you?"

"I guess not, but I thought about it. Real hard."

"But you didn't, so no foul, no harm."

"No harm, no foul."

"Yes, that's right."

"You said…never mind." She shook her head. "Lauren had to have known."

"Do you want her to know?"

"What?"

"Do you want her to know that you like her and want to kiss her?"

"No." That sounded horrible. What if Lauren rejected her? What if she threw her out of the apartment? What if she accused her of sexual harassment? Sam could think of so many reasons she didn't want her to know. "We work together," was all that came out of her mouth.

"I'm pretty certain that never stopped anyone. Workplace romance is a whole category of novels."

"Have you seen her? There is no way someone as put together and…and…beautiful would want to be with someone like me."

"Hold up. Where is all this 'she's too sexy' shit coming from? You're always 'so-and-so is not my type' or 'so-and-so is too clingy.' When was the last time you wanted to kiss someone and didn't?"

"Never. But…" Oh, this was bad.

"They didn't mean anything. Because you have to spend more than one night with someone for it to mean something."

Ouch, that burned.

As if reading her mind, Olivia said, "*Chica*, you are in big trouble but not because you did anything wrong. Because you *like* Lauren."

Sam hung her head. She did like Lauren. A lot. "It doesn't matter because I think she got a booty call from Seth Madden."

"The ex who cheated on her?"

"The same one."

"I'm changing my recommendation. Go get laid."

"Not helpful. I gotta go."

"Oh no, you don't. You can't call me up and make me ditch the team and then say you have to go." Though her words were serious, her tone was light and playful.

"I'll text you after the tournament."

"You better. I hate when they cancel the series before the story ends."

Sam frowned.

Olivia added, "A metaphor, Sam. I need to know the rest of the story. You know. Did you, didn't you?"

"I can already tell you the end. Nothing is going to happen."

"Spoiler alert would be nice. Good luck tomorrow. You got this."

"Later."

With Discord closed, Sam stared at the desktop background: a screen grab of one environment she'd made for her virtual reality headset home screen. She could live online and never feel alone. Why did she feel so alone in the real world? Maybe Olivia was right. Maybe she needed to find some stranger to fill her emptiness. Even if she had kissed Lauren, chances were, they wouldn't make it further than a night at best and a kiss at worst, and she didn't like that idea.

Chapter Eighteen

The morning of the Indianapolis tournament finals, there was a knock at Sam's hotel room door. She opened it to find Lauren looking fresh and perfect, wearing a monochrome silk blouse and skirt. Her heels even matched. She moved past Sam and entered the room. "You ready for this? Big day. Your first match final as a pro."

Sam blinked a few times. Lauren was backlit by the sunlight streaming through the window. Sam could see the outline of her legs through the skirt she wore. Wasn't that what a slip was for? So someone like Sam wouldn't lust over the silhouette of Lauren's legs? No surprise that Seth regretted leaving Lauren and tried to get back with her last night, if even for only a little while. What was confusing was why Lauren would want him back? At least after what she'd told Sam about their relationship.

"Come on." Lauren walked to the closet and pulled out the wig. "Let's get you dressed."

Sam knew her face had fallen into resting bitch mode as she looked at the wig.

Lauren bumped her gently. "Pretend you're in costume."

Wasn't she in a costume every day? Who was she really?

All pimped out and ready, she followed Lauren through the crowds to the pregame room. Even in a wig, she didn't get the stares Lauren did. She felt protective of her. She wanted to tell the guys off. Put an arm around Lauren and claim her as her girlfriend. But she knew that wasn't ever going to happen.

Perry whistled when she entered the team room.

Dylan looked up. "What the hell, O'Brian? I still can't get used to you looking like a real girl."

Perry laughed.

She didn't answer. Of course the only compliment he could pay her was about the way she looked. She flopped in the nearest chair and swiveled around a few times. Luke brought her a Coke. "Thanks." He'd turned out to be a good guy. Once they had gotten over the fact that he was the backup, he'd been eager to talk to her about strategy. He was at the end of his career, having been a mediocre *Call of Duty* player. He wanted to keep playing as long as he could. She got it. At twenty-five, she probably only had a year if she was lucky enough to stick around at all.

Will entered the room. "You bastards better play your hearts out. I'm counting on you."

"Okay. We're up." Alec grabbed his tablet and rounded them all up.

Sam bounced nervously as she waited to take the stage for the final. She wanted to pull up her hoodie, but they still wouldn't give her a hooded version of the jersey, and it wouldn't matter anyway because the damn wig would shift if she did. Why had they picked the longest braid she'd ever seen?

Lauren grabbed her and said, "Good luck. You can do this." Then, she smiled, and Sam's stomach did a little flip.

Dylan's comment was a little less encouraging. "Don't fuck it up," he said as they walked to the stage.

She had no intention of it.

She wasn't the only one who seemed out of sorts. As the first game started, the entire team seemed off. She tried her best, but each time she died and respawned, she thought of Lauren watching her somewhere in the crowd or on the stream.

"Get in the game, O'Brian," Dylan said over her headset.

She moved out, this time trying an underwater route to the checkpoint. Not her favorite thing to do, but this was hardcore. No extras, no heads-up display. No map. No heat sensors. No radar advantage. Nothing. Only straight-up strategy. Usually, nothing entered her mind but paths and angles and play style and the ways the other team was using the maps. Like math equations in her head. She knew where they would be and where they expected her to be. This was what made her a good player. What she had worked on since she was ten years old. Watching the best of the best play on their streams and breaking down their performances in slow motion, repeatedly, looking for patterns, quirks, and the things that made them better than everyone else.

Now, as she moved through the map, her thoughts wandered to last night. To the look on Lauren's face when Sam put her on the ground and still held her waist. How she had wanted to lean in and kiss her. What it might have looked like from the outside, like a camera circling them, capturing it all. She could hear music playing in her head. But none of what was racing through her thoughts had anything to do with the buttons she was pushing on her keyboard.

She was playing this game on autopilot, and anyone watching who knew anything about *Siege Encounter* would be able to tell. She should not have been here. She should not have been on this team. She was not contributing anything to this final. She ripped off her headset.

Alec leaned over her. "What are you doing?" he asked.

"Nothing. I'm fine."

The noise of the crowd cheering and the sound of the announcers talking about their play filled her head. Without being able to hear her competitors' footsteps in game or the commands of her teammates, she'd be playing at a disadvantage. But what she'd been doing wasn't working. She needed to play unpredictably and without concern.

And that was what she did.

They won games five, six, and seven, tying the final at 4-4. One more game would decide the tournament. One more win would mean the team would split a twenty thousand dollar prize. Five thousand dollars for four days of playing a game she loved. Except she didn't care about the money. Sure, she knew she could pay off her student loans with it. But it wasn't the reason she wanted to win this last game. This was what she was born to do. This was what she loved to do. It was all she had dreamed of when she'd first explored gaming as a kid. It left her mind so preoccupied, she didn't think about all the things that left her feeling alone in the real world.

Her father lived in his own world. Damaged from eight tours in Afghanistan to the point she worried about him when he was home alone for too long. And her mother...how could she ever explain how she felt about the death of her mother to anyone, especially to people who had never known her? Why would she want to get involved with someone like Lauren? Someone who would surely tire of her morose ways and her lack of sophistication.

Dylan threw her headset on her lap. "Put it on. I need you to hear what we need from you. This game is too important for you to play diva."

Sam laughed. No one had ever called her a diva. Not once. A robot. Unfeeling. Cold. But a diva? She slipped the headset on.

"This is it." Dylan's voice was clear. "I say we vote down the last map."

Perry disagreed. "We just won on it. I think we should stick with what is working."

"By the slimmest margin of points ever. Vote down this map."

So far, Sam had said nothing in any of the games. She'd kept her mouth shut and played her game. They had little to say to her and asked her opinion exactly never. But if they wanted to win, they needed to stay with the previous map. This week, she'd repeatedly watched the other team's game streams. And even though her mind had wandered to Lauren multiple times, somewhere in her subconscious, she had been able to identify their opponents' patterns.

"They will be better on the second map," she said.

"What do you know?" Dylan snapped. "You've been a pro all of six weeks. I'm the team captain, and I say we vote down this map."

She should have stayed quiet, let him accept the consequences, but she thought of Lauren. How she tried to tell them things they needed to hear in ways that would get them to listen. "I might be wrong, but I believe they will play better on the second map." The words lay heavy on her tongue. The rest of them she made clear and factual. "I watched their last twenty tournaments. They love flat maps with fewer obstacles, less height, and three clear lane layouts."

"I agree with Sam," said Perry.

"What the hell? We get an amateur with boobs, and now you fucking go rogue on me?"

Well, so much for trying to be nice. "What do my boobs have to do with anything? I used my brain. I spent hours watching their gameplay."

The next voice was their manager. He'd pulled on a headset. "All right, I don't know what got everyone losing their minds, but people can hear you even if you aren't on the live feed. Cut out the language, now. Make your votes, or we're going to get disqualified for delaying the game."

Sam pushed her vote. She watched as the votes totaled. Perry had voted with her and against Dylan. She let out a sigh. One hurdle down. Six minutes of stress to go.

She heard someone say her name. She looked to her side. Lauren stood there in her pencil skirt with her lanyard. Next to her, one of the tournament social media team held a phone in the air, taking a photo. Sam didn't take her headset off. Lauren's voice was muted, but she could read her lips. "Good luck," she said and stepped away from the stage.

Sam watched her go. Her heartbeat pounded in her chest the same way it had when they were in the stairwell last night. Lauren was a distraction.

The game was the longest six minutes of her life. If this went bust, she'd be persona non grata with the rest of the team. Even so, it was a team. She wasn't the only one playing. If they lost on this map, they would have lost worse on the other one. She was certain of it.

She wiped the sweat from her hands on her pants and reseated her headset, careful not to move her ridiculous wig. The noise-canceling deadened the outside crowd noise. A lot of team chatter filled the silence quickly. The others were excitable and talked a lot when nervous. She'd never been that way. She went into her zone. No smiles. No reactions.

She knew that was why the team had nicknamed her the "glacial goddess." They meant it as in she was cold and heartless. But she wasn't. She didn't feel the need to show every emotion on the outside. Most of the time, she was more interested in the world of computers than in making friends. There was so much to create. And now that she was here, a pro in her sport, she was wondering if this was what she wanted at all?

But she played as if her life depended on it. She wouldn't be the reason they came in second. She would play her absolute best. Focused, fast, aware, consistently accurate, able to change her game plan to meet the other teams' threats and style of play. And when it was over, she looked up at the big screen above them as it ran an animation of their team's name, declaring their win.

She laid her headset on her keyboard and let out a long breath. They'd done it. They'd won. She'd won. Her first professional in-person competition was over, and she was a member of the winning team. She wished she had her phone. She'd take a selfie and send it to Olivia and the others. Hopefully, they were watching and would give her grief about her play later tonight.

"Good game," the other team's captain acknowledged her.

"Good game," she replied. The rest of the players shared congratulations. They were respectful, not rude like the amateur teams she'd played in Baltimore. Joining the team now felt like the right decision after all. Even Dylan grudgingly slapped her shoulder in excitement.

The crowd was excited for them, too. With her headset off, the cheers from the mostly younger crowd were loud. She stood and waved with the rest of the team. Then, she saw Lauren, and she smiled for real. Lauren smiled back and looked away as if she was embarrassed but not in a bad way. In a sweet way that captured Sam's heart. She was the biggest distraction ever.

"Good job, O'Brian," said Alec.

"Thanks." Relief flooded her. She'd proven herself on her first big test. One small step to the world championships. Her probationary period would end soon. She hoped they'd keep her after this. Would that mean she'd move out of Lauren's apartment? She looked for her in the crowd as the tournament staff moved them to where the announcers waited to ask them to break down the post-gameplay.

As she moved through the crowd, she saw Ahn Ji-ho with a group of sponsor VIPs. He watched her carefully, like a large predator assessing its prey. The Koreans were in the Western division, while the Barrage was in the Eastern division. They wouldn't meet in competition until the finals, if either team got there. She almost wished Alec would schedule a scrimmage against them as a test. She'd have to ask.

CHAPTER NINETEEN

The lights on the announcers' set were bright. When Sam took her seat at the end of the row, she couldn't see anyone in the audience, only the blinding lights. An audio guy rushed up and slid a lavalier mic up Dylan's shirt and clipped it in place. Then, he looked at her and frowned. He thrust the mic at her, and she took it, but as she was about to try to clip it on, Lauren appeared at her side.

"Let me." She took the battery pack and clipped it under Sam's shirt on her waistband. Then, she took the microphone and pulled her shirt away from her body. "I'm going to run this up inside your shirt. You good with that?"

Sam swallowed hard. "Yup." Lauren's fingers tickled where they touched her. As Lauren fed the mic over her chest, the closeness made Sam breathe faster. It was impossible not to. Lauren was beautiful, and she smelled clean and sweet. She was so close that if Sam turned toward her, they'd touch foreheads.

Shit. She was definitely aroused. She had gotten turned on by how Lauren put a lavalier microphone up her shirt. Who did that?

Lauren looked up from her handiwork. Could she tell that Sam was having a hard time not letting her know she wanted to finish that almost kiss in the stairwell? She leaned closer and spoke in a soft whisper. Sam thought she might combust. "Don't forget to treat the mic as if it is always hot. Meaning, it is always recording what you say. Watch out for the get-to-know you chitchat. It's a great way for them to get something to use that you didn't intend to say."

Sam nodded. All she could think about was how beautiful Lauren's eyes were. How she had perfect eyebrows. How did someone have perfect eyebrows? And why did Sam care about them?

Get it together, O'Brian. "I'm cool." She didn't know what to expect. What if she said something stupid? *Ugh.*

As if reading her mind, Lauren said, "You'll be fine," and stepped away, leaving Sam nervous and aroused.

Sam glanced at her teammates. None of them looked anxious at all. They were laughing and smiling. Perry was randomly punching Dylan's shoulder lightly. Neither of them had to worry about being the first or only anything today.

When the countdown for the postgame live stream started, she turned her attention to the cameras and smiled. Holding a smile for more than a few moments felt unnatural. She didn't care what the announcers were saying. It was all a rehash of the match. What were you thinking at this point? Why did you choose this map and this type of gameplay?

The attention made her feel vulnerable and exposed; she hated it. Lauren had warned her not to roll her lips inward or risk getting lipstick on her teeth. Now she sat still and stiff. Afraid to relax. She hated the smell of the foundation and the taste of the lipstick, and she was certain her eyes were going to be red when she was done. And this wig. She kept wanting to scratch her head.

She was a mannequin. It was fine because Dylan did most of the talking. He obviously enjoyed his role as team captain. He liked the spotlight.

The first few questions for the rest of the team were easy. How long had they played video games? What were their favorite games? *Siege Encounter*, of course. What was life like as a pro? Being a professional meant sacrificing personal time and constantly striving for excellence. What was the favorite team snack? Perry took that question. Utz chips, of course.

Not that she expected the team to be asked about world peace or foreign affairs, but could these questions be any inaner?

"Why Seven?"

She realized the announcer, a guy with a greased up wavy hair and small eyes, was speaking to her. "Sorry." She'd missed the context of the question.

"Samantha, why is your gamer tag Seven?"

She cringed at the use of her full name. No one seemed to care that she wanted to be called Sam. She rubbed her neck around the collar of her shirt. "One of my online friends is a sixty-year-old guy who loves Star Trek. He suggested I be called Seven of Nine, the Borg character. She was in the *Picard* show recently. But Augustan doesn't allow you to use names that are property of other creative companies, so it became Seven."

"But *why* Seven?" he asked. "I mean, you're not wearing a skintight onesie." He and the other male announcer laughed. Even her teammates chuckled.

She kept her smile painted on and answered as calmly as she could. "Because I stay cool and logical under pressure, and I assimilate the best of competitors' gameplay."

"But none of us would object if she wanted to cosplay at the team house," said Dylan.

She felt her smile drop. Way to take her answer about her strength and turn it into a sexual joke.

"You were unstoppable in the final game," said the only woman on the panel. A former semi-professional player who ran a Twitch stream, she was dressed in a blousy dress with bare shoulders. Sam was thankful for the change of subject. "You were on fire. Your K-D was amazing. You couldn't miss."

From the corner of her eye, she could see Dylan shifting uncomfortably in his chair. He wanted all the credit for the win. The attention on her was irritating him. He wasn't the only one. She didn't want any of the attention. She wanted to slip from the stage and track down Lauren. To talk to her about what had happened last night.

"How does it feel to be the top point scorer of the tournament?"

Sam looked around. Surely, she was asking one of the others, but with everyone on the panel staring at her, it was obvious they were waiting for her answer. "Um. I didn't know."

Some forced laughter from the others.

"A number of fans and pundits say that your success is doubly important because you're a woman, proving that women players can compete head-to-head with men in the top ranks. What are your thoughts on that?"

She wanted to say the same thing she'd said to Dylan earlier. What did her boobs have to do with anything? She knew she was taking too long to answer, but her mind had gone blank. "I'm here to compete."

Why hadn't she come up with something, anything, that was better than that sucky answer?

"What's it like being the first Korean American player in the league?"

The question caught her off guard. She should have planned for this, knowing someone would eventually ask. She swallowed and looked around. She felt like a teenager again, unable to speak on behalf of a community she had never felt a part of. Strangely, her gaze fell on Ahn Ji-ho, who was barely visible on the edge of her vision, watching her with interest.

Thank goodness the announcer asked a different question when she froze. "Will we see you in Pittsburgh in three weeks?"

She didn't know what the team had planned for her.

Alec stepped in and answered for her. "Samantha will absolutely be in Pittsburgh. We wouldn't leave her behind. Not after that showing."

Sam, she wanted to scream.

Dylan still looked miffed, and Perry had crossed his arms. Clearly, they didn't like all the attention on her. She wondered what Lauren was thinking about her performance. The thought made her want to finish strong.

"I'm a newbie on the team," she said. "These guys made my job easy. They've been playing together for months. And Luke stepped up to assist me with lots of practice games." She pointed to Luke standing off to the side of the stage. He looked surprised. "Without their teamwork, I'd have had nothing."

The team's supporters in the audience liked that response. Her jaw tensed. She had repeated something she heard Lauren say in an interview. Lauren was a pro at redirecting everyone's attention to the guys and their fragile egos.

Sam didn't care about the attention. She didn't play the game for announcers from a streaming broadcast to stroke her ego. She'd have been happy to review the stats in a day or two and enter them in the Excel file she kept for tracking her performance. What she wanted was to play and win.

There were a few more questions for Alec but none for her, thank God. She pulled on her smile again and held it frozen in place until someone said it was a wrap.

While she struggled to get the lavalier microphone off, the woman announcer came by and congratulated her on the win and wished her good luck. Sam thanked her, and then, she was up and moving. She watched Ahn Ji-ho step away from the stage. She wondered what he thought of her. Was he from the same place as her grandfather?

Lauren stood at the side of the stage in conversation with an older man in a button-down and a light sweater vest. Who wore a sweater vest in the middle of the summer? Sam didn't like how his gaze fell to Lauren's body more than once. Granted, she'd taken more than one look herself, but it seemed different when it was someone else. Anyone else. Ugh. She had to stop thinking that way. Lauren could take care of herself.

When Sam stopped to wait for Lauren, Dylan bumped her shoulder. He didn't slow or apologize, meaning it was intentional. She firmly believed that he would never accept her as part of the team. Luke passed by, casting her a sympathetic look that hinted at an apology for Dylan's behavior. He shouldn't need to apologize. It wasn't his fault.

Lauren appeared to excuse herself, and when her gaze fell on Sam, Sam's heart skipped a beat. Could anyone be more beautiful? "Hey, great job," said Lauren when she got closer.

Sam shrugged. "You know I looked as nervous as I felt."

Lauren waved off the comment. "Trust me. You did great. I couldn't keep my eyes off you." Was she blushing? She pointed to her tablet. "FYI, it was one of the most watched matches for any of the Barrage teams this season. You were amazing."

Sam tried to stay focused instead of nervous. She was going to do it. She was going to ask her to have dinner with her. "I was wondering…" Her question drifted away when she saw Seth Madden approaching. He wore a cheesy grin, and he seemed to strut.

"Lauren." He glanced at Sam.

No, not your type, buddy.

Lauren's demeanor turned cool. "Seth."

He threw a thumb over his shoulder. "I was wondering if you had time for a drink before you head back to Baltimore."

Lauren glanced nervously at Sam. "Sorry. Sam and I are heading out for a late dinner. Then, I have an early flight in the morning."

Sam tried not to look surprised.

He gave Sam a bit more scrutiny, then stuck out his hand. "Seth Madden." She shook it. "You're a damn good player. Especially for a girl."

She clenched her jaw so hard, she was certain she was about to break a tooth. She spit out a thanks.

Will called to him. He walked away. "Let's catch up later," he said to Lauren as he went. Sam could see his pleading gaze. He was a like a puppy.

"I'm very busy," said Lauren. She looked relieved when he turned away.

"You sure you don't want to have dinner with him?" Sam asked hesitantly. She flashed back to seeing him enter Lauren's hotel room last night.

Her eyes went wide. "Not in a million years."

"But...um..." She didn't know how to put this delicately.

Lauren squinted at her. "What?"

"I saw him...go into your room." Sam wanted to melt into the floor. Saying it out loud was unbearable.

"My room? Oh." Lauren looked surprised and a little embarrassed. "Not what you're thinking. He'd had a few drinks and got all nostalgic and weepy. I gave him a couple of glasses of water, listened to his sad story, and sent him back to his own room with a warning that he shouldn't come back again."

Sam was relieved. She rubbed the back of her neck. "Sorry, I jumped to conclusions."

"I'm glad we cleared that up. I wouldn't want you thinking I'm hooking up at every convention." She bumped her hip. Then she added, "Or at any convention."

"No judgment if you were."

Lauren gazed at her as if trying to see what was in her mind. If she could read her mind, she'd see that Sam wanted to be the one in her room last night, not Seth.

Lauren scrutinized her. "I'm pretty sure you were judging me a little," she said lightly.

"A little," she admitted. "But only because he was a dick to you, and I wouldn't want you to be treated that way again."

"That is sweet of you to defend my honor." Lauren cast her eyes in a different direction before asking, "You sure that's the only reason?"

Sam felt short of breath. Was Lauren asking if she was jealous? Because she was.

Lauren pivoted the conversation before she could answer. "Looks like I made us a dinner date without consulting you. If you need to do something else, I completely understand."

"No." Sam's reply came out so fast, even she was surprised. "I'm starving. There's a food truck out on the street selling pulled pork sandwiches. I'm down with that if you are."

"Sure. I'm easy to please."

Sam's imagination went ballistic at that statement. She replayed the moment in the stairwell last night, but this time, she kissed her in the memory.

"I need to do a couple of things first. I can meet you outside in a half an hour," said Lauren.

Sam nodded agreement. "Yeah, sure." She watched Lauren walk away. Relief flooded her. Lauren hadn't had a late-night booty call with Seth. Now the question was, did she feel the same way about their moment in the staircase as Sam did?

A tournament assistant handed back her cell phone. She turned it on, her regret immediate. Her DMs were full.

Hey, sexy, DM me when you're in Chicago. We'll have fun together.

Here's what you need. The message included a photo she wished she could unsee. There were more, each one as disgusting as the next. Then there were the ones that didn't make any sense at all.

Go back to China!

You call yourself a pro. You're a loser.

And it wasn't only the message content. Someone had doxxed her, providing access to her massage scheduling software. Now her work schedule was full of fake appointments and disgusting comments.

I hear you do Asian style real good. Long time.

Do I get a happy ending with my massage?

There were strangers telling her to own her Korean heritage and others saying she was too whitewashed to be Asian. She sat on the edge of the stage. This roller coaster of a day was getting out of control. She'd lost her appetite. She texted Lauren:

Hey, not feeling well. I'm going to go to bed.

Oh no! Text me if you need anything. She sent a nurse's cap and a bowl of soup emoji.

Sam wanted to smile, but she couldn't. She leaned over and hung her head between her knees. What could possibly happen next?

CHAPTER TWENTY

Lauren rubbed her eyes. She hadn't slept well last night. Her mind had drifted to thoughts about Sam. How Sam would move out soon and how Lauren was attracted to her. How she was thinking about her all the time. As she sat in the meetings while Will droned on about his latest ridiculous idea for building appeal. While she stood in the bathroom brushing her teeth. While she ate dinner alone. Honestly, all the time.

She'd been staring at this press release for the past thirty minutes, and all she could think about was Sam. How she should own up to her feelings. Tell her that there was something there. But she didn't have any experience with something like this. What should she say? *Hey, I think I'm attracted to you? I'd like to kiss you. Do you feel the same way? Yeah, I know we work together.*

She'd barely seen Sam since they'd returned from Indianapolis. Their schedules had been different: one sleeping while the other was working. She missed her. Obsessively, she thought about the moment in the stairwell when she'd thought about letting Sam kiss her. She wasn't sure what would have come next, but she wasn't against it. Thoughts warred inside her. She'd been so certain that she didn't want to date a gamer again, but Sam was different.

Though Lauren had nothing to do with Sam's success, she was proud of her. Sam was a talented player, one who should have been mentored and trained when she was younger. Watching a woman take the top points spot at the tournament had been a dream come true. Sam had proven that women could compete at this level and win. How many little girls might watch the game streams over their brother's shoulders after being told they couldn't play a game like *Siege Encounter*?

Like so many other equal opportunity sports that didn't rely on strength—racing, equestrian, and shooting sports—esports were still dominated by young men because they wouldn't let the girls play, not because the girls weren't able to play. She'd been thinking about that for a while now, especially after she'd gotten Sam to tell her about the doxxing incident. Lauren had had to research what doxxing was. Someone had released Sam's personal information on the internet as retaliation for some perceived slight. In this case, it was most likely fans of one of the opposing teams.

Lauren had spent the last couple of weeks perusing online chats and message boards, collecting as much information as she could. The vitriol directed at Sam horrified her, and she planned to speak to Will about it.

Her phone showed a video call incoming. "Hello, Mother."

"Hello, sweetie, how are things in Charm City?"

"Fine. How are you and Father?"

"You'd know if you ever came to see us."

Lauren looked at the ceiling. "I've been busy."

"Yes, I understand that. I had a job once as well, you know. But you need to prioritize your mental health and your family."

"Thanks for the pep talk."

"How's it going with the new roommate?"

"She's great." Her thoughts drifted to an image of Sam smiling.

Her mother narrowed her eyes. "That's all? Great?"

She had definitely just caught Lauren daydreaming. "She's a brilliant player, and she's kind, and she's an amazing cook. I've put on five pounds since she moved in."

"I'm glad to hear that. You can use a few pounds."

"Mother."

"What?" Her mother tried to feign innocence, as if she hadn't just criticized her. "When do you get your office back?"

Sadness washed over Lauren at the mere thought of Sam leaving. "I'm not sure. We haven't talked about it. A few weeks, I suppose."

"You don't sound happy about it. I thought you enjoyed having the place to yourself."

Lauren ran her finger across the sofa cushion, drawing a circle on the fabric. "I do. Sam is nice to have around," she admitted. "If this was a true two-bedroom, I'd consider asking her to stay."

"Get a bigger apartment," her mother said matter-of-factly.

"I have a lease for another four months."

"Break it. You can afford it."

Her mother was right. She could afford it, and if Sam helped pay the rent, they could afford a three-bedroom if they needed it. Her brain screeched to a halt. She couldn't ask Sam to live with her. What about Toronto? What if she got a job with Augustan? She changed the subject. "I've been thinking about something. The city high schools have begun getting donations for esports teams, but I've done a little research, and I rarely see girls participating. I think it's a combination of the choice of games and the barrier to esports created by…"

"Bullying?" suggested her mother.

"I'm sure some of it is unintentional. But whether intentional or not, boys are trained to be competitive, and they don't seem to take the smack talk as personally as a fourteen-year-old girl. I want to suggest that the company sponsor some sort of coaching for girl gamers. Have some of our players go out into the community and encourage girls who want to play competitive games but feel ostracized."

She could see her mother's mind working. "I think that is a great idea."

The response surprised Lauren. Her mother had never understood her obsession with games as a teenager. "Really?"

"I have no earthly idea why anyone wants to spend several hours playing games, but I think giving back to young people is a noble gesture. If you think there's a need for this, I think you should do it."

"Watching Sam's journey these past couple of months has opened my eyes. I used to think women didn't like the same games as men, but I don't believe that's always the case. The toxicity to Sam's ascension in the ranks is astounding. I don't know how she hasn't given up before now. I would have."

"Why not make that part of the program? Educating young players on how to handle the abuse. I know an amazing therapist who works at the Johns Hopkins Children's Center. I'm certain she would discuss how you might manage something like that."

"Wow. That would be great."

"Sometimes, having a mom is useful," she teased.

"I wonder if Sam would be up for helping me." Creating something worthwhile felt right. She'd always been driven by money, trying to live up to her parents' expectations. But if she could create something valuable as her legacy, that would feel a lot better. Certainly, a lot better than a Towson University blurb that read, "Alumna helps sexist douchebag change his public image." She was an accomplice to the destructive behavior in gaming, writing stories that redeemed Will and the team.

"Why don't you come down on Saturday, and bring Sam with you?"

Lauren shook a finger at the screen. "This was all a ploy to get me to come to the house, wasn't it?"

"So? We'll see you then?" her mother asked, her voice filled with hope.

Lauren heard the door lock beep. The thought of seeing Sam excited her. "I'll text you later and let you know. Love you."

As she ended the call, her mother's face lit up with surprise, having heard the words, "Love you." Lauren didn't say it nearly as often as she should.

Nervous excitement coursed through her. She liked the idea of Sam meeting her parents. She liked Sam, and she hoped they liked her, too. She stood and faced the door. When it opened, she smiled. "Hey. How was your trip? I watched a replay of the final. You did great."

Sam dropped her key chain in the bowl with a clunk. "Long. Flight was delayed." She set her backpack on the floor. "Alec insisted I wear that damn wig the entire trip back." Obviously, she'd taken it off as soon as she could since she had on what looked like a brand-new Baltimore ball cap, probably from the airport.

Lauren wanted to talk to Sam about her idea, but she realized now wasn't the time. Sam looked tired. "Can I get you something to eat?" She gestured to the kitchen.

Sam made a half-smile. "You mean reheat something I made last week?"

"I'm getting amazing with the microwave. I haven't overcooked anything in weeks."

"You and my dad." Sam shook her head with a slight smile on her face. "Let me put my stuff away."

Lauren nodded and prepared the dinner. When Sam returned, they sat together on the sofa and ate in silence. Lauren cast a quick glance at her. Even tired, she was still incredibly attractive. Ever since the first time they'd bumped into each other, her body reacted to Sam's presence like a switch was turned on inside her. Initially, she'd attempted to control herself, but now she'd completely given up. "Excited about New York?" she asked.

Sam shrugged. "I guess."

Lauren elbowed her, mostly for the comfort of her touch. "You guess? You must be excited. You're the highest point scorer in the league behind Ahn Ji-ho. The team is in third place in the division. Win at the event in New York, and you're going to the world championships in Toronto."

Sam shrugged. With her mouth full of chili, she asked, "What are you going to watch tonight? Anything new?"

Lauren pointed with her spoon. "A show about two young men who ice-skate. I got it from the library. I'm excited about it."

"The guys are in love?" Sam asked, her eyebrow raised.

Lauren nodded. "Love is love. Right?"

Sam stared at her.

She swallowed. She could feel the heat building in her chest. They were sitting close but not close enough. She wanted to move closer. Instead, she sat rigidly while they continued to eat. She'd told Sam that she'd had a girlfriend when they'd gotten caught in the rainstorm together. She figured Sam understood she was bi, but she hadn't told her explicitly. If she said it directly, she couldn't keep pretending that she didn't want more.

They hadn't spoken about the almost kiss either, but she thought they'd flirted a bit after the fact. They could pretend it had never happened, but it had. She'd felt it. She still felt it. What if Sam did too?

She grabbed the remote and put on the show. They watched the first episode together and finished dinner.

Sam checked her phone and then said, "Seriously?" She tossed it on the coffee table, stood, and walked to the windows.

Lauren paused the show. "What's wrong?" She followed Sam and stood beside her.

Sam seemed reluctant to respond. Then, she took a deep sigh and said, "A journalist at the tournament kept pestering me about online trolling. I mentioned that I got doxxed. Alec just texted me and said that Will told him not to let me talk to anyone else about it."

"I'm surprised no one has called me about it." It was her job to deal with exactly this kind of issue. She reached out to touch Sam's back, to comfort her, but her fingertips hovered in the air. She pulled her hand down. If this was what Sam needed to talk about, she would be fully present for her.

"And suddenly I'm benched for the online match on Thursday."

"Why?"

Sam shrugged. "Something about my play not being up to par this weekend. They aren't wrong. I was sluggish." Sam still gazed out the windows at the darkening sky. "I've thought about quitting."

No, she couldn't let these guys win. And Lauren was certain they were guys. The emotionally stunted ones who spent hours making AI fake nudes of girls who had refused their advances and putting them on the internet or sending them to their work colleagues.

"I'd been keeping my massage therapy software active in case one of my long-term clients wanted to get ahold of me. The trolls filled up all my appointments with garbage, so even if a regular customer wanted an appointment, they couldn't schedule one. Being online has been the best thing that ever happened to me. I'm getting paid to play games. But I'm also a massage therapist, and that is how I'm going to make my money when this ends. And we both know it will end. Why should they be allowed to destroy my livelihood with no consequences?" Sam flexed her hands.

"They shouldn't." Lauren slipped her hand in Sam's and pressed her cheek against her shoulder. She liked how it felt. Sam glanced at her. She wanted to tell Sam that she saw her as a strong, beautiful, and sensitive woman. No matter what anyone thought of her. "I do think we need to make a statement about the sexism and the racism you're receiving. It might not help stop this, but it could help bring attention to the issue. Other young players would see that they aren't the only ones dealing with something similar."

"I might quit, but I'm not going to stay silent about it. If Will wants to fire me, so be it."

Lauren clutched her hand tighter. "I'm glad, but I want you to succeed, so don't quit yet. Give me a chance to talk to Will. Actually, I have something to tell you that might help convince you to stick around." She led Sam to the sofa and sat her down. She held her hand and turned toward her. "Would you be willing to help me create a gaming program for young women?"

Sam looked a little surprised.

"I know it's a lot to ask. Your schedule is crazy enough as it is, but I spoke to my mother about the idea. She's keen on it, which usually means it's a good idea, believe it or not. She knows a woman at Johns Hopkins who could help create the program."

Sam nodded, acknowledging she was listening.

"Anyway, we can talk about the details later. Especially since I don't have any details yet. I'm going to approach Will to see if he'll fund a pilot program, but ultimately, we make something replicable that schools and others can use anywhere." As she spoke, Lauren leaned closer as she got more excited. "What the program really needs is women gamers, and well, you're a gamer." Lauren's cadence slowed, and her voice lowered. "And you're a woman."

Sam's eyes traveled around her face and finally fell on her lips. Lauren's hand felt sweaty. She'd been in Sam's grasp the whole time she'd spoken. The silence made her nervous.

Finally, Sam nodded and said, "I think it's a great idea. Teach some internet literacy. Play some games. Talk about how to treat others. Give girls the ability to voice their concerns so people will listen. Talk to boys about why what they hear older boys saying to girls is not okay. I have a lot of questions and ideas myself."

Lauren wanted to touch Sam's cheek, but she held herself in check. "I'm going to my parents' house on Saturday. I'd like it if you came with me."

Sam narrowed her eyes and cracked a smile. "Taking me to meet the parents? That's a big step."

Lauren took in a sharp breath. She knew Sam was joking, but Lauren's cheeks heated. "My mother is a superb cook, so there will be plenty of food."

Sam's gaze traveled to her lips again, making her heart rate increase. "There you go, trying to lure me into doing things with offers of free food. What are you going to do when I move out?"

She didn't want to think about that. "I don't want you to leave," she said. "I mean, you can't live in my office forever. I'm certain we're breaking the lease agreement, but I like having you here."

Sam nodded and looked at their joined hands. "I enjoy being here."

"So," Lauren said more lightly, "are you interested in hearing more about my idea?"

Sam looked up at her with those beautiful eyes. "Yes."

Lauren's knuckles hurt, she'd been squeezing Sam's hand so hard waiting for her answer. She let go reluctantly and grabbed her laptop. "I want to get some thoughts collected, and I'd love your help with this." While she created the document, they sat so close that she could feel the heat from Sam's knee against her leg. She wanted to talk to Sam about her attraction, but talking about it after discussing the dark side of their industry didn't seem right. There would be a better moment soon.

CHAPTER TWENTY-ONE

Sam lay in the loft bed and stared at the computer lights flickering against the ceiling. What was she doing? She had desperately wanted to kiss Lauren. As soon as she had talked with so much enthusiasm about her plan for a gaming program to combat bullying, all Sam could do was watch her lips. It hadn't mattered what she was saying. She would have said yes to anything. Luckily, it was something she wanted to say yes to.

Now, images of Lauren spun through her mind. The first time they'd met on the convention floor. Nights of watching anime together. Staring at her seated several rows ahead on the plane to Indy. The times when Lauren had stood behind her as she prepared dinner. The little moments. It couldn't be one-sided.

Why hadn't she kissed her? When Lauren had taken her hand earlier, she'd felt like she was going to jump to the ceiling. If she didn't say something soon, she might implode. She lifted the sheets, slid down the ladder, threw open her door, and strode across the hall. She grasped Lauren's bedroom door frame so hard, her fingers hurt. With her fist suspended in midair, she took a deep breath, preparing herself for what lay behind the door. But right when she was ready to tell Lauren that she liked her, a wave of doubt washed over her.

She dropped her hand and leaned her head against the doorjamb. She wasn't brave enough to reveal her true feelings. A fear rushed up from deep inside her. She liked Lauren a lot, and when she cared for someone, they left her. Her mother had left her when she'd needed her. Yes, she'd died. It wasn't her fault, but still, she had abandoned Sam. Her father had left her when things had gotten too hard for him. When would Lauren choose to leave?

She stepped away, intent on going back in her room and forgetting all about this, but the door to Lauren's bedroom swung open, and she instinctually apologized. "I'm sorry. I didn't mean to wake you."

Lauren didn't say a word. She grabbed Sam's hand and pulled her into her room. She closed the door and pushed her against the wall, pressing their bodies together. At the unexpected action, Sam inhaled sharply.

"I take it you're not straight," said Sam. She cringed at her own comment. What did it matter what Lauren was? She was pressed against her and making her body ignite like fireworks.

"Bi." Lauren touched her cheek. "You good with that?"

Sensations coursed through Sam's body in response to the touch. She stumbled around for words. "Totally, but you said you don't date gamers. Not that I'm saying this means we're dating." She tried to be smooth, but her voice trembled with nervousness.

"Sam." Even in the dim light from the window, she could see Lauren smile. For a moment, they stared at one another. Lauren ran a hand along the back of Sam's neck, and Sam could see the desire in her eyes.

"Are you certain about this?" She should've been asking herself that question. Nothing ever went right for her with women, and she really liked Lauren. What if this screwed things up for them?

"Absolutely." Lauren leaned in to kiss her.

Things were going to change, but she couldn't help herself. As soon as her lips collided with Lauren's, she had no hope of changing the course of action. Her body took the lead, and her concerns and worries were smothered by the overwhelming desire that drove her for the rest of the night.

❖

In the morning, Sam woke to Lauren stroking her hair. Her scalp tingled at the touch. The room was bright with sunlight. Was she really lying naked in Lauren's bed?

"Waking up to you is much better than my alarm," said Lauren.

"Aren't you going to be late for work?" Just saying the word work let the reality of the day creep in to her thoughts. She had to go to work later and potentially see Lauren there and pretend they hadn't slept together last night.

"Unfortunately, I already am." Lauren snuggled closer.

Sam wrapped Lauren in her arms. Waking up every day to someone as beautiful as Lauren was something she could handle. She ran her hand down Lauren's stomach until she reached her tattoo. Seeing it after so many weeks had been incredibly satisfying. The art was so much lovelier than what her imagination had conjured. The curved branch of a flowering cherry tree pointed from Lauren's hip to her pubis. Sam followed the line of the branch with her fingertips.

Lauren grabbed her wrist. "If you start that, I'm never going to get to work."

There was that word again, trying to remind her that their moment together might not have been such a good idea. She wanted to leave reality in the future and keep enjoying the now.

"Would that be so terrible?" she said with a smile. She moved down and kissed the curve of Lauren's abdomen.

"Maybe if we were independently wealthy," said Lauren. She shimmied out from underneath Sam and got out of bed. "Seriously, I love your enthusiasm, but I really do have to get to the office. Considering I walk there, I can't really claim traffic was an issue."

Sam lay back against her pillow and watched Lauren move around the room. "Your tattoo is strikingly beautiful."

Lauren stopped dressing and sat on the end of the bed. "It reminds me of my grandfather. When I was a little girl, he used to take me to see the cherry trees blossom in DC. After he died, I saw a painting at a museum of a man with a child beneath flowering trees, and I knew it was my grandfather's way of telling me he was all right." She paused as if she might be reminiscing. "Anyway, when I got to college, this was my one and only tattoo, and I don't regret it."

Lauren was lucky to have something beautiful and meaningful and not just a drunken college dare. Was there something she'd get tattooed if she had the chance? Thoughts of her mother swirled, but she couldn't think of any one thing that would represent their bond, not in the way that Lauren's tattoo represented her bond with her grandfather.

"You shouldn't regret it. It's amazing, and so are you."

"Thanks." Lauren blushed. "I really have to go, but maybe we can take up this discussion again later?" She came around the bed and kissed Sam. "Maybe you can wear the same outfit then, too?"

Suddenly aware of her own nakedness, Sam pulled the sheets up. "I'm sure that could be arranged." When Lauren left the room, Sam grabbed her pillow, drew it to herself, and pressed her nose to it. It smelled like Lauren, and now that she knew what Lauren smelled like, she wanted to bottle it and keep it with her.

CHAPTER TWENTY-TWO

L auren dragged herself to the coffee shop across the street and stood in line, looking at the handwritten choices for the day. She'd struggled to pull herself away from Sam, and it had taken all her might to get ready for work. She'd have been happy to lie in bed for the entire day, not bothering to do anything except kiss and touch Sam.

Last night had been so much more than she could have imagined. Her body had responded to Sam as if they had been together for years. When Sam had slid her fingers inside her, she had fallen into a moment of pure bliss where her mind had gone blank. No coherent thoughts, only pleasure and frenzied movement. And when she'd come, she was unprepared for the intensity of the orgasm that had ripped through her. She'd felt nothing like it in her life. Overcome by the emotion, she hadn't been able hold back her cries of ecstasy.

The guy in front of her had on a motorcycle jacket. It reminded her of the one she'd bought for Sam weeks ago. She hadn't found the right time to give it to her. Maybe now would be appropriate. Or maybe it would feel too much like a thank-you-for-the-great-sex gift. Perhaps she'd wait a little longer.

Her favorite barista was behind the counter, and when it was her turn to order, she dropped a hint the way she had promised she would.

"Latte or a café au lait today?" the girl asked with her characteristic cheerfulness.

"I'll take a flat white and a black coffee."

The girl arched an eyebrow. Lauren could feel the blush on her cheeks.

"Congratulations." The barista stuck the order slip on the counter for preparation. "Do I get any details?"

"Only that I'm about as happy as I have ever been," replied Lauren.

The girl placed a hand on her heart. "Aw, that's so great." When the drinks were ready, she handed them over. "Here's to happiness."

Lauren saluted with her flat white cup. She stepped outside in the morning sunlight and decided today was a good day, and she was going to make a difference.

Two hours later, she was beyond frustrated. She'd been showing Will and Raymond the printouts of the doxxing and trolling that had been raining down on Sam for the past month. Pittsburgh, Atlanta, Memphis, now Philadelphia. The better the team did in the tournaments—Sam in particular—the worse the attacks had become.

"We can't be responsible for every wacko out there who wants to psych-out our players," said Will. "This game is about aspirations and comradery. If the fans think someone doesn't belong, they don't belong."

"What you're telling me is that gaming fans want to believe they can be as good as the players, but they can't picture themselves as a female player. Consequently, they try to bully her off the team?"

"No. I mean..." He looked flustered. "You just don't understand the minds of gamers."

"I lived with Seth for three years, and I am a gamer. That's why I'm here. Because I love gaming, too."

"That's not the same thing." He turned away and looked at his phone.

She slapped the table to get his attention. "What do you plan on doing about what's happening to Sam?" She pinned him with a stare.

"Nothing. There isn't anything to do. We can't turn off the internet. Tell her to ignore it like the rest of the guys do."

She would not let him brush her off this time. "How does she *ignore* doxxing? They literally leaked her home address and phone number this week. Last week, someone created a potential schedule showing where she would be every day of the tournament in Philadelphia, and the guy asked people to send him geotagged photos if they saw her. He also encouraged attendees to let him know what hotel room she was staying in. His screed included threats of implied violence, and when someone called him out on it, he said he was joking around."

"It comes with the territory. Online trolls shitpost about everyone. Including me," said Will.

"No one else on the team was doxxed. Not to mention, she was targeted for both being a woman and being mixed-race."

Frank Moore, the operations manager, chimed in, "All the guys are getting threatened these days. Especially now that sports betting is legal in most states. When people lose money on the games, they take it out on the players."

"Even more reason for the team to stand behind her. Say you don't condone this kind of behavior. We can do a series of online PSAs about violent rhetoric and toxicity in gaming. We can shoot some videos and post them about how to participate in fair play. You can bring the Barrage to the forefront of the movement instead of sitting back and waiting until something dreadful happens." Her mind went to the thought of something happening to Sam. "Don't just go along with everyone else in the industry, Will. Do the right thing and lead."

"Wow. Calm down. I've never known you to be so emotional."

Being assertive wasn't being emotional, but this was personal. "Sam's used to the sexism. She's lived with that since she began gaming online." Lauren wanted to say her whole life, but what was the point in telling that to a roomful of men who did not understand what it meant to be a woman in a man's world? "But the rest of this is disgusting and threatening, and we need to address it because it is affecting her mental health."

Will threw an arm in the air. "Then she isn't tough enough to be a pro."

"That's your response?" She was dumbfounded. "You'd prefer to lose the highest-scoring player on your team right before the semifinals than do the right thing and support her?"

He looked away. "Let's move on to other things."

"Fine. Let's start with allowing her to talk about her experiences to the media as long as she doesn't disparage the company."

"That's not what I meant," he said.

"You've turned her into something she's not. You've allowed her to appear weak because of it. She's not that person, Will. She's Sam, not Samantha, and she has things she wants to talk about that are important to women gamers. If you aren't going to support her, she has the right to support herself."

"Lauren, you work for me. Not the other way around." His face was beet red.

She was embarrassing him in front of Frank and Raymond, who were doing everything they could to blend into furniture, and she was doing everything she'd ever learned not to do in this business, and yet, she was glad to do it. "Here's one more item for the agenda," she said. "If you force her to continue to wear the skirts and makeup, we'll both walk, and you'll have to answer questions from Augustan about why your team can't seem to keep women in the workforce."

He held out a hand like a stop sign. "Hold on. You're getting worked up about nothing."

"Nothing?" Her voice was as calm as ice when she said, "I do not call being threatened with rape nothing."

He blanched at the statement.

Raymond jumped in. "I'll talk to one of my law enforcement contacts and see if there is anything we can do."

Will shook his head. "We are not going to get the cops involved. One police report and every journalist and wannabe journalist will plaster it all over the internet."

Lauren interlaced her fingers and leaned forward. "Then I won't continue to talk to my contacts at Guarantech any longer. You can send Bob to negotiate with them."

Will stood and walked to the glass wall of the conference room. He put his hands on his hips and looked through the glass into the office. "Fine. Tell her she can wear whatever she damn well pleases from now on."

That had gotten his attention. Of course she should have led with the money trail. "And?" she asked.

"And what?"

"What about a press release regarding the doxxing?"

Will pointed to Raymond, who looked like he wanted to be anywhere but under Will's gaze. "Ray and I will discuss the legal ramifications of something like that. You just make sure she stays on the team."

His response didn't satisfy her, but she nodded. It was the best she was going to get from Will today. She'd have to come up with another way to address the issue later and hope this was enough of a compromise to satisfy Sam. She picked up her tablet and purse and moved toward the door to the conference room.

Sam stood outside the partially open door, staring at her. How much had she heard? "You didn't have to do that," said Sam.

"I couldn't not do it. I'm only sorry I couldn't get them to commit to a plan of action on the press release." Regrettably, Lauren was also now convinced that Will would never provide funding for their program aimed at girl gamers. She'd have to find some other way.

Sam looked around before she stepped closer. Lauren couldn't suppress her libido. It had taken over from her conscious thoughts and become nothing but instinct today. She didn't even care if anyone in the office saw them. Her body betrayed her, and she sank back toward the wall like an invitation. Sam leaned a shoulder against the wall next to her and ran a finger along Lauren's wrist and the back of her hand.

"I'm glad to have you in my corner," said Sam. "Sometimes, it feels lonely here."

Lauren knew exactly what she meant. "I'm here for you, Sam."

"I'll be home during dinner tonight if you think you'll be around." Sam's intense gaze conveyed the mutual desire that was palpable between them. She ran her fingers across Lauren's before moving away. She looked back over her shoulder, her expression serious. "I owe you one for sticking up for me in there, and I intend to repay you."

Lauren thought she would melt on the spot. A lot of competing thoughts danced in her head about what form of repayment that might be. All of them would feel good. She didn't know where this was going. It was probably not the best idea, but so far, Sam was everything she wanted in a partner. Unbelievably sexy. Polite. Focused. Conscientious. And thoughtful.

And yet, their paths were eventually going to diverge, and what then? She pushed that thought to the side. Right now, she was going to enjoy what was happening.

CHAPTER TWENTY-THREE

Sam woke on Saturday, drowsy, spooning Lauren with an arm around her waist. Her face was against Lauren's neck. "You smell so damn good," she growled and pressed herself closer.

"We need to get ready."

Sam groaned. "Do we have to go? I'm not sure I'm ready to meet your parents. Especially after..." She snuggled closer and placed a kiss on Lauren's neck. "Call and tell your mom you're sick."

"I already called in sick to work once this week." Lauren gently pushed Sam away and flung off the sheets. She moved around the room, laying out clothes for the day. Sam couldn't take her eyes off her. She could lay in bed and watch all day. "And you missed ranked play last night. Alec sent me a message at midnight. I told him you had a flat tire at your dad's."

"Thanks." She leaned across the bed and inhaled Lauren's scent on her pillow, then sat up and leaned against the headboard. "I just wanted to get to know you better." Her thoughts wandered to everything they had done together this week. The intimacy of their actions.

"I think you know me better than anyone at this point," said Lauren. "As much as I love the sound of that, I promised my mother we'd come to the house. She already texted that my brother and his family will be there."

Sam threw off the sheets. "You're right. We can't disappoint your mom." She would kill to have her mom back to disappoint.

Sam had worried all week about meeting Lauren's parents. Originally, she'd said yes, thinking she'd merely be the gamer roommate tagging along. Now she was…what? The fuck buddy? The girlfriend? Either way, she was still sleeping with their daughter, and that would feel awkward even if they didn't know.

Lauren had told her she should wear something casual. She'd put on her summer cargo pants and a T-shirt. She should have known that her idea of casual and Lauren's idea of casual were not the same thing. Lauren wore a pair of capris, a pastel green tank top with a white sweater tied around her shoulders, and a pair of dock shoes.

Lauren drove her to Havre de Grace and let her drop off some food for her dad. He wasn't home, which was odd, but she left him a note asking him to call her. This wasn't the first time he hadn't been at the house since she'd moved out. The fact that he was out might be a good thing, but she wasn't sure.

On the drive across to the Eastern shore, Sam spent most of the time staring at Lauren's profile, looking at her hands on the steering wheel. The stress of the past few weeks diminished when they were together. She didn't dare check her phone and ruin it. She'd seen enough threats for a lifetime.

"Let It Go" from *Frozen* came on Lauren's playlist. She broke out in a forceful sing-along. She sang at the top of her lungs, with an occasional flourish of a hand. She was fantastic.

When the song ended, Sam clapped. "Your singing is amazing."

"I used to sing in show choir in high school."

"I would never have known."

"Not exactly something useful for my job. I save it for the shower."

Now Sam had an image of Lauren naked in the shower. "I'd like to be in the audience for that sometime." She surprised herself with her assertiveness.

Lauren glanced at her with a look that said she was thinking the same thing. "Your turn." She pointed at her phone. "Pick something."

Sam frowned. "Nope. Not happening."

"Come on," Lauren pleaded. "There must be something you sing along to when you're alone."

"Nope." She was not going to embarrass herself. "I'm the world's worst singer."

"You can't be that bad."

"Oh, yes, I can."

"At least pick your favorite song. One you like to dance to." When Sam refused again, Lauren whined. "Please."

"It's embarrassing."

Lauren touched her playfully on her thigh. "Oh. You're too cool, I see."

The touch made Sam's breathing shallow. It reminded her of all Lauren's touches last night. If Lauren hadn't been driving, she would have reached out and run her hand along the inside of her thigh.

"Fine. I'll show you how uncool I am." Sam made her selection and sank deeper in her seat as it began to play. Her mother had loved "Girls Just Want to Have Fun." She remembered dancing around the living room with her as a little girl. That memory was one of her favorites. When they had been together, happy and without care.

Surprisingly, Lauren knew the words, and by the time the chorus started, Sam joined in. Not loudly, since she couldn't keep a tune, but enough to feel lighter. When the song ended, the farmland speeding by outside the window calmed her.

In Chestertown, they pulled down a tight street lined with mature trees, where all the houses sat up against the sidewalks. Lauren parked on the street next to a large property that took up the equivalent of three or four of the other house footprints. Sam had seen enough historic homes in Maryland to know the house was from the late 1700s and sizeable for the period. A symmetrical brick facade, dark green shutters, a pitched roof, dormer windows on the third floor, and a well cared for garden wall. This was an expensive home.

As Lauren headed for the front door, Sam felt nervous. Not only because they had slept together but because it hadn't occurred to her that Lauren's parents might be rich. She looked at her scuffed sneakers and her well-worn cargo pants. What would they think of her?

Lauren turned and drew closer to her. Standing close enough to touch, she said, "I don't know how I'm going to spend all afternoon not kissing you."

Sam felt like she was melting, and it wasn't from the warm summer temperatures.

Lauren opened the front door and yelled, "We're here."

The inside was even more daunting than the exterior. High ceilings, a long straight staircase, rooms off to either side. A woman who looked to be Lauren's older twin, in a summer-weight wool sweater and a long flowery skirt, popped her head out of a door at the end of the hall. "Finally, the prodigal daughter returns." She gave Lauren a hug and a kiss on the cheek. She turned her attention to Sam and took her in a warm hug.

Sam stiffened. Her family weren't huggers, especially not with strangers.

"I've heard so much about you, Sam. Lauren thinks you're the best roommate ever. She can't stop talking about your cooking."

"Mother." Lauren gave her a warning look.

Sam's cheeks warmed.

"What?" said her mother. "You do."

Sam choked out a few words even though she was nervous. "You have a lovely home, Mrs. Johanssen."

"Call me Barbara." She waved them to follow her into a more modern extension at the back of the home, only half as wide as the original house.

Lauren grazed her fingertips against Sam's and gave her a mischievous grin. It was going to be hard to hide her desire all afternoon. They hadn't spoken about it, but sharing their status with Lauren's parents was Lauren's decision to make. Telling her family they were dating was more likely to occur after a few months not after a few days.

The extension was an enormous kitchen with a casual dining area and a den beyond. Outside the window was an interior courtyard crisscrossed by gravel walkways. A man with thinning, sandy-gray hair dug in a flower bed. He sat cross-legged in a long-sleeve shirt with horizontal stripes, a pair of dark blue cotton pants, and a pair of simple white sneakers. "That's my husband, Harald. He loves taking care of the plants. Says it clears his mind."

Lauren must not have inherited that gene. Sam hadn't seen a green plant in their apartment.

Barbara pushed open a screen door and called, "Harald, your daughter is here."

He pushed up slowly and carefully and walked stiffly toward the door. Sam couldn't help but think of how she might try to help loosen the muscles that were obviously giving him trouble. Lauren was already digging into a professional-looking charcuterie tray that was set out on a table in front of a long banquette. With a mouthful of food, she turned and gave her father a kiss on his cheek.

Lauren's father directed his attention to Sam. "Harald Johanssen."

She returned the greeting. "Sam O'Brian."

He turned back to Lauren, smiling. "Tell me about work. How's it going?"

Sam pushed her hands in her pockets and stood off to the side of the room, watching and listening to their interaction. She could feel the warmth between them.

"Can I get you anything?" Barbara asked her.

"I'm fine, thank you."

"Grandpa." A girl about nine, with dark blond hair, rushed into the room and grabbed Harald around the waist. "Auntie," she added excitedly. Lauren kneeled and gave her a bear hug.

"Sorry, the bridge was backed up," said a tall thin man with the same hair color as Lauren's. Behind him, a well-appointed dark-haired woman with a perfectly coifed hairdo brought up the rear. She dropped her purse on the counter. Though Sam couldn't tell a luxury purse from a knockoff, she couldn't help but notice the two interlocking Cs on the latch. Her hair, her nails, her outfit, her deep tan. There was something flashier about the woman than Lauren and her parents.

Lauren let go of the little girl and approached Sam. "This is my big brother, Harry, and this is his wife, Angelika. And this"—she reached out and ruffled the little girl's hair—"is Bunny."

The girl rolled her eyes and sighed. "My name isn't really Bunny. It's Elizabeth."

Sam nodded toward her. She understood how important it was to be called by the name you wanted. "Nice to meet you, Elizabeth."

Elizabeth smiled at the acknowledgement.

Angelika gave Sam the once-over. Her squint told Sam all she needed to know. Angelika's gaze had traveled up and down, and she wasn't checking Sam out for a date. She was judging her outfit, her hair, her otherness, or all the above.

The conversation quickly turned to what Lauren's niece had been doing on her summer vacation, and Sam slipped to the far end of the room. She stood completely still, afraid to accidentally bump into something valuable. She could see a fountain in the garden. The statue was Asian. Perhaps Thai, with the sharp shoulders of the outfit. It seemed out of place. Like her.

Barbara approached. She looked so much like Lauren, it was uncanny. The only difference was the deep laugh lines around her eyes and the softness of her jawline, both the lovely effects of aging. Sam didn't mind it at all. On entering the home, she had expected Mrs. Johanssen to have a Botox forehead and the telltale signs of plastic surgery, but she had none of those things, and it was relieving.

"Come with me," said Barbara.

Sam was curious why Lauren's mom wanted her to follow her, but she did so pliantly, not asking questions. O'Brians didn't ask questions. When someone older said to do something, you did it. More residual Catholic guilt. They passed through a short, uneven doorway, and the change was immediate. The ceiling was low, the room small, the far wall was river stone with an old fireplace, and in the corner, a narrow staircase led to the floor above. The wood floors creaked as Sam walked. This had to be an older building.

"Do you drink?" Barbara asked.

"Only on special occasions."

"Consider this Christmas in July." Barbara stepped to a small bar and fixed drinks for them both.

The furniture in the room was simple. Thin-legged chairs and tables with clean lines. Sam ran her hand along the drop leaf table under the window. She wasn't sure how much the things in the room cost, but she knew it was more than anything she'd bought at IKEA. She'd seen pieces like it in a museum before. Someone had made this table by hand, and just feeling the wood felt like a connection to the past. Touching it felt like she was doing something she shouldn't.

"Do you like antiques?" asked Barbara.

Sam found the question funny since no one in her family had ever owned one. "Only the ones I see through a shop window."

"You have a good eye," she said, pointing to the table. "That's the best piece in the house."

"The wood is beautiful."

Barbara handed her a glass containing a thin line of gold liquid and no ice. Sam remembered that Lauren liked scotch. A family tradition, it seemed.

"I don't know a thing about scotch." Sam swirled it around and took a sip. It burned.

"Should have warned you, the first swallow burns, but the second gives you the flavors. This one was aged in a sherry cask that will give you sweet notes." Barbara sat and motioned for Sam to join her. "The house has been in my husband's family for over two hundred years. The original owner was the customs officer on this side of the bay."

Sam nodded and took another sip of scotch. This time, it was exactly as Barbara had said, warm and a touch sweet. She fidgeted with the glass when she finished, uncomfortable under Barbara's gaze.

"But I come from more humble beginnings. My dad worked on the Cape May ferry up in Lewes," she said, matter-of-fact. "Farmers, fishermen, seamstresses."

Sam thought about the difference between her and Lauren. "Was it a big change for you?"

"Yup." She gestured around the room. "I didn't know a Duncan Fife from a Chippendale when I married Harald." She sipped her drink and gave Sam a pointed look. "I noticed you were uncomfortable, so I thought we could come in here and relax for a minute." She put a hand on Sam's wrist. "Don't let Judgy McJudgerson get under your skin."

Sam nearly spit out the sip of scotch she'd taken.

"She's harmless, and she's a kind mother. Give her a few years, and she'll stop caring so much about all that external stuff."

This was not at all the conversation she had expected.

"And relax. There is absolutely nothing in this house that my husband can't replace. And if he can't, so be it. Someone else's version will be worth more." She gave Sam's arm a pat as she laughed.

Sam could see where Lauren got her gentle demeanor.

"Have you considered Lauren's offer yet?"

Sam wasn't certain what offer she meant. Currently, most of the offers were sexual in nature. She suddenly felt warm with embarrassment.

"I think assisting with creating a seminar or program to reduce the issues facing girls who enjoy gaming is a great idea."

Sam relaxed. At least Lauren's mom didn't know they were sleeping together. She polished off her drink before answering. "Yes. I'm excited about it."

"Good. Lauren's been grasping for meaning in her life for a long time. I'm sure you understand how it is with mothers. We think we know what's best for our children, but they never want to hear what we have to say."

Sam's chest tightened. What would her mother have wanted for her? She wasn't certain her mother had been given the best life. Had she been happy? Would that be what she would want for Sam? And what would her mother have thought of Lauren?

"Did I say something to upset you?"

Sam forced a smile and stumbled for a response. "No. Not at all." She just didn't have any idea what her mother would have wanted for her.

"If you have any influence, I hope you'll talk her into following through on her idea. I'm certain it will be good for her." She touched a small photo on the butler's table beside her seat. Even from here, Sam could tell it was the family on a beach, probably when Lauren was young. All four of them wearing white. All smiles. A pang of jealousy hit her. She sat back in her chair. She was already feeling the effects of her drink.

Lauren hadn't had to fight for attention in a big family or sleep in a room with two cousins or wait for a weekly video call to reassure her that her father was still alive in Afghanistan. She tried to shake the feeling. Gaming was the one constant amidst all that. "Absolutely. I want to help in any way I can."

It wasn't Lauren's fault that she seemed to have had an idyllic childhood. This was about her own life, not Lauren's.

As if conjured from her own thoughts, the door opened, and Lauren poked her head inside. "Here you guys are." Maybe it was the scotch or maybe Sam was no longer able to suppress her feelings, but she couldn't take her eyes off Lauren. "Everyone is getting hungry. Especially me."

"I hope you have ice cream," Sam said to Barbara without looking away from Lauren. "She's addicted."

Lauren smiled.

"Always has been," said Barbara. She looked at Lauren and back at Sam. Then, she spoke to Sam in a low voice. "You wouldn't have a Karmen Ghia by any chance, would you?"

Sam wasn't sure what that was. "Sorry, no."

The late lunch was delicious. The family was gregarious and obviously loved each other. This was what it was like to be in a roomful of cheerful people. Sam thought back to her mother's Shaw family in North Carolina. So much of the time was spent focusing on the boys. They were the ones to be paid attention to. They could go explore and get dirty, but she was expected to stay close to the house, help fix food, and clean.

Then there were her O'Brian grandparents. With such a big family, they couldn't be warm to everyone. Instead, they showed their love by rounding everyone up and herding them off to church or a street party or to school. She'd only hugged her grandmother once she'd become an adult, and only when they were alone. With the entire clan together, she could barely get near her.

When she had entered Lauren's family home, she had feared not fitting in. But the more the day drew on, the more comfortable she became. Especially when Elizabeth found out that Sam was a professional gamer. She'd made Lauren switch seats with her so she could sit next to Sam and wouldn't talk to anyone else at the table. When the meal was over, she'd asked to be excused and dragged Sam away to watch her play a game on her Nintendo Switch. And Sam was happy to do it.

Lauren found them on the patio. "All right, Bunny. Enough of monopolizing Sam. Time for you to head home."

"Okay." Elizabeth did as she was told, but she obviously wasn't happy about it. "Will you be here next Saturday?"

Sam looked at Lauren. "I don't know."

Lauren pushed Elizabeth toward the door. "I'll bring her back soon. I promise. Now get going."

Lauren might want her to come back again. That was reassuring.

"You could have excused yourself," said Lauren.

Sam waved it off. "I liked it. She's good at that game."

Lauren sat on the arm of the chair, her side against Sam's shoulder. Sam wanted to wrap an arm around her waist. "Ready to head home?"

Home. She liked the sound of it. "Sure." She looked around to make sure no one heard her. "There are things I'd like to do back home. Specifically to you."

Lauren ran a hand through Sam's hair and whispered, "I can't wait."

They said their good-byes. Barbara made sure Sam would promise to come back again. When they left the house, the shadows were long on the street, and a breeze was blowing up from the river. Sam closed her eyes and let it move across her face.

"Pretty evening." Lauren unlocked the car doors.

"Not as pretty as you."

"Wow, that was the cheesiest line I've ever heard."

Sam shrugged and opened her door. "Hey, what's a Karmen Ghia?" she asked as she took her seat.

Lauren squinted at her. "A vintage car. Why?"

"Your mother asked if I owned one." She shrugged.

Lauren rolled her eyes. "My ex-girlfriend owned a convertible one. My mother misses that car more than the girlfriend."

"You don't think she knows about us, do you?"

Lauren ran a hand along her arm. "What would it matter if she did?"

Sam's heart rate soared at the touch. She put an arm around the back of Lauren's seat and leaned toward her. Lauren's eyes stayed on her lips as she drew closer.

There was a loud knock. She jumped back in her seat and found Barbara standing outside the car. Great, this felt a little like the time she'd gotten caught at her grandparents in the closet with the Christmas presents. She'd been looking for the power cable for the family computer and ended up knowing what everyone was getting as gifts that year. Sam rolled down the window reluctantly.

"You forgot your leftovers." Barbara handed her a bag with several Tupperware bowls in it. She smiled. "Safe trip back." She walked to the end of the sidewalk, turned, and waved with a little smirk on her face.

"Well, she knows now," said Lauren. "The text messages should begin arriving before we hit the bridge."

Sam scratched her head. That was unexpected. What was it like to have a mother know about her being gay? Did Barbara think Sam was a fling? Was she going to be good enough for their little girl?

She remembered watching her mother wave to her, framed through a school bus window. What would she be thinking of what Sam had become? In her memories, Sam held on to the moments of love she'd felt from her mother, but the inability to ask her important things like this left doubts. It was time she asked her father instead.

CHAPTER TWENTY-FOUR

Sam fell asleep in the post-scrimmage meeting. She awoke to an almighty racket. Seemed her teammates had balanced an assortment of Ping-Pong balls on her while she slept. Everyone had a good laugh at her expense, but she couldn't be mad. It was hard to be mad when she was having sex as many times as she could fit into a day. But it was wearing her out.

"You feel all right?" asked Alec.

She ran her hand along the back of her neck. "Yeah, sorry. Just tired."

"We need you at your best for New York this weekend. Why don't you go get some rest? I'll see you tomorrow at eleven."

She nodded her thanks, threw her stuff in her backpack, and headed out. She should have gone to the apartment and slept for the rest of the day. Lauren was on a trip to Miami with one of the other teams and would meet her in New York on Friday, so it wasn't like she'd distract Sam from sleeping. Instead, she worked on a thank-you gift for Lauren that would let her know how much Sam appreciated her standing up to Will at the office. She should have stood up for herself, but she wasn't even off probation yet, and she knew it would have been futile. She had almost walked away from it all instead.

She'd considered bringing Lauren flowers and Bomboy's and making her a special dinner, but none of those seemed right. It had to be something she hadn't already done. Lauren might not like what she settled on, but she'd try anyway.

It required her home computer, so off she went to Havre de Grace, and now she was staring at her father's car in the driveway. She only hoped he was okay seeing her as he hadn't been there the last three times she'd driven up.

She'd tried calling him, but instead of his landline ringing incessantly, she'd gotten a busy signal. She didn't even know busy signals still existed. He had call-waiting. Whatever was going on, she only hoped he hadn't had a bad episode while she was gone. With her hand on the doorknob, she wasn't sure if she should use her key or knock. What if he freaked out? She opened the front door an inch and yelled into the house, "Pops, it's me."

"In the kitchen," came the reply.

That was reassuring. He sounded clear, and dared she say, upbeat. As she walked past the staircase to the half wall that separated the single great room and the kitchen, she saw her father at the kitchen table with a calm, full-grown yellow lab wearing a service dog harness sitting at his side.

"What's going on?"

He reached down and scratched the dog's ears. "This is Scout. She's a service dog for folks like me with PTSD."

That was the first time he had ever said the word out loud to her. He'd been diagnosed with PTSD seven years ago and retired with full disability since he'd served for over twenty years. She only knew anything at all because he'd left the paperwork around the house from his doctors, but he'd never spoken to her about any of it.

They'd both known something was wrong the first time he'd run through the house in a thunderstorm, yelling about taking cover as if they were under attack from mortar fire. He'd scared her enough that she'd called her grandparents, and it had scared her every time since. Her grandfather had come and taken her dad's guns and locked them in a safe at her grandparents' house. Her dad had never complained.

She pulled out a chair and sat.

"I decided it was time for me to learn how to get around on my own again," he said.

"You know, you could have called me."

"I can't have my daughter taking care of me when I can do it myself with time." He continued to gently rub the top of Scout's head.

Her gaze fell on the kitchen phone. The handset lay unplugged on the counter, disconnected from the base. "What happened to the phone?"

"A few days ago, the phone started ringing and wouldn't stop. Every time I answered, it was a weird sound like your computer used to make. So I unplugged it."

Sam knew what it was. Someone was using the phone number that had been leaked on the internet. They'd probably set up an old computer or an app to dial the number repeatedly. What was wrong with these assholes? "That's my fault, Pops," she said. "Somebody is trying to harass me, and they put your phone number on the internet. They probably haven't figured out a way to social engineer someone to get my cell phone number."

"Mmm." He nodded thoughtfully. "Bums."

"I'll take care of it. I'll get the number changed."

"I'll handle it myself."

"You sure?" she asked.

"Certain." He stroked Scout's head gently.

As she watched, she experienced a sudden pang of envy. She'd wanted a dog after high school, but he'd been adamantly against it.

"Is that all they're doing? Tying up my phone line?"

Should she give him the whole truth or a sliver? She stretched her legs and leaned back in her chair. How could she tell him what she was feeling? Explain things to a man who had literally faced death for years? She'd sound like she was whining. "It's not only the phone number. Some guys online have been giving me a hard time. Way more than I'm used to. Some days, I don't think it's worth it."

"I was running around in the yard in my underwear a few months ago, thinking I was under attack. I'm the last person who can give you advice, Sam. But the best thing I did was walk in the VA and ask for help. If what's happening to you is hard, find someone to talk to." He motioned with his hands. "A good therapist."

Who was this man, and what had he done with her dad? She nodded. "I'll think about that."

"But don't let those bastards force you to quit doing what you want."

"Pop, I'm more worried someone will hurt you." She choked on her next words. "You're important to me. I love you."

He stood and did something out of character for him. He took her in a hug and held her tightly. Tears she'd been holding in for a long time rolled down her cheeks. After a few moments, he returned to his seat. She wiped the tears from her cheeks. "I should have been here for you after your mother died, but I was too covered in my own grief. The only way I knew how to manage it was to go back to where things were too out of control for me to stop and think about it all."

Sam tried to keep her bitterness from overwhelming her. He'd gone back to a war zone rather than stay with his eight-year-old daughter. Then, she felt guilty for thinking badly of him. Her throat tightened as she said, "I needed you."

An anguished expression came over his face. "I know that now." He hung his head. "I miss your mother every day. When she died, it was like someone reached in and cut my heart from my chest."

Sam thought about Lauren, how she couldn't stop thinking about her. Was that how it had been for her dad?

"My VA therapist would like it if you would come to a session with me sometime. Do you think you could do that? If not—"

"Of course I will." She looked at her hands. "But I might say things. Things that might hurt us both."

He nodded slowly. "If we're going to make our bond better, we need to be honest with each other."

She'd never thought things were bad, merely difficult, but now, she had a lot to think about. "If we're being honest, I need to know something." She looked in his eyes. "What would mom have thought about me being a lesbian?"

He looked surprised. "She wanted nothing more than to be a mother, and she was never happier than when you were born."

Sam shifted uncomfortably in her seat. Wanting to be a mother more than anything else felt foreign to her. So different from her life goals.

"She wouldn't have given a damn, Sam. If you're asking how she would've handled your grandma Shaw and the rest of the family in North Carolina, she would have chosen you over them if it had come to that."

"I'm seeing someone," she blurted out.

"That woman who came here?" he asked.

"Yep."

"Are you happy?"

She thought about how Lauren made her feel. Complete. "With her, yes. With everything else, not so much."

"I watched a few of your games with Jarek."

Jarek? He'd been here with her dad? Why hadn't the shithead called her lately?

"I had to watch with classical music playing. The sound was too much for me. Jarek explained how good you were and how many guys wanted to be just like you, including him."

Scout nudged him with her head. Did she sense he was nervous or anxious? He looked directly at her and said, "I'm proud of you. I'm glad you're going for your dream."

Talking about feelings had never been easy for either of them. It overwhelmed her. This was the longest conversation they'd ever had. Second only to the time he'd tried to talk to her about sex and had given her the army version of the venereal disease lecture. *Talk about cringe.*

He leaned forward in his chair, giving her a hard stare. "Your hair is long."

"Yeah, about that. Do you have your clippers?"

He nodded.

"I think I need a new haircut."

He walked off wordlessly to find them.

Later, Sam moved to the basement and tinkered with the files on her computer, taking the textures she'd requested from her friend and adding them to the mesh objects in 3D. She was adding motion now, setting keyframes, making leaves drop from the trees. The final product would have taken her weeks if she hadn't already had similar files to mod. She rubbed her freshly shaved undercut.

She heard the familiar footsteps on the stairs to the basement. Jarek dropped his backpack on the floor and sat on the sofa. "Hey, I saw your car outside. What are you working on?"

"A new home space for Lauren."

"Nice. Is there something going on with you two?"

She felt flushed. "Yeah," was all she said. "What have you been up to? I've tried to reach you a few times, but you seemed to be ghosting me."

He shook his head. "It wasn't about you, O'Brian. I was jealous is all. Olivia gave me an earful recently. Made me see that you didn't make this happen. If they'd wanted me, they would have picked me."

"I'm not sure they wanted me, either."

"Things not going the way you expected?"

"I'm assuming you've watched the gameplay?"

"You talkin' about how they femmed you all up?" He laughed. "Believe me, Olivia, Ashton, and I chatted about it more than once. That must have been sending you."

"Oh, it was making me crazy all right, but I'm done with the cosplay." She changed the subject. "Hey, thanks for hanging out with my dad."

He looked embarrassed. "That's nothing. He stopped by the store one day with Scout. I was surprised he had a dog. We got to talking, and he asked if there was a way to see you play."

"Still, you did me a solid." He'd done more than that. but telling him what it really meant to her would only embarrass them both. She was always worried about her dad when she wasn't around, but it was comforting to know that Jarek was watching out for him.

"Well, if you need me, hit me up. Your dad's a good guy. He doesn't scare me as much now."

"Thanks, Jarek." She wanted to tell him how much she'd missed talking with him and hanging out, but he'd just get all weird about it.

He stood and lifted his backpack over his shoulder. "I've gotta get to work." He looked back over his shoulder. "Why don't you play with us later tonight?"

She shook her head. "I've got something I have to do, but I'm off probation now, so I'll be getting my own place soon." She didn't dare say she didn't *want* a place of her own.

"Wicked. Ashton will be jealous of that, seeing as he's still living with his mom."

Sam laughed. "Well, here I am in my dad's basement, and I might be back here before long."

"Hell, no. You have to do it for the rest of us." He started up the stairs.

"Good to talk to you, Jarek. Don't ghost me again, loser," she yelled after him jokingly.

He gave her a big smile. "Wouldn't think of it."

She stared at the screen. It was reassuring that Jarek was okay with her. She'd hated how distant they had been these past few months. Bad enough that everything in her life had changed so quickly. Some things needed to stay the same.

When she finished the files, the clock on the computer said 12:08 a.m. The box with the brand-new headset sat at her feet. She opened it and did a software update. This home was a present for Lauren, a thank-you for everything, and she didn't want to give it to Lauren on her old spare headset. Although she was certain Lauren wouldn't care if she got a used one, she'd bought her the latest one with last week's paycheck. Afraid it would arrive with its original box showing what was inside, she'd sent it to a package locker at the bodega down the street from the apartment. Not that Lauren would know it was for her, even if she had seen it.

Now that it was all complete, she worried that Lauren wouldn't like it. *Get out of your own head, O'Brian.* What else could she do? Buy her some more romance novels?

She opened the program on her computer, connected the headset via USB, and sent her APK files to the device. She disconnected it and put the headset on. A few more settings to make her new custom home be the default startup environment, and then it came to life before her eyes. So much pink. Oh well. Lauren seemed to like pink, and that was all that mattered. This was all about her.

She pulled off the headset and ran her hand through her hair. There had been moments when she'd thought she was being selfish. How many people had to wear things they hated for work? She needed to rephrase that. How many women wore things they hated or clothes that made them uncomfortable, just so they could make a living? Perhaps she was being too sensitive, but why was it so hard for the world to let her wear the same thing that the guys wore? If Dylan wanted to wear heels, she wouldn't stop him.

Her dad had waited up for her. She gave him a long, tight hug. "I'll call you when I get back from New York."

Scout moved close to his leg. He reached down and stroked her head. "Give 'em hell, O'Brian."

"Roger that." She smiled. The way they parted might have sounded silly to others, but she knew it meant he loved her and that she loved him, and that was all that mattered.

CHAPTER TWENTY-FIVE

The whole flight to New York, Lauren thought of nothing but seeing Sam at the hotel. She'd even daydreamed about if she'd been on the flight with her, doing it in the bathroom for a mile high club membership. Yes, it would have been embarrassing to be caught, and no, there wasn't enough room in the lavatory, and ew, who did it in a bathroom? But she was addicted to Sam's touch. It was like nothing she'd ever experienced.

She was glad Sam had come to her door that night. She had been too frightened to initiate the first move. For days, she had been waiting and thinking, Sam constantly on her mind. When she'd arrived in New York, she'd texted Sam, telling her she'd be there soon.

But the drive from Kennedy to midtown Manhattan had taken over an hour and a half. As her cab pulled up to the hotel, she had watched a Princess Leia and someone dressed as Garfield leave the lobby. Once again, the *Siege Encounter* tournament was in tandem with a large pop culture convention at the Javits Center, taking advantage of cross-promotion.

And inside the lobby, she saw Sam lounging in a chair, waiting for her. She had on her signature hoodie and noise canceling headphones, but the moment Lauren looked at her, she seemed to know it and looked back. And Sam smiled at her like no one else in the room mattered, and maybe they didn't because now they had a secret between them. She didn't know what it meant for them.

Every so often, the thought that Sam was a professional gamer would intrude in her happiness because she had promised herself she wouldn't get involved with a gamer again. But Sam was not Seth, and they had yet to talk about the future. For now, it was the best sex ever.

Normally at a work thing, Lauren would have been making calls or writing press releases or meeting with journalists, but Sam had worked her way into Lauren's heart, and her charming smile, along with a hug she could feel all over and a longing look, meant work was the last thing on her mind.

Sam tilted her head toward the elevators. "Want to check out my room with me?"

Lauren nearly wilted. Yes, she wanted to do anything Sam asked. "After you. I'll check in later."

Surprisingly, Sam didn't take the stairs. She rode the elevator, standing close to Lauren, gently running her fingers along her behind. As soon as the door closed on the hotel room, Lauren let go of her luggage and threw down her tote. Sam swept her into her arms and kissed her like they had been apart for a year, not a few days. Then, Sam lifted her off the floor and carried her to the king-size bed.

Sam hovered above her. "I have something for you, but it can wait." Then, she kissed her again. Clothes were thrown to the side, and all Lauren's daydreaming went with them. Because the reality was so much better.

Afterward, Lauren lay against Sam's chest, listening to her breathing. "As much as I'd like to stay like this for the rest of the day, I'm starving."

Sam got up and pulled on her T-shirt and boy shorts and opened the tiny hotel refrigerator. She withdrew a paper bag with a blue Greek key design along the edges. "I saw a Greek diner across the street and got you a sandwich when your flight landed."

Lauren slipped on her shirt and looked inside. "Oh my God, I love egg salad." She pulled out half the sandwich and took a giant bite.

"Your mom told me."

"When did she tell you that?"

Sam gave her a shy look. "Um. When I texted her to tell her your flight arrived?"

Lauren closed her eyes and shook her head. "I knew I shouldn't have given her your phone number."

Sam laughed and withdrew a to-go cup with a straw. "And she mentioned you'd probably still like a black and white."

She took the offered milkshake, took a long sip, and sighed with satisfaction. Best day ever.

Sam then proffered a large, gift-wrapped box.

"If that's donuts, they'll have to wait. This is fucking fantastic."

"Did you just say the f-word?" Sam asked.

Lauren shoved another bite in her mouth. "I did, and I won't take it back. Fucking amazing. I'd say I'd like to learn to cook, but that would be a lie. I enjoy eating food cooked by other people."

Sam held the package out again. "I've been working on this for a few weeks as a thank-you for all the stuff you've done for me. You know, disrupting your life, having to buy furniture, sharing a bathroom with someone not as tidy as you."

Lauren swiveled to face her. Everything Sam had brought to her life had been worth any disruption. She was the happiest she had ever been. "You didn't need to get me anything, Sam."

"Oh yes, I did. I've been difficult about all the changes, and you took all my complaints in stride. And then when you stood up for me with Will..." Sam looked as if she might get a little teary-eyed. "Yeah, anyway, you deserve a thank-you." Inside was a VR headset. One that looked like the one Sam had for herself. "I know it may not be exactly your thing, but I made something for you inside."

Lauren opened the box and removed the headset and controllers. Now she was intrigued.

"It's already charged." Sam stepped closer. "Let me help you put it on." She pushed a button.

Lauren heard a characteristic beep. Sam slid it on Lauren's head and walked her through how to set the safe zone.

Then, something amazing happened. She stood in the garden of a traditional Japanese house with a thatched roof, open veranda, latticed windows, and sliding doors. Beside her was a Zen garden with perfectly curved lines in the gravel and a standing stone in the middle. In the distance was an open gazebo, and all around her were blooming cherry trees, occasionally dropping delicate pink petals.

The sounds of wind rustling the branches accompanied the leaves falling. A gentle ringing sound played in the distance, a bell or a wind chime, and if she moved closer to the pond, she could hear the water burbling. Several large orange and white koi swam lazily in the pond. "This is amazing. It's like I'm in my favorite show."

"That's what I was going for. You can even pick up the rake and redraw the Zen garden if you want. But be careful, you might run out of room to move in here."

"You made this?" She was stunned by the detail. Everything was so real.

"I put it together and did the rendering. I have a friend who makes custom textures, so I asked her for a favor. And I bought some stock imagery for the background mountains. The thing that took the longest was making all those little 3D polygons to lay those pink flower petals on."

Lauren pulled off the headset and set the controllers on the bed.

"The headset company makes it easier by allowing tools to upload the APK files for public use—"

Lauren moved closer, not thinking about what she was doing.

Sam's eyes went wide. "You don't want the details, do you?"

"Nope." Lauren stepped closer. She dropped her voice lower. "As a matter of fact, I'd prefer you keep it to yourself and let me imagine you used magic to make that happen." She stopped inches away. She could see the desire in Sam's eyes. "Magic," she repeated and reached around the back of Sam's neck and pulled her forward.

There was no resistance. Sam's lips met hers with the same interest and ferocity as their first kiss. That first kiss had happened so fast and so unexpectedly, Lauren hadn't had time to think about anything other than feeling good and being wanted. This time, she noticed more. Their lips fit together. Sam's were soft, and her tongue was smooth. She felt the kiss through every nerve in her body.

It wasn't long before the room felt like it had melted away, and all she could think of was the pink leaves falling all around them like gentle rain. This was, without a doubt, the best kiss she had ever had. Nothing could touch it. Nothing at all.

She felt Sam's hands around her waist. Every finger sent separate signals low in her belly. So much sensation. So many tastes and smells. She was overwhelmed in a good way. In the way where she did what she felt like doing instead of doing what her brain told her to do.

She didn't know how long they stood there kissing, and she didn't care. She would have stayed in the same spot forever, but her body wanted more, and she was all about letting her body drive. "I think it's my turn to give you a gift," she murmured against Sam's lips. She felt her smile.

The next morning, Sam woke to a light knocking at her door. She rubbed her eyes and opened the door to find Lauren on the other side holding two coffees.

"Big day." She set one cup on the desk and opened the blinds. Lauren gazed at the New York skyline and sipped her coffee while Sam slipped into her team gear.

"Give me a hand." Sam held out the wig. "Alec said this was nonnegotiable."

Lauren frowned.

Sam held up her hand. "Before you get worked up about it, I'm too happy right now to be upset. I decided to treat it like cosplay. Whatever the reason for making me into a doll, I don't blame you. I'm just thankful you got them to change my name."

"You shouldn't have had to do any of it. You should've been yourself from the beginning. Confident. Charismatic. Handsome."

Sam raised her eyebrows and gave a shy smile. "Handsome. I've never been called that before. I like it."

"You are handsome and beautiful at the same time. You should see how the girls giggle and stare at you from the gaming floor."

"You sure they aren't doing a mean girl routine?"

Lauren shook her head. "Oh no. They stare at you the same way my friends admire movie stars."

"You're the only one I want looking at me."

Lauren set her coffee down and assisted in putting the wig on. She put her hands on Sam's shoulders when she was done. Sam noticed the little extra touch Lauren made before she released her. "You ready? You win this, and you're guaranteed a spot in the World Championship."

The World Championship. The inaugural edition for *Siege Encounter*. With a prize of one million dollars to the winning team. She could pay off a lot of her dad's bills with her share of that money. He'd texted her last night from a phone number she didn't recognize. She'd finally called back to verify it was really him. He had gotten a mobile phone. She took a selfie and sent it to him, though she didn't expect him to become chatty in one week.

She glanced at Lauren, who was as put together as always. No wrinkles in her clothes. Not a hair out of place, her outfit sleek and trim. Sam's hands itched to massage her calves. Her gaze traveled the length of her until they stared at each other. Lauren didn't hide her desire. Why should she? Lauren looked amazing, and Sam wanted her to know it.

Lauren coughed and stared into her coffee. "Time to go." She strode to the door, but Sam captured her hand and turned her. Careful not to bump her coffee, she leaned in and kissed her. Lauren gave a slight smile.

The next hour was a whirlwind of last-minute strategy discussions with the team, a few photos with fans, a quick sound bite with the streaming media team, and finally, Sam was standing ready to go onstage.

Lauren leaned close as they moved to take their seats. "Good luck."

Something about Lauren's expression filled her with confidence about the games. She followed the rest of the team onstage.

"You better bring it today, newbie," said Dylan as she settled in her chair. He shoved her headset at her. "Don't take it off."

She didn't tell him to eat shit, though she wanted to. Instead, she played the best match of her brief career, ending the tournament atop the leaderboard once again. The team was going to the world championship. She didn't wait to find out where they wanted her to stand or if she was even needed at the postgame show. Instead, she rushed from the stage and took Lauren in a bear hug. Everywhere they touched, she buzzed with energy. When they broke apart, she took her by the hand and dragged her down the corridor until she found a stairwell.

"What's going on?" asked Lauren.

"I want to do something I should have done in Indianapolis." Before she could overthink it and stop herself, she was kissing her.

They broke apart. and Lauren ripped the wig from Sam's head and flung it on the stairs. Then, she took Sam's face in her hands and kissed her back. "Yes, you should have."

When they returned to the gaming floor, Will was angry. "Where have you been? We need Samantha on the set now."

"I had something I needed to do," said Sam. She gave him a pointed look and added, "By the way, my name is Sam."

"What happened to your wig?" he asked, ignoring the discussion of her name.

Lauren shrugged. "Malfunction. It happens."

With a smile, Sam moved away to join the others. She was going to the world championship, and she had a girlfriend. Could it get any better?

CHAPTER TWENTY-SIX

Toronto at the end of August was cooler than Baltimore. This was it, thought Lauren. The Baltimore Barrage would clash with the sixteen best teams in the world, including the Seoul Daggers, for the inaugural world championship. Seoul's participation had been practically guaranteed from the beginning of the season, but the bet makers had ranked the Barrage much lower. They were ranked sixteen out of sixteen going into the tournament. Most of the gambling apps had one of the two Chinese teams going up against the Daggers in the finals. Even Sam's arrival on the team, which had boosted their ranking, seemed to receive an inordinate amount of pundit hate. They seemed to see her as the weak link, even though her statistics showed a different story.

The hotel lobby was crowded, the room filled with backpack-wearing teens and twenty-somethings, most of them guys, but there were a few groups of girls scattered around the room. Most of them standing together. One or two of them yelled at Sam as the team entered with their rolling luggage.

"Is this normal?" Sam asked her.

"For the world championship tournament? Back in March, the *Legends* one was much crazier." She moved to the side while Frank dealt with getting all the room codes. "But I am a little surprised at all this interest in a new game."

"I didn't realize the Barrage was in the finals of *League of Legends*," said Sam.

"They lost, but it was great recognition for the team, and I got to go to Warsaw." Thinking about it made Lauren sigh a little. Traveling internationally for work had been her dream.

Sam's attention turned away from her to the entrance. The sound around them had increased to a cacophony of screams. The Seoul Daggers had arrived dressed in their bespoke suits.

Lauren would have agreed with Sam that Ahn Ji-ho looked like the lead singer of BTS arriving, but now that she and Sam had watched one or two K-dramas together, she felt like she was watching the start of a TV series. Some inept girl was going to stumble in front of the main character. He would find her intriguing, and away they'd go.

The Seoul team's operations manager was already waiting for them near the elevators, so they breezed past Lauren and the Barrage team members at the front desk. The last one leaned over and said something to Sam. Her expression changed from awed to confused.

"What did he say?"

Sam shook her head. "Same thing he said to me the last time I saw him. *Hon* something. I don't know."

"Could it be a greeting of some kind?"

Sam shook her head. "I don't think so."

Lauren rubbed Sam's arm. "Don't worry about it. He's probably trying to intimidate you."

"I know he is," said Sam, still watching them as they got in the elevator.

"Here ya go." Frank handed each of them a room card. "Scan that card, and you'll be able to use your phone app after that. I put you in adjoining rooms like you asked."

Sam's head whipped around at that. Lauren tried not to grin. "Thanks."

Once in their rooms, Lauren knocked on the connecting door. Sam opened it and invited her in. The room was modern, with clean lines and warm brown furniture. A rain shower stood between the bed and the bathroom, encased in glass. Her mind went to imagining Sam showering in there. "You'd think Nate could have splurged for a little better room," she joked.

Sam gestured to the king-size bed and smiled. "Who needs anything else?"

Lauren let out a startled gasp as Sam grabbed her and laid her on the mattress. She slid on top of her, pressing against her. Desire flooded Lauren in response. Sam kissed her, and she deepened the kiss. She could have stayed like this for the rest of the day if they didn't have places to be.

Lauren reluctantly pushed Sam to the side. "I have something to give you." She hurried back to her room and retrieved the motorcycle jacket from her luggage. As she returned, she held it out.

Sam's eyes went wide, and her mouth dropped open. "Wow, when did you get this?" She helped Sam into the jacket. She looked amazing. "I've had it since the day you tried it on," she said coyly.

Sam ran her hands along the sides. "I thought you said we couldn't buy it."

"The team didn't buy it. I did," she admitted.

Sam seemed to be trying to work that out in her head.

"I was trying to find the perfect moment to give it to you."

Sam looked at herself in the mirror and back at Lauren. "I don't know what to say."

"Say you'll wear it."

"Of course I will."

"Good." Lauren kissed her cheek.

Sam wrapped an arm around Lauren's waist. "But if you bought this for me when we went shopping, does that mean you liked me then?"

"You're trying to embarrass me, aren't you?"

"I liked you the first moment I saw you striding through the convention center in Baltimore."

Lauren felt the flush of heat on her face. "The first moment I found you attractive was when you were at the bar in your hoodie. I couldn't see all of your face, just your jaw and your lips." She ran a hand down the sleeve of the jacket. "And I must have a thing for bare forearms. Something about you called to me."

"If we're admitting things, I should tell you that I followed you in the bar." She put up a hand. "Not in a stalker way. I just figured it was a good time to check out the hotel bar and maybe check you out."

The thought was titillating, not strange at all. "I'm glad you did."

Sam lifted the front of the jacket. "I love the smell of leather."

Lauren leaned in as if she was smelling the jacket and then kissed Sam's neck instead. "I love the smell of you." She could see the desire in Sam's eyes before Sam leaned in and kissed her. Lauren sank into the kiss. When they broke apart, she said, "We need to be at the arena for the first of your matches in thirty minutes."

"Plenty of time." Sam put an arm around her waist and pulled her closer. "Should I leave the jacket on?" The seductive timbre of Sam's voice sent pulses of arousal through her.

Lauren gave in to her desire. "Absolutely."

The first match went exactly to plan. The French team fell in five games straight. Later that night, Sam and her teammates had moved on to the round of eight. This time, they played the Argentinians, an unexpected underdog like the Barrage. Sam appeared to be as happy as Lauren had ever seen her, and her play reflected it. Her movements were fluid and easy. Her intuition for the movement of her opponents was like watching a talented soccer player. Unlike when Sam had first joined the team, it was Dylan who was showing weakness, but Sam and Perry played well enough to cover for him.

Lauren and Sam spent most of the night in bed but not sleeping. It was exciting to be in a new place. Sam seemed pumped from her games, and Lauren benefitted from the extra energy with multiple trips to the edge of ecstasy. The heat between them was like a furnace.

Day two, Lauren stood with several of the Barrage investors in the VIP section of the arena and watched the large screen above the stage. She twirled her drink mindlessly and smiled when she thought someone said something she should have been listening to. The team was playing in the semifinals against one of the two Chinese teams still left in the competition. The Barrage fell in the first three games, not winning a single map.

Lauren worried. How would Sam take it if they lost the next two games? As if knowing she was being talked about, Sam found her in the crowd and smiled at her, looking as if nothing was wrong. It was comforting.

The noise in the arena was deafening as the fourth game began. Lauren knew the Chinese teams playing in other leagues had a rabid fan base in China, but the number of fans who had shown up here in Toronto overwhelmed her. This game was consistently compared to *Call of Duty* and called too slow by players used to the frenetic pace of other games. Yesenia's job trying to market *Siege Encounter* around the world seemed daunting, but that was a challenge Lauren would love to have.

As she watched game four unfold, she held her breath. She could see Dylan saying something to Sam. From his expression, whatever it was seemed to make Sam go cold. Sam hadn't told her much about the dynamic with the other players. She seemed to compartmentalize well, keeping the internal politics to herself. But Lauren had seen it for herself multiple times: Dylan didn't like her.

"Come on," Lauren muttered to herself. She'd never been this invested in one of Seth's competitions. Then again, she hadn't worked for his team. But this wasn't only work. Her heart was falling fast for Sam, and she wanted her to do well. She was also proud to see a woman player on the stage. There only needed to be more.

The Barrage found their groove. They won games four, then five, lost six, won seven, and won eight. They hadn't needed to go to a full nine games yet in the tournament, but here they were, one game and one map from the world championship final. The scores went back and forth, but in the end, Sam and the others won.

That was when Lauren noticed how many women and girls were in the arena as their higher-pitched screams filled the air. That gave her an idea.

She called out to one of her assistants. "I need you to do me a favor. I need you to find a contact for me."

"Sure thing," he replied.

Postgame, she waited in the meeting room at the hotel where the press conference would be held. Nearly an hour passed before the Korean and the second Chinese team finished their semifinal. It came as no surprise that the Seoul Daggers would be their opponents in the final. Lauren moved around to the side of the group of journalists, trying to get a better view as Sam took her seat at the long table with her teammates. She wore the jacket Lauren had given her, and she looked bold and self-assured. A warmth traveled through Lauren when she thought of what Sam had done to her yesterday while wearing that jacket.

"I see you cut your hair," said one of the male journalists to Sam. For a moment, all Lauren heard was the clicking of the digital cameras and their flashes.

Sam gave a deadpan reply. "Thanks for noticing."

Lauren let out a deep breath. Sam wasn't taking the bait, thank goodness. She looked amazing, and a gaggle of screaming fan girls off to Lauren's left seemed to agree.

There were a few questions to Alec about team coherence and how they would counter the Seoul team's almost perfect gameplay tomorrow in the finals.

"Samantha, how does it feel to play your people?" asked another guy. Lauren tried to see his credentials. Looked like he was an internet content creator.

"It's Sam, and by people, I assume you mean other highly skilled gamers?" she retorted. A chuckle ran through the crowd. Oh, she was on fire tonight. Will should have let her be herself from the beginning.

The guy wouldn't give up. "I meant you're playing the Koreans, and you're part Korean."

This time, Sam's eyes narrowed. She looked around until she found Lauren in the crowd. Lauren smiled reassuringly. "These"— she motioned to her teammates on the stage—"are currently my people, and we plan on showing out tomorrow."

A woman reporter raised her voice. "What do you have to say about the online attacks you've received?"

Sam's expression darkened. "We've all received some awful online hate, but I don't understand guys who put people's livelihoods at risk. I'm playing a game. This isn't a war or a rebellion. We're here to entertain people and to show others they can play these games and have fun, too. The industry has to do better. I hope to have a kid someday, but right now, I'd be reluctant to let them play online knowing the abuse they'd face."

Lauren wasn't surprised by the fact Sam wanted children, but she was surprised by the fact that she envisioned herself and Sam having them together. When had her feelings for Sam become that strong?

"Any thoughts on how to make the industry safer?" asked the woman.

Will answered from his position standing off to the side, "How about we get back to the tournament?"

"I'll talk to you about that after we win." Sam gave her that rogue smile that melted Lauren's heart. She knew that smile was meant for her, not the reporter. Sam threw a thumb at Luke. "Ask Luke about how it feels to get the abuse he gets as the backup to a girl."

Luke looked startled, but he answered honestly. He had nothing to lose by being honest. At first, he'd been hurt, especially by the comments that implied he wasn't man enough to play professionally. But he realized that didn't matter. What mattered was that he was a good teammate and a decent human. After hearing what he said, Lauren wondered if he might be interested in helping her and Sam with the program she was developing.

The tone of the questions changed to what the team had seen in Toronto so far, what they would do with their winnings, and other less serious topics. When the press conference ended, Sam walked up to Lauren and took her hand. "Man, that was a crazy match. I can't believe we did it."

Lauren pretended to straighten the jacket. She leaned in close to Sam's ear, knowing her breath would play across her skin. "I'd really like to kiss you right now."

Sam shivered, and her eyes conveyed her desire.

Lauren leaned away and winked at her. "I thought I'd leave you with a little something to think about."

"If you could see my mind right now, you'd be the one blushing."

Lauren laughed. "Somebody got a haircut and a sexy jacket and became a heartthrob."

Sam stood straighter and put one hand in her coat pocket. "It's hard not to feel amazing when you're dating the sexiest woman in the room."

Lauren felt the heat of her blush.

"Lauren, sweetie." Yesenia waved and gave her air kisses. "Sam, so nice to see you." When she gave Sam her air kisses, Sam went stiff and looked like someone had handed her a grenade she shouldn't drop. "I've been following your progress. Everyone at Augustan is pleased to have you representing our game."

"Thanks." Sam seemed to have lost all that swagger she'd mustered on the dais. Lauren understood. Yesenia's powerful presence could make CEOs wither.

"Augustan wants to make some adjustments for the winter season. And we're interested in hearing more about your experience with bullying. We're listening." Yesenia grasped Lauren's hand. "And I'm so excited for you, darling."

For a moment, she thought Yesenia knew she and Sam were together, but she hadn't told her yet. "About?"

"About? Don't you read your emails? I can't wait till you move here. There are so many great restaurants we can go to."

Lauren was excited for about a half a second as the realization came over her. She'd been offered a job at Augustan Gaming. Then, as quickly as the excitement had arrived, she felt like she'd been kicked in the stomach. She glanced at Sam, who'd gone pale, meaning she had reached the same conclusion.

Lauren took Yesenia's arm and walked her a few paces away. "Can we talk about this later?"

"Of course." Yesenia looked between them. "Officially, I can't take sides, but good luck tomorrow, Sam."

Sam was standing very still, her expression pensive. Lauren grasped both her hands to try to reassure her. "I haven't even seen the offer. Even if it seems like a good move, maybe I'll only do it for a year or so. And it's only Toronto. I can fly back anytime."

She could fly back anytime, but the thing was, she didn't want to leave at all. Not now. Not when she'd found someone so perfect for her. She'd done this before, traveling and long-distance dating. It hadn't worked for her. Well, it hadn't worked with Seth. However, Yesenia and Bodhan managed to be together. Surely, she and Sam could make it happen as well.

The feeling of abandonment swarmed over Sam like a heavy cloak. She realized that her grief was about to overwhelm her. Grief that had little to do with Lauren and more to do with her mother's death. She started moving and put a hand up in a small wave. "I need some time alone."

Lauren followed her. "Sam, please, let's talk about it. I don't have to take the job."

Her throat tightened. "I can't talk about it right now. I need some space."

This time, Lauren stopped and let her move away.

Sam shouldered past several fans who were trying to get her attention. She couldn't stop right now, or she'd break down. Until she stepped through the revolving doors of the hotel onto the street, she hadn't even known where she was going. She looked around at the unfamiliar city.

"Well, hello," said an elegant sounding male voice, like a British TV actor or a BBC announcer.

She turned to find the man standing next to her was Ahn Ji-ho. "Hello," she replied, then returned to looking intently interested in her phone.

"I've been meaning to introduce myself. I'm Ahn Ji-ho."

"I know who you are," she replied dryly. "We're playing against each other tomorrow,"

"You're Samantha O'Brian with the Barrage."

"Just Sam. Listen, I'm not in the mood—"

"I wanted to apologize for my teammate's behavior the other day." His diction was exquisite, as if he was teaching English rather than speaking it. A little haughty, but that might be his posture and immaculate wardrobe.

"It's all right. I don't even know what he said." Embarrassment flooded her. "I don't speak Korean."

He lowered his voice and leaned toward her. "He said *honhyeol*. I apologize for even repeating it. It means half-breed."

"Ah, well, he certainly didn't want to go out for drinks, then."

Ji-ho looked quizzical.

"One of my friends was certain he was asking me out for drinks."

"Well, then I should do that." A black car pulled up in front of the hotel. Ji-ho motioned for her to accompany him. "Join me?"

Having drinks with the best player in the world was dumb. He was her opponent tomorrow. What if her teammates saw her? What if Lauren saw her? What did that matter? Lauren was leaving her. Her mind was a twirling mess of thoughts, and none of them were about tomorrow's match. What the hell? She hopped in beside him.

He asked the driver for the best Korean restaurant, and within a few minutes, the driver dropped them at what he assured them was a traditional Korean bar. Her heart pounded. She knew nothing about Korean food. She'd tucked away all the parts of her that reminded her of her mother and the grandfather she had never known. All the things that hurt, like being abandoned. Exactly what Lauren was about to do to her.

Inside, most of the tables were group style seating, six to eight seats at long tables with a cooking unit built in the center. They took one of the only two tops in a corner.

She laced her fingers together and leaned against the tabletop. "So why are you apologizing for your teammate? Shouldn't he be doing it?"

Ji-ho adjusted his watch slightly, setting it in a different position on his wrist. The timepiece shined when it caught the light. It looked expensive. "He is highly competitive. When he sees someone he knows will be a threat, he does not hold back with his intimidation."

"I'm a nobody. We both know I'm an aging newbie who isn't going to last a season. And while your teammate yells slurs at people who don't understand Korean, you stand around in sunglasses and give the stare down?"

"Stare down?"

"Evil eye?" He still didn't seem to understand. "A mean look."

"Ah." He smiled and nodded. "I do not need to give anyone the evil eye. My gameplay speaks for itself."

She wished that could be the same for her. Instead, she had been wearing long wigs, short skirts, and makeup for most of the season. Intimidating to some but nothing but uncomfortable for her. She had tried to feel as relaxed as Lauren looked in her traditionally feminine clothing, but she was a tomboy at heart and always would be.

A server approached. Ji-ho ordered a drink Sam had never heard of, and the server walked away before she could order herself a Coke. The woman returned with a small green bottle and two shot glasses.

"How old are you?" asked Ji-ho.

Did she appear that young? "Old enough to drink."

"Korean traditions are based on age. Generally, the elder or host must serve the soju first. I'm twenty-four."

Her lack of knowledge embarrassed her. "Twenty-five."

"Then you are the elder. In this case, I will serve as host though since it is your first time." He swirled the bottle, banged the bottom on his palm, removed the cap, and did a little flicking thing with two fingers that spilled some on the table. He told her to hold out her glass with both hands, and he served her a shot, holding the bottle with two hands. He then asked her to serve his drink. Luckily, she didn't need to swirl and bang it.

"Now we drink, but I must turn away since you are the elder."

She squinted. "A lot of rules in this drinking game." She turned up the shot and drank the whole thing. The flavor was nearly imperceptible, with a light crispness and the cold burn of alcohol. Ji-ho filled her glass again. She'd regret this later.

"What brings you out on the night before you play in the final of the world championship?" he asked.

They didn't know each other. What did it matter if she told him the truth? "A broken heart," she muttered. "What about you?"

"Pre-competition nerves," he replied without a hint of humor. She knew she was giving him an I-don't-believe-you expression. "I have anxiety."

"I find that hard to believe."

"It's true," he said. "Ever since I played in my first tournament."

"This would be the moment in the K-drama where the female lead would help you overcome all your fears." She cocked her head. "Too bad for you, I'm not the female lead."

"I read online that your grandfather was Korean. Where was he from?"

She shook her head. Damn online articles. She wished the journalists would leave her alone. "I never met the man. I don't even know his name."

"I'm sorry."

She critiqued Ji-ho with his unblemished skin and his perfectly smooth black hair. His features were much more stereotypically Asian than her own. His suit had a sheen to it, not a wrinkle in it, and it fit him perfectly, not all baggy and oversized like her clothes. Was this what had happened to her grandmother? Had her grandfather been a beautiful man who'd asked her to have soju with him?

The server returned with two menus. Everything was in Korean, with English translations underneath in a smaller font. "Can I ask you a question?" Sam said.

"Certainly," he replied.

"How many years have you been a pro?"

"Ten."

She was surprised. She'd liked to game at that age, too, but she couldn't imagine handling the pressure she felt now at fourteen. "How did you manage that?"

He nodded thoughtfully. "It wasn't easy. My parents required me to stay in school. So between gaming, day school, and seven hours a week of *hagwon*, which is a cram school where I mostly got extra tutoring in English and Math, there wasn't much time left for sleep."

"How long did it take you to learn English?"

"In Korea, we are required to learn English in school for twelve years."

Her voice rose. "Twelve years?" She'd taken three years of Latin in Catholic school and thought that was commitment. "How long do you think it would take me to learn to speak Korean?"

He smiled and shrugged. "I am not a language teacher. A few years. I doubt you would ever get rid of your American accent, though."

"Hey." She took mock offense. "I might surprise you."

"Perhaps."

When the server returned, Sam deferred to Ji-ho's choices for their meal. She wasn't hungry anyway. Her stomach had been doing somersaults since she'd heard Yesenia tell Lauren about the job offer.

"How do you like playing with the Barrage?"

"How do you like playing for the Daggers?" she replied.

He nodded. "I like it a lot." Four small dishes containing a series of foods of all different colors arrived. When she admitted she wasn't very knowledgeable about Korean dishes, he pointed out what they were as he grabbed each one deftly with his chopsticks. "Traditional kimchi, which is cabbage. Cucumber kimchi. *Gat*, a mustard leaf, and *gamja jorim*, potatoes in soy sauce."

Sam looked at the food and realized she wished Lauren was here trying everything with her. She blurted out, "I'm a lesbian. If this"—she motioned between them—"is some sort of come on, you're going to be disappointed and out some cash."

He laughed. "I learned a long time ago that it is not good to mix business with pleasure."

An image of Lauren popped into her mind. It wasn't a good idea, was it? The dark wave of grief clawed its way around her again. "Then, if this is your way of sussing out the competition, I'll take your food, but I won't talk strategy with you. I plan on winning tomorrow."

"Fair enough." He poured more soju into her empty glass.

She drank the second glass as quickly as the first. He filled it again. She took the cubed potato and placed it on her tongue. Though it tasted delicious, she struggled to swallow the bite. She should call or text Lauren. She shouldn't have run away. "Tell me something truthful."

Ji-ho set his chopsticks down and waited for her question.

"What are the chances of someone like me going pro if I was Korean? As a woman and a lesbian?"

He threw back his drink and placed the glass carefully on the table. "There are almost no professional female players in Korea."

"So it isn't just over here." She had guessed the answer before she asked the question. "And my sexuality?"

"Korea is quite conservative." He seemed to consider his words carefully. "You might find it difficult."

"Are women players there subjected to the same harassment as they are here?"

He wouldn't meet her eyes. "Perhaps even more so." He ate. "Explaining the cultural differences between your country and mine would take us much longer than a single dinner. And I am not certain I would be best suited to do so. You should come and experience it for yourself."

She had way too many things to think about right now to consider something like that. Like, what was Lauren doing right now? Was she disappointed in Sam's reaction?

A few hours later, Sam stumbled as she stepped from the cab at the hotel. Ji-ho steadied her gently. "Thanks for dinner. We should do this again sometime. Except let's skip the soju. That stuff is like drinking water. If I lose tomorrow, I'm blaming the national drink of South Korea."

"Fair enough. Will you be all right from here?" he asked as they entered the lobby.

"Totally fine."

He gave her a small bow. "Good luck with healing your heart."

He walked away, all tall and lean. And that suit. If she had a suit like that, she'd get all the girls. Actually, all she wanted was one. One woman. She scolded herself for letting her mind wander back to Lauren. She shook her head, trying to clear it. Drinking, contrary to the hope that it would dull her pain, had done the opposite and intensified it. Now she was drunk and sad and wanted to do nothing but knock on Lauren's door and either cry on her shoulder or kiss her. What a conundrum.

She stumbled up the stairs to her floor. It was ridiculous to be so upset about something she had known might happen. Lauren had been honest with her all along. She'd even fixed her computer knowing full well that Lauren was trying to apply to the job at Augustan. But at that point, it had been a crush on her roommate. Now it was…much more than that.

Back in her room, she swayed in front of the connecting door, trying to decide if she should knock. She wanted to talk to her. Explain why she had walked away. What she was scared of. But she decided talking when she was a little drunk wasn't the way she wanted to do it.

When had she fallen in love with her? And how was she going to tell that to Lauren?

Chapter Twenty-seven

Lauren sat on her bed. She read and reread the job offer from Augustan. The money was fantastic. The benefits were great. They'd handle her work visa, pay all her moving costs, and give her three weeks of vacation, plus the nine days allocated by law for holidays. She'd be working with Yesenia. There was ample opportunity to travel. What was there to not like about this?

Sam.

She pulled out her phone, hoping there would be a text or a missed call from her, but there was nothing. Well, at this point, she had no shame. She opened her video app. She couldn't believe she was about to call her mother for romantic advice. At least it wasn't too late in the evening to do so.

"Hello." All she could see was the top of her mother's head down to her eyebrows with a great view of the den ceiling.

"Can you tilt the phone down a little?"

"Oh. Can you see me now?" Her mother broke out in laughter. "I don't know if you remember the commercial with the guy walking around all over the place saying, 'Can you hear me now?' Who would have thought we'd be video chatting a few years later?"

"Who'd have thought?" Lauren said without enthusiasm.

"Well, I know that sound. You sounded like that the time you lost out to the horrible girl, Stacy Whatever, when she tricked you into giving her your solo at regionals in high school."

"Tracy."

"Stop telling me her real name. I've been trying to forget for fifteen years. You were devastated, and she was such a piece of work."

"I heard she got married after high school."

"A shotgun wedding?"

"Mother."

"I'm saying she was on a mission to find someone to take care of her, even at sixteen. How could you have possibly had a crush on her?"

"I did not have a crush on her. I thought she was my friend."

"As the saying goes, with friends like that, who needs enemies."

"Can we move on from this walk through my most embarrassing moments?"

Her mother sat back on the sofa, and the video became jerky. "Fine. What's wrong?"

"Augustan offered me a job."

"What are the terms?" Here came Business Barbara rather than her mother. She imagined other moms started the conversation with, "That's great." Not her mother.

She rattled off the benefits, the salary, and the opportunities. "But I would need to move here. To Toronto."

Her mother flinched and then settled into her more schooled business expression. "The offer sounds competitive. What are your concerns?"

Her concern was that Sam made her want to consider turning down her dream job. "I'm not sure if I should take it."

"Sweetie, that's not a list. What exactly are your concerns? Are you afraid your father and I will be upset? Because I'll miss you terribly, but you can fly home anytime with that salary."

Lauren nodded. "That's what I told her."

"Told who?" Her mother squinted. "Ah, so there isn't a long list of concerns. Am I right?"

Lauren nodded. Aggravated when the tears flowed against her cheeks. "Sam got upset and hasn't spoken to me since."

"Did she tell you not to take the job?"

"No. She said she needed some time alone."

"Let her have the time to think things through. It doesn't mean she's going to break up with you. You don't want her to break up with you, do you?"

"God, no. She's amazing. Caring. Sensitive. A great cook. Gorgeous." She sighed and wiped her cheeks. "But Augustan is the job I've been wanting for months. I reread the offer, and they even mentioned that part of my job would be communications about changing the culture of gaming."

"Speaking of, did you get in touch with Anita at Johns Hopkins?"

"I did. Thanks. She had so many good ideas. I think Augustan would be open to helping me find funding for the program." She felt awful for being excited and desperately anxious at the same time. "How do I decide what to do?"

"Do you like the job you have now?"

This was her mother; she could be honest with her. "No. I feel like I've spent months banging my head on a brick wall."

"And we've already established you can come home anytime you want, or we can come see you."

"I think I'm in love with Sam." She blurted it out without thinking about it for too long.

"Does she know this?"

Lauren sniffled and shook her head.

"I'll give you my last piece of advice for the night, mostly because your father just pantomimed that he wants to watch *House of the Dragon*. I've worked at a lot of places in my career. You can find other jobs and make other friends at them, but when you love someone, sometimes, their needs come before yours and vice versa. Let Sam have the time she needs to consider what this change means for her. When she's ready, she'll talk to you. Then, tell her how you feel about her. She may surprise you."

Lauren smiled. "You like her, too."

"I saw the way you looked at each other. Why would I want to deny you happiness?"

Lauren heard her father's muffled voice offscreen.

"I'm coming, Harald." Her mother covered the screen with her hand. "Tell me how it goes. Love you."

How was it going to go? She felt guilty for getting involved with Sam and then running off to take a job in another country. She couldn't ask her to wait. They'd only just begun their relationship. That wouldn't be fair to Sam. But the job was the one she'd been hoping for and turning it down wouldn't satisfy her either. She wished someone else would make the decision for her.

Soju, it turned out, was a clean drink. Sam was tired the next morning but not the hungover mess she'd expected. She so rarely drank; she was convinced she was going to have the hangover of all hangovers this morning. Thank goodness they had eaten plenty of food. Sam squinted at the bright light that met her as she pulled the curtains aside in her room. The glass and metal canyon of the street drew her eye to the CN Tower in the distance.

She hated drinking. She felt like her mouth was sandpaper. Gross sandpaper. She grabbed a bottle of water from the mini-fridge.

She pulled on her jersey and retrieved her jeans from her luggage. They were the ones Mimi had picked for her at the vintage store in Baltimore. She'd driven back and bought them for herself after the fact, the look on Lauren's face when she'd stepped from the dressing room still etched in her memory. She put some mousse in her hair to lift it away from her undercut. Now she looked like herself. The jacket Lauren had given her yesterday lay over the back of the chair. She grabbed it and threw it on. The smell of the leather was heady. Now she was ready to face both the match and hopefully, Lauren.

She was still struggling to decide how she would handle the knowledge that Lauren was going to move here to Toronto. If she hadn't been too scared to leave her dad alone, where might she have gone after high school? Would she have met Lauren in that alternative life? She pulled out her phone and dialed her dad's new cell number.

"Hello?"

She was relieved to hear her father's deep, gravelly voice. "Hey, Pops." She sat on the edge of the bed. "Whatcha doin'?"

"Sitting here in my tighty-whities. I thought Jarek told me you have a big game today."

"I do. We're playing the best team in the world. Can you believe that?"

"You needing a pep talk? You know I'm not good at that."

"No. I'm okay." The silence stretched on a little. "Hey, Pops. How did you know Mom was the one?"

She heard the scraping of his chair as if he'd sat at the kitchen table.

"I just did. She was the only woman I'd met who didn't make any demands of me. I mean about being in the Army, going to Afghanistan multiple times. She took it all in stride. Never complained."

"What if she had? What if she'd said, I need you to come home and stay home this time?"

"That's a big question. I don't know what I would have done then, but I know what I would do now. I wouldn't have volunteered for another deployment, but she would never have asked me to give up the military. I guess we would have compromised."

She rubbed her eyes to keep from crying. "Thanks, Pops. That helps."

"I guess you have something going on besides the game?"

"A definite maybe."

"Mmm. Well, give 'em hell, O'Brian. Make me proud."

"Roger that. I love you, Dad."

"I love you, too, Sam."

Downstairs, she strode into the Barrage team room at the arena. When she sat at the table, Luke nodded at her. "You ready?" she asked him.

"If I'm needed." He took a swig of canned tea. "I'll just be happy to be part of the winning team before I retire."

Was she starting her career, or was it coming to an end? She tried to see her future, but all she could think about was Lauren staying here in Toronto.

The others filed in, but Lauren was noticeably missing. Sam glanced at her phone. There were multiple texts, but they were all from Olivia, Jarek, and the others. There was a one million dollar payout for the winners. Two hundred and fifty thousand dollars for the runners-up. A nice income for playing a game she loved. But her mind was everywhere but on the match. This had never happened to her before. She'd always been able to focus.

Alec looked nervous. He fiddled with his glasses, taking them on and off and wiping them at least three times. His inspirational speech fell flat. Too many ums and ahs. What was he nervous about? They were the ones playing today.

She glanced at her phone again. Should she text Lauren? See if she was okay? She shoved it back in her pocket. Whatever they needed to say to each other needed to happen in person.

A guy in a staff shirt with a headset leaned in the doorway. "We're ready for you."

Sam stood and followed Luke from the room. Dylan came up on her right. "If you make any mistakes, I'm going to ask Alec to slot Luke in. I swear to God."

She didn't have time for his shit today. She stopped and turned to him. "What is your problem, Dylan?" A few attendees in the hall watched with curiosity, their phones out. "Seriously, man. What have I done to you? I've showed out for every game. What is your fucking issue?"

Alec tried to usher them forward. He grimaced rather than smiled at the fans. "Let's keep this to a minimum today, guys."

"No. She wants to know why," said Dylan. "Fine. Because this is our space. You come along, and now we can't talk the way we want. We can't do anything fun because someone might be offended. *Siege Encounter* is for guys. You don't belong here."

"When you say someone might be offended, you mean women players? So you want to bully and intimidate each other and pretend it doesn't bother any of you when other guys call you names and shit talk about you?" asked Sam. "What does my being a woman have to do with anything? I haven't complained once about your behavior. I just suck it up and play."

"Women don't belong in foxholes."

"Tell that to the woman medic who pulled my dad off a road in Afghanistan during a firefight. I'm sure they'd both disagree."

She moved on. Yes, she was short-tempered today. Partly because of the drinks last night, partly because she'd been taking shit from Dylan since she'd arrived, and mostly because she had yet to hear or see Lauren today.

They all quieted as they entered the arena. Sam tried to put on a smile for the fans, but the argument in the hall had deflated her. Dylan didn't like her because he couldn't say and do things that would insult people and hurt their feelings? That was fucked-up. This was a job, not a bachelor party.

As she stepped on to the stage, Ji-ho gave her a slight bow. She returned it, though she felt odd doing it. While she was sorry she'd run away from Lauren last night, in a way, the time with Ji-ho had made her realize she had so many things she wanted to know about herself. It wasn't too late to experience her heritage for herself and her mother. Sometimes things happened for a reason, right?

As she settled into her seat, Dylan continued telling her his opinion. "The Barrage only hired you to check the diversity box."

"Hey," she said with a defiant tone. "I'm here to play. We have a chance to win this, but they're going to bury us if we can't get our shit together." She pointed at the Korean team already settled in their seats and ready.

"You took Luke's place on the team. He should be sitting in that seat, not you."

Luke stepped in. "Dylan, shut up, bruh. Don't use me as an excuse for giving her crap. If you don't have anything inspirational to say to all of us before we play the biggest game of our lives, then shut up and let her play."

"You trying to get in her pants? You're too late. She's fucking the marketing director."

They hadn't been discreet enough, obviously. Was he jealous? "I don't care who she's sleeping with, and I don't want to know who you're sleeping with," replied Luke. Perry had his headset on and was trying to stay out of the fray.

Was this all worth it? Was this what she'd be going through every day while she played for the Barrage? "Fine." She stood and stepped away from her station. "You can win this match without me."

Alec returned from talking with his counterpart on the Korean team. "What's happening?" he asked. Before anyone could answer, Will was on the stage, enraged.

"Why are you not in that seat?" he asked.

"Ask your team captain," she replied.

Dylan seemed to have lost his desire to mouth off.

Alec looked at Sam. "Are you refusing to play?"

"Yup."

He nodded. "I'll let the tournament officials know. Go ahead and take the seat, Luke."

Luke stepped to Sam's side and crossed his arms. "I refuse as well."

At that, Will took hold of Luke's jersey and pushed him toward the game station. He stumbled against the chair. "Sit down."

Luke stood up. "No. Sam's right. None of this is okay. This is the worst team environment I've ever played on. I didn't say anything because I was happy to be on a team at all. But you know what? Sam is a good player. As good or better than any of us. She deserves respect. I deserve respect. If you can't give her that, then I'm retiring right now."

A security guard and the tournament director approached. Sam assumed they were going to tell them time was up, and they needed to sit or forfeit. She couldn't let Luke forfeit on her account, though she appreciated everything he had said.

"You need to leave the arena," said the director to Will.

He appeared dumbfounded. "What? I'm the president of the Barrage."

"I don't care if you're the president of the United States. The rules clearly state that we do not tolerate any physical abuse on the premises."

"This is a misunderstanding." He pointed at Luke. "He tripped while taking his seat." He looked at Luke and Alec. "Tell them."

None of them spoke.

"Follow me, sir," said the security guard.

Will seemed to grasp the severity of the situation and left reluctantly, still calling out instructions to Alec.

"I've let this go on too long," said Alec. "I'm sorry, Sam. This is on me. Dylan, you're backup. Luke, Sam, take the seats. They're yours."

"What?" Dylan looked shocked.

"I'll inform the tournament officials."

For all his earlier bluster, Dylan stood and stepped away, looking shell-shocked.

Luke slid into his chair. Sam took hers, surprised by the turn of events.

Perry slipped his headset off one ear. "With that settled, who's captain?"

"Take the stick, O'Brian," said Luke. Perry nodded.

Wow. This had not been what she had expected. She'd been certain they would let her walk away without a bit of hesitation.

The moment she saw Lauren motioning to her from behind the ropes, Sam instantly regretted walking away from her last night. She'd needed the space, but she should have at least told her why she needed the time alone. Explained that it wasn't about her but about something she couldn't control in herself. She'd make it up to her as soon as the match was over. She'd stay and listen to her and tell her that she cared about her.

"I'll be right back." She slipped out of her chair and made her way to the edge of the stage.

Lauren bent closer to her. "I have something for you."

Sam barely heard a word she said, her heart beat so loudly in her ears. She wanted to reach out and take her head in her hands and kiss her.

Lauren pressed play on her phone. A video appeared. It was Quinn and her parents. They told her to win and that they were watching. Then, a second video played. Too close to the screen was Omar. Several family members sat on the floor behind him. His message was as brief but no less emotional for Sam.

She stared into Lauren's eyes. "Thank you."

"You're welcome," Lauren replied. "See you after the match."

"Yes, I have stuff I need to tell you."

"Me too. Good luck." Then, Lauren strode off the stage.

Luke leaned close. "If Dylan was telling the truth, you're a lucky woman."

She smiled in reply. "I am." She set her headset on her ears. "Let's do this."

Perry's leg was bouncing. He was nervous. She was, too. Her underarms were sweating even though the air conditioning in the convention center was set to freezing. She glanced at Ji-ho. He was in a huddle with the other players and their coach. His face looked tight, indicating his concern.

She had assumed that losing Dylan would give the South Korean team a boost of confidence. Dylan might have a complicated personality, but he was their best player. His only weakness was that he wasn't an intuitive player. He tended to plan a tactic and use it over and over again, thinking he'd get a different result through shear doggedness. Maybe Ji-ho and the others had planned for that and were now trying to determine how Luke would play.

"Don't let them get into your head," said Luke.

She turned her attention to him.

"The only thing they have going for them right now is their overconfidence." Luke looked surprisingly relaxed for a man about to either become a world champion or be berated for losing in Dylan's stead.

"Any other nuggets of wisdom?" she asked.

Initially, he appeared concerned, but then he showed a smile. "Nope. We have absolutely nothing to lose. They were already the favorites coming into the tournament. We should just enjoy the games."

Enjoy the games. She hadn't done that since she arrived on the team. What the hell. She could try and do that. The tournament announcer began pumping up the crowd, and before long he was saying her name, Sam O'Brian. Not Samantha. She could see her new team photo on one of the big screens around the room.

That was Lauren's doing. She'd arranged a new photo with Sylvia. An over the shoulder shot in a hoodie, but this one had her name across the back in the team colors. She loved it. She scanned the audience and the wings for Lauren but couldn't see her.

Game one went to the Daggers. The audience erupted in applause and excitement. Even the announcer seemed to get excited by the win. He called out each of their names with the enthusiasm of an MMA announcer, as if they had just punched Sam and the others in the sides of their heads.

"That didn't go well," said Perry.

Alec leaned in over them. "Give the strategy a chance. We have a plan. Stick to it."

Sam could already see the strategy wasn't going to work. Clearly, the Koreans had done their homework. With Luke trying to play like Dylan, albeit a bit slower, he was an easy target for them. He was a fluid player when he'd played *Call of Duty*. She'd watched his old gameplay online. If he was let off the leash, he played better. Unpredictable.

Game two was nearly identical to game one. The Daggers shut them down in standoff on the bridge map. They never even got close to the goal. Game three was the same map and gameplay but reversed, with the Barrage doing the defending.

A smoke canister obscured the target. Sam moved forward to meet the oncoming attack, while Luke did long coverage, and Perry moved along the side of the map to try to catch the Daggers in a crossfire.

"Oh. It's a feint," she heard Perry say in her headset before she saw his marker go red. "I'm out. They're coming around."

The smoke was a ruse. They weren't coming from the other side of the bridge at all. It was too late when she saw Luke's marker go red. She went prone behind the target and waited. The only chance she'd have was to take them out as they arrived. She got the first one, but Ji-ho took her out almost as quickly.

Game three was another loss. Two more and the South Koreans would be the world champions.

She looked at Alec. "Can we change up the plan now?"

"Give it one more game."

She frowned. "I think it's a mistake. They play a predictable game. If we keep playing as if Dylan is here, they're not going to drop a single map."

He shrugged. "Your call."

Luke and Perry stared at her expectantly. She didn't have much time to think it through. She didn't want to lose every game. One game at least. They had to win one. The next game was going to be destination on the mall map. A great place to catch the Koreans in tight corners. They tended to stick close together on this map in previous matches. It was a respawn game that would time out after six minutes. Plenty of time to try to take them all out at once before getting eliminated.

"Luke, pretend you're back in *Call of Duty*. Let yourself go. No more strategy. Perry, stick close to me, but stay just out of range in case they toss grenades. Play corner to corner and let's move counterclockwise."

Perry nodded. "Seems reasonable to me."

Luke cracked his knuckles. "Now you're talking."

The announcer did his usual schtick hyping the crowd by making them aware that the Koreans were only two games from the win. Sam wondered how many of the guys in the audience had bet against them now that online betting was legal in Canada.

Once the game was underway, she and Perry moved as one through the rooms of the mall with precision. They had caught the Koreans off guard with Luke playing like a maniac, running around with no strategy in mind. He was distracting them, and that meant she and Perry were able to eliminate them over and over again. When the timer ran out, the audience sat in stunned silence. Two hundred twenty-five points to sixty-five. Sam had to reread the numbers to be sure.

"What the hell?" Alec stared up at the big board. "Whatever you all just did, do it again."

Three games for the Seoul team. One for them. It was a start.

Whether it was the shock of the defeat or the aftereffects of the soju, Ji-ho was not his usual perfect player. In game five, Sam saw his patterns as clearly as if he was drawing lines all over the maps. No longer having to stick with the strategy designed for Dylan, Perry, Luke and she were able to make decisions quickly and adjust to everything the Seoul team tried.

Three games to two. Luke's gameplay probably hadn't been part of their opponent's preparation. The unexpected change seemed to work in their favor. Sam began to have fun with the games. Without Dylan and his threats and without Will misnaming her and asking about her wig, everything felt right.

Until it didn't.

Game six was back on that damn bridge map. Single elimination. No respawning. They had moved slowly and carefully through the game, but it didn't matter. This was Ji-ho's perfect play.

With the game lost, Sam knew the championship was slipping from their grasp. One more loss and the tournament was over. Would the Barrage want her back for another season after that? She'd caused a lot of trouble for them. Trouble they'd brought on themselves but problems nonetheless. If they lost, would the shit start again about girls not being good enough to play at this level?

Luke started humming.

"What the heck, dude?" said Perry. "Are you humming the theme from Rocky?"

Sam liked it. They were underdogs. They had nothing to lose. She started humming along.

Perry shook his head. "Oh my God, you're both nuts."

The announcer started his pregame hype. The countdown clock ticked down from ten to one. And they were off. Sam didn't say anything to either of them. She just kept humming along with Luke as they played. And they got to one hundred points in destination in the fastest time of the tournament.

Four to three. It seemed like momentum was in their favor. Even the crowd seemed to sense the change. Some disbelieving murmurs and the announcer was no longer as obviously biased to the Seoul Daggers. Another match game, this one on another favorite map for the Daggers. The humming became more intense. "Cross fire in the bus station, stay in the outside lane," Sam said between hums.

"Got one," said Luke.

When the game ended, they were tied, four games each. Sam couldn't believe her luck. One more game would decide it all. Bragging rights. Money. A woman world champion?

Luke and Sam stopped humming this time. "Communicate," was all she said to Perry and Luke before it started. They both nodded.

"Ji-ho is up top," said Perry before he was eliminated and respawned.

"Stay low," Sam replied.

"Shit." Luke respawned. "He's got great positioning."

The score went back and forth. Sometimes they were ahead, and sometimes the Seoul team was ahead. Sam's palms were sweating. Time was running out. Twenty seconds left. Fifteen. Ten. Sam moved from her position and came around a corner just as Ji-ho arrived in the same spot. He had the angle on her, but he didn't have enough time to make the shot.

The game ended. Their avatars hung still on the screen.

They'd won by a single point.

A millisecond longer, and Ji-ho would have won the tournament with her elimination.

As the win sank in, Sam threw off her headset and rocked back in her seat. Perry screamed and jumped up and down over and over again.

One point. She dropped her chin to her chest and closed her eyes. How was it possible to go from playing with her friends to winning the first world championship in less than a year? She could only imagine what Olivia, Jarek, and Ashton must have been doing right now. Spilling their beers and screaming at their screens, she hoped.

Luke clapped her on the shoulder. "Thanks for making my retirement one to remember."

"You sure you want to quit? You're a world champion now."

He nodded. "Go out on a high, dude."

She'd just earned more money in this one tournament than most professional women gamers in their entire careers. Maybe she should go out on a high as well. Then, she thought of Quinn and other girls watching. They deserved to make a living at gaming if they wanted. She needed to stick around if just to get photos of a woman champion out on the internet for a few days, showing the world that women could game with the guys.

The Korean team filed past. Each of them gave a small bow and said, "Good game."

Ji-ho stopped to speak to Sam. "Next time," was all he said.

"Soju is on me," she replied.

He smiled and shook a finger at her before walking away.

Sam didn't remember the next few minutes of other people congratulating her. She kept looking for Lauren. This was the biggest moment in her life, and she wanted to share it with the person she loved.

"Come on. We've got to do the postgame interview." Luke guided her gently through the throng of people that had surrounded them.

She scanned the crowd for Lauren as she moved forward. Where was she? More people called out congratulations and good game as she passed. She should be excited, but now she felt anxious, worried the inevitable social media backlash would begin. With Dylan being sidelined before the match, she was certain blame would fall on her. If she could just find Lauren. Having her beside her would reassure her and help her get through the media circus that was about to befall her.

Once she was mic'd up on the video set, Luke leaned toward her. "Relax. You've got this. We just won the first world championship for *Siege Encounter*. We're going to be famous for all of fifteen minutes."

Sam laughed. Yeah, she was probably worrying about something that would last as long as a day or two. She could make it through this. Eventually, trolls got tired and moved on. Still, she really wanted to talk to Lauren. They had a lot to discuss. Mostly about their future together. Now that the game was over, her thoughts were filled with how she should tell Lauren how she felt.

The interview was bland. As excited as she was for the win, the questions were similar to every other interview she'd done since joining the team. How did she feel being a champion? Was she looking forward to the start of next year's season in a few weeks? Her answers were as bland as the questions. She really wanted to hurry up and go find Lauren.

Finally, the main lights shut off, leaving her able to see the faces of the folks still watching from the audience. Her heart leaped when she saw Lauren's smile. She couldn't get the mic off fast enough. Sam didn't care that an entire audience was still milling about in the center. She leaned in and kissed Lauren and kept kissing her until she heard a few catcalls. She gently disentangled herself, a bit embarrassed by the attention. "Do I have lipstick on me?"

"Yes, it's a terrible shade." Lauren wiped it away with a smile and wrapped her in a hug. "Congratulations." Sam relaxed into Lauren's arms, her touch comforting. "I'm glad you're here."

"Where else would I be?"

Good question. Somewhere not with Sam. Suddenly all the worries about the postgame trolling seemed to drift into the distance, replaced by the realization that she was going to be left behind. Exactly as she'd always feared. *Love someone and they leave you.*

She thought hard about her next words. She wanted to be selfish. To ask Lauren to stay in Baltimore. To stay with the team. Stay in their apartment together. Put up with Will's shit for another season. But that wasn't right. She loved Lauren, and Lauren deserved to have the success she wanted. She should have her celebration, too. She'd fought for Sam. She'd protected her against the team and tried to change things from the inside. She'd rooted for her to be the best player in the world and had helped her achieve that. Sam couldn't make her stay in Baltimore. She had to let her go.

"You should take the job."

"What?"

"I love you, Lauren. I'm not going to be the reason you put your dream on hold." She felt like someone had clenched her heart in a vise as the words came out, but she wasn't going to take them back.

"I love you, too," Lauren replied. "So, maybe I need to rethink what I want. Maybe the job isn't that important."

Sam didn't believe a word she was saying. Lauren wasn't going to throw away a plan for her future that easily. Not for love. Sam wasn't going to let her. "You're going to do it. It's what you've wanted since I met you." Sam didn't know if what she was saying was true, but she had to try to sell it. Lauren deserved something good after all she had sacrificed to get here. "What about your plan to start the program for gamer girls? Won't Augustan be a better sponsor than Will?"

Lauren took a few moments before answering. "Are you sure you're okay with this?"

"I'm being practical," said Sam. "I'm not sure what I want to do now that I'm a world champion. I'm twenty-five. I'm ancient in the team's mind. I think I can play longer, but you know they want the latest greatest thing. You also know I'm not going back to wearing skirts and wigs, so there's that. So while you do your thing at Augustan, I'll figure out my own shit."

Lauren searched her face, no doubt looking for the weakness she was trying not to show. One of the Barrage assistants motioned for Lauren, and Luke was waving to Sam to join him in the spotlight for an interview. "Can we discuss this a little later? I need to get a lot done now that you and the team are world champions."

Sam nodded. She knew they both had a lot to think about.

"How about a walk? Must be a late-night coffee bar around here somewhere," Lauren said as she moved away.

Sam gave her a thumbs-up. She took her phone from the tournament usher and turned it on. She could feel the text messages buzzing, but she didn't look at them. The only thing she cared about was the ringtone that would tell her Lauren had sent a message.

❖

It was nearly midnight before Lauren texted. Sam had already done her research. She called a rideshare and paced in front of the hotel. She looked at the time. Eleven forty. She hoped they would make it before the place she had selected closed.

Lauren rushed out the doors. She'd changed into some sweats and a soft sweater. "I thought I'd never get out of there. The shit is already flying about both Will and Dylan, as you can imagine."

Sam kissed her. "Don't care about either of them right now. Just you." She got a notification that their ride had arrived. She took hold of Lauren's hand in the back seat.

"How does it feel?" asked Lauren.

"Your hand?" she teased.

Lauren gave her an exasperated side-eye.

"Surreal." She looked out at Toronto's night skyline moving past. "Most people don't give a shit, but I got a handful of calls from my dad and my grandparents, Olivia and Jarek. It matters to them. A couple of scummy *financial advisors* approached me at the hotel wanting to help me invest my winnings. My family may not have as much as yours, but my grandparents are pretty savvy about retirement stuff, so I think I'll talk with them when I get home."

"Does it bother you? That I didn't tell you that my family was well off?" It was clear that Lauren was feeling uncertain.

Sam thought back to the day at Lauren's parents' house. She'd never be fully comfortable in that environment, but her parents had been welcoming and unexpectedly warm. "Your mother called me a little while ago to congratulate me. She said she had no idea what was going on in the game, but that Elizabeth was very excited and wanted me to come visit next weekend."

Lauren squeezed her hand. "You sidestepped the question, Sam."

She looked at their entwined fingers. "You didn't owe me any explanations. I could have guessed it if I'd been looking for it. I'm more worried that I'll do something to embarrass you. Like, not use the right fork or some shit."

Lauren leaned as close as her seat belt would allow. "You think I'll dump you because you used the wrong fork?"

"I don't know." She slumped a little in her seat. "I think people will know that I'm not the same as you. In lots of ways."

"That's a good thing," said Lauren. "I really don't want to date myself. I'm way too high-strung and definitely a workaholic."

Sam laughed. "And I'm a slacker?"

"No. Nothing of the sort. I think you're just right." Lauren put up a hand to stop Sam from saying anything. "I know I complained about gamers having strange hours and being on the road all the time, but I don't care. It isn't forever. If things work out, we'll have plenty of time together in the future."

Future. Sam's heart jumped. Lauren was talking about far future, not the next couple of months. She'd never thought further out than next week. The car stopped at their destination, allowing her a moment's reprieve.

On the street corner, Sam stood and stared at the recommended ice cream place. The exterior of the building was decorated with giant ice cream cones, cows, and painted milking canisters. A small line of patrons was out the door. She checked the time. Eleven fifty. Ten minutes until they closed. She took Lauren's hand and rushed her to the end of the line.

Lauren craned her neck to look inside. "Look at all the kitsch on the walls."

Sam bit her lip and looked at the time again. "I hope we make it before they close."

Lauren stepped in front of her and took her hands. "Sam, even if we don't get anything, I'm still enjoying being with you, and we can take a few selfies with these giant cones. It's fine."

Still, it felt a little like a metaphor for their relationship. *Can't get the ice cream. Can't be in the same city.*

"Besides, if you really meant what you said earlier, we can come back again when you visit me."

The line moved them closer. Oh yeah, that discussion. She had told Lauren to take the job here in Toronto while Sam stayed in Baltimore. Five hundred miles away.

"I want to take the job with Augustan." Lauren looked at the waffle cones in the case, not at her. "But I don't want to do that if it means losing you."

The line moved again. They were next. So much pressure. She wasn't going to take back what she'd said. Lauren deserved to do the thing that would make her happy. Lauren had said it on the ride over, this wouldn't be forever. Sam had waited before. Months on end for her father to return from deployment. Her mother had done it. And this wasn't even a military deployment. They could see each other as often as they wanted as long as they could afford the plane tickets. Sam had already checked. Three hundred dollars nonstop out of Reagan in DC.

The line moved again, and a teenager called out, "What will you have?"

They'd made it. Just in time. The employee cut off the line behind them. They took their ice creams outside. She needed to be clear with Lauren. She took a deep breath. "I love you. I'm pretty certain I've never loved anyone before. I have no idea how a relationship works, and I don't know what I'll be doing in six months. But I do know that if you'll have me, I want to be doing whatever it is with you." It felt good to get it out.

"And what if, after six months, I decide I want to be wherever you are?" asked Lauren.

Sam secretly hoped that would be the case. "What if I'm back in Havre de Grace in my dad's basement? You sure you want that?" She was half joking, but there was a chance it might happen.

"I'm certain we can negotiate something that works for both of us."

"Always the diplomat."

Lauren put a hand on her hip and smirked. "I haven't tried that as a career. I'll have to think about it."

Sam took her hand. "Then you'll take the job at Augustan for now?"

Lauren became serious. "As long as this isn't good-bye."

Sam leaned in and kissed her. Despite the coldness of Lauren's lips from the ice cream, her body radiated warmth.

The ride back to the hotel was tinged with melancholy. Sam had no idea what would happen to them, but she was willing to try. Lauren made her feel loved. Real love. Adult love. The kind that made her want to go to the roof of the hotel and shout it to all of Toronto. Somehow, she'd make it work. She was certain.

CHAPTER TWENTY-EIGHT

L auren sat at the conference table with the leadership of Augustan's business development team. Nearly six months had passed since she'd moved to Toronto. Six months where she'd thrown herself into her new job. Late nights. Early mornings. Lots of ultra-processed food and a half dozen cups of coffee a day.

She'd presented the Women in Gaming program plan two weeks ago. Now she waited patiently for either additional questions or a final decision. This was the moment that would either make it all worthwhile or leave her questioning her choices.

She rubbed her hands together to warm her fingers. They were still cold from the walk to the office from the subway station. She hadn't adjusted to winter in Canada, but Toronto was a great city to live in, surprisingly cosmopolitan and amazingly clean. She'd seen so many things she wanted to take photos of and send to Sam, but she'd saved them, hoping someday soon, they would see each other again.

"Lauren, I speak for everyone here when I say that your presentation was thorough and well thought out."

But? She waited for the shoe to drop.

"And I'm happy to tell you that Augustan will finance the entire budget for the next twelve months."

Lauren couldn't believe it. The entire budget?

"After that, we'll reassess how the program is performing. We'll expect surveys of the participating groups, and for those children under eighteen, surveys with their parents' approval only."

"I can't thank you all enough for believing in this project." Lauren felt humbled. "I promise, you won't regret this decision."

There were handshakes and congratulations, but all she could think about was how she longed to call Sam and tell her. The program they had discussed, the one helping make gaming safer for girl gamers and others who were vulnerable, including boys, was about to become reality. Her mind was already returning to the first test case. The regional tournament in Toronto had a safe space for girl gamers where they discussed issues with trained moderators. They had discovered that boys wanted to talk, too.

Now they would have a session for girls and boys to talk to each other as well. A space with no judgment, where they could discuss miscommunication, why they saw the gaming world in such different ways, and why they felt differently about it. Next steps would be to determine how to best integrate sessions for trans and nonbinary players as well.

She checked her Instagram for the tenth time. There was Sam. Hair short, the tips dyed purple, and she wore a moto style jacket with the Boston team logo on it. They had leaned into her androgyny rather than trying to make her something—someone—she wasn't.

Though social media still had a loud contingent of trolls complaining about Sam's participation in *Siege Encounter*, a surprisingly vocal grassroots backlash had taken place. And the source of the support came from women and girls who had almost never taken part in the discussions before. The turning point had been a video of Sam that had gone viral.

Lauren had already reached out to the media outlet and the Boston team to get approval to use the video clip in the campaign for girl gamers. Now she rewatched the reel for the twentieth time, mostly to look at Sam.

"The reality is that female gamers are going to be exposed to more online abuse than guys. We need the tools to stop the worst of the behavior, like doxxing, swatting, and threats of violence. But we also need resources to support those being bullied so they don't take that hate and internalize it. And the industry needs to step up and help.

"Changing people's behavior is hard. We do things the same way over and over, and it works, right? Or you want to fit in. So if you grew up watching your older brother intimidating others in games by calling them names and threatening to come to their home, you think, okay, that's what you do to win. Which is why we need safe spaces for young gamers where they can learn acceptable behavior without the influences of older, more mature gamers who are resistant to change.

"We need to focus on younger gamers, making sure they know the rules and understand why those rules are in place. Make sure it's okay when gamers do the right thing and call out bad behavior. Gamers have accepted toxicity as part of gaming for too long. That needs to stop."

Lauren paused it there. Sam looked so serious and so beautifully handsome.

Her office door flew open without a knock.

"Did you hear the news?" Yesenia asked.

Lauren looked up from her desk. "Can you give me more of a hint? Local news? World news? Office gossip?"

"Will Campbell is out at Baltimore."

"What happened?"

"Since you never kiss and tell about your former employer, I heard through other sources that he was less than stellar at financials?"

Lauren tried to keep her face neutral. She knew not to gossip about a previous work environment. How many times had Nate warned Will in their meetings about his knife edge control over the team?

Yesenia continued when Lauren said nothing. "A minority partner bought out enough of the other investors to take over a controlling stake. First thing he did was replace Will as president."

"Good. Couldn't have happened to a better guy."

"By the way, congratulations! Your assistant told me the news about the women in gaming program. I'm so happy for you."

"Thanks."

An appointment reminder rang. She moved to turn off the alarm. Her phone's lock screen displayed a captivating image of Sam sporting futuristic wraparound glasses adorned with LED lights and sticker strips that mimicked innovative VR technology. Shot as a low, angle three quarter profile of her looking to her right and out into the distance. No smile necessary. It was perfect and so very Sam.

Yesenia peered over Lauren's shoulder. "How's she doing in Boston?"

Lauren slapped her phone facedown on her desk. "She's doing great. The team is a better fit for her than Baltimore."

"Have you talked to her or only texted?"

"We promised each other we'd give each other space to follow our careers without influencing one another. I don't want to make her think twice about her choices. Or about my choice."

"Why don't you go down to Boston and spend some time with her?"

Lauren shook her head. "That wouldn't be a good idea." That was the truth. She missed Sam terribly. If she went to Boston, she might not come back.

"Did I tell you that Bodhan is applying for a job transfer?"

"No. When did that happen?"

Yesenia looked casually at her nails while she leaned on Lauren's desk. "Last week. He says if it comes through and things work out, he'd like to make things official."

"Official? As in married?" Lauren jumped up and wrapped Yesenia in her arms. "That is so exciting. Congratulations."

"Don't get too excited. I'm due to go back to Spain first. It would be a lot easier for him to move to Spain anyway. EU and all."

"You want to go home?"

"I miss it. Especially the weather."

"What will I do without you?"

"Probably take my job," she teased. "Now that you're in charge of the youth program, you can work from the Boston office. Most of the conventions and tournaments are in the US anyway. That's the nice thing about a global company."

"Jumping a little ahead of ourselves, aren't we? Sam's been super busy with the winter season. I've gotten a few emojis and a selfie or two of her in different arenas."

"What did you send back?"

"Some emojis and a couple of selfies of me in my sleeping bag of a winter coat."

"Have I taught you nothing, padawan?"

"Now you're pulling out *Star Wars* references. That does not fit your vibe."

"Give me your phone." Yesenia took it from the desk and held it up, facing Lauren. "Unlock it please."

Lauren did as she asked but worried about what was about to happen. Yesenia leaned down and aimed the phone at Lauren's legs.

"What are you doing?"

"Sending her a selfie of your heels with a little ankle and calf showing."

Lauren tried to take the phone, but Yesenia stood and backed away.

"She likes you in heels. Written all over her face when you weren't looking." Yesenia swiped a few more times on the phone and handed it back.

Lauren groaned. "What is she going to think?"

"She's going to think you're propositioning her, which is exactly what you should be doing."

"I want to do what's right."

"Do you want to be with her or not?"

Lauren sighed and looked up at the ceiling. "I do. More than anything."

"There is your answer," said Yesenia as she headed for the door. "Talk to her and put in your request to move. I'm going to be in sunny Spain with Bodhan. You should be in Boston with Sam."

Lauren thought about what it would mean if she reached out to Sam and told her she felt more strongly about her than she had thought possible when she'd left for Toronto. Would she want her in Boston? First, she needed to have a conversation with her boss's boss to determine the feasibility of a potential move.

Her phone beeped. Sam had replied to the photo with an emoji of a smiley face with heart eyes. A text message followed:

When can I see you?

Guess that answered that question.

❖

Sam checked the weather in Seoul for the tenth time on her phone while she waited to board the plane. The temperature was the same as in Boston. She unzipped the pocket on her backpack for the third time and checked for her passport. Going to Korea seemed surreal, and on St. Patrick's Day of all days. Her grandmother had found that endlessly funny when she'd told her.

This was the trip of a lifetime. Augustan had arranged all this. She was going at the invitation of the Seoul team to play some friendly matches with them, meaning she'd be playing with Ahn Ji-ho rather than against him. It was all thanks to Lauren. She'd convinced Augustan to cover the costs for this goodwill tour, to open the doors for women gamers around the world.

Some days, Sam was happy, and others, she was lonely. She'd made the choice to move to Boston. The team was the best. The owner was a woman, and she was committed to finding another female player for the team besides Sam. And still, she'd wake up in the morning, touch the vacant half of her bed, and remember what it had felt like to live with Lauren. Her apartment seemed empty in comparison.

And Sam was certain that she knew what she wanted now, and it wasn't this life if it meant being without Lauren. Hell, that was why she'd become a massage therapist. Massachusetts had issued her a license since her Maryland one was current and met their standards for educational hours. She was ready to find clients as soon as this dream job ended; that could be at any moment.

She'd already looked to see how hard it would be to move to Canada and if they'd take her licenses. Turned out, they'd recently made it easier since they wanted people in her occupation to immigrate. That seemed lucky. But it all depended on whether Lauren wanted her in Canada. They hadn't seen each other since New Year's. Spending the holidays with each other's families had been fun, though awkward at times. The best part of Thanksgiving with Lauren's family had been a late afternoon sail on their boat. What had made it so special was the look on Lauren's face while they were on the water. Her expression had reflected sheer joy as she'd helped her father sail. Sam had spent most of the time seated and hanging on to a railing, but it had been worth it. It still seemed surreal to have a legit girlfriend.

Video calls were fine for spending time with friends, but it wasn't the same with Lauren. Not to mention, their schedules had been very different the past few months. Sam had some time off now that the winter season had ended, and she'd looked at flights to Toronto, but she hadn't reserved one yet. She couldn't decide if she should ask Lauren if she could come visit or if she should show up unexpectedly.

As she shuffled along behind the other passengers, she kept her headphones on to drown out the dull hum of machinery. She'd never left the country before, and everything about the trip made her nervous. Her seat was in the center aisle with a separator between hers and the one beside it. She played with the controls, laying herself flat, then pulling the seat back upright. They hadn't even taken off yet, and she was already reading the duty-free shopping magazine. So much perfume and makeup. This was going to be a long trip.

What would she find when she got there? A little girl smiled at her as she walked past with her mother. She smiled back. Might that have been her and her mother in another time?

After takeoff, Sam looked through the selections on the TV screen in front of her. She spotted a familiar pink title. The first romantic anime she had watched with Lauren. She pulled up the main screen and took a snapshot and sent it to Lauren while she knew she still had Wi-Fi. There was a ping to her right, as if the person in the seat next to her had also received a message.

A reply came almost immediately, lots of heart eye emojis.

Then there was a knock on the barrier. "Think we could watch together?" asked the voice.

Sam slammed the divider down. Lauren smiled back at her. Her heart beat so fast, it felt like it might burst. She was here. On the plane. "What? How?" She leaned over the divider and kissed her. She didn't care what anyone in the cabin thought.

Lauren made her sit back in her seat and put on her seat belt. "I'm not sure I like this big half wall between us."

Lauren pointed at the ottoman where her feet rested. "You can come visit me at any time on the flight. It even has a seat belt."

Sam pursed her lips in a questioning way. "Not what I had in mind."

"Aw." Lauren gazed at her over the divider. "Can't take being apart for fourteen hours?"

"We've been apart eleven weeks. I can do it. I won't like it though." She stared at her, still amazed that she was here on the way to Seoul with her.

"You were counting."

"You weren't?"

Lauren's laugh was soft and sweet. "Why else would I ask my boss to make me your plus one on this trip?"

"I still can't believe you're here. I'm so happy."

"I won't get in your way, but I thought maybe we could do a little exploring together."

"That sounds great." she reached across the seat and grabbed Lauren's hand. "I missed you."

"I missed you, too."

Sam lowered her voice. "Do I have you all to myself in Korea?" Her thoughts were already moving to what the hotel rooms were like in Seoul.

"Some of the time. I do actually have to do some work while we're there." She smiled shyly. "I'll be meeting an interpreter and going to the Ministry of Culture as a representative of Augustan Gaming. My guide is supposed to help keep me from making any terrible faux pas. Did you know you shouldn't carry a to-go coffee to a meeting?"

Sam suddenly felt underprepared for this trip. What if she did something really stupid and embarrassed herself and Lauren? "Now you've got me worried."

"I'm sure Ahn Ji-ho will take good care of you."

Ji-ho had turned out to be an all right guy. He'd reached out to offer his assistance while she was in Korea. He'd even mentioned helping her look for her grandfather if she wanted. She wasn't ready for that yet. Maybe she'd change her mind once she got there, but for now, she just wanted to enjoy the trip and learn about the culture.

Part of her wanted to know why her grandfather had never acknowledged her mother, but she wasn't sure it would mean anything. Her mother had lived her whole life without him, and knowing why wouldn't help anyone now. But it did put in stark contrast how dedicated her mother had been to Sam's dad. She'd put up with long deployments and the lack of comfort from her own family, all because she'd loved him.

Being apart from Lauren had been hard. Mostly, she wanted the little things. Hanging out together over breakfast. Sleeping next to each other. Admiring her when she wasn't looking. Feeling proud to be out in public with her. Listening to her recount her day.

"I've been thinking. Maybe after a season with Boston, I could try to join the Toronto team. If you want me to be closer."

"Aww, that's really sweet." Lauren shook her head. "But if you approve, I'd like to take a job transfer."

Sam's heart sank. Would that mean they'd be closer or farther away from each other?

"To Boston."

Sam nearly crawled over the divider. She leaned as far over as she could. "Really? You're not sending me, right?"

"Facts." Lauren smiled. "I'm going to help craft the messaging for Augustan's new campaign to encourage girls to play our games. And they've agreed to fund the anti-toxicity program. The best part is, the new office for youth in gaming will be in Boston."

"That sounds amazing and difficult."

"Luckily, I have an offer for the best woman gamer in Augustan's *Siege Encounter* league to assist me with both. If she'll do it."

Sam had to think about that statement for a moment before realizing Lauren meant her. "I'd do anything for you."

Lauren smiled and leaned closer. "Is that a yes on my move to Boston? I'll need a place to live."

Sam was never going to say no to Lauren moving to Boston. As a matter of fact, it was the best St. Patrick's day present she could get. She could hear her grandmother saying, luck of the Irish. "A two-bedroom apartment recently opened up at my building. I can text the manager and let her know I'll take it. As a matter of fact, let me do it now before I lose the Wi-Fi."

Lauren touched her arm. She shivered in response. "Shouldn't we talk about what this all means first? Do you have any concerns?"

Did she? Sure, plenty of them. Would they last as a couple? Would Lauren want her as much as she wanted Lauren? Would their different backgrounds eventually cause some kind of rift? "Here's my answer: I miss cooking for you. I miss your face, and I miss your smell. And damn, I miss your legs. Don't make me beg you to move."

Lauren ran a hand through Sam's hair, sending tingles throughout her body. "Then you've got yourself a new roommate."

Roommate. That didn't sound strong enough for how she felt. What made someone know for certain that they'd found the one? She'd known Lauren for almost a year now. They'd lived together in a tiny apartment and survived unscathed and enjoyed their time together.

Lauren had a way of making her feel good about herself. She believed in her. Believed she could be the best at what she was doing. And even when things had been difficult, she'd never taken out her aggravation on Sam. Not to mention, she'd eaten everything Sam had ever cooked and hadn't complained once. She'd definitely gotten points for that with Grandma O'Brian. So if roommate wasn't the right term for what she wanted, what was?

"What if I don't want a roommate?"

Lauren spoke cautiously, "Are we moving too fast? I can move into my own place—."

Sam wasn't sure what she was going to say next. She wasn't thinking this through the way she would've done with a game. Maybe she should take some time to analyze the pros and cons.

No, there weren't any cons. The hell with it. She'd been analyzing her way through life. Maybe this was one thing that didn't need to be examined from all sides. Maybe she should go with her feelings.

She unbuckled and went around to the aisle next to Lauren. She kneeled beside her seat and took her hand. "What if I want a partner?" she said more seriously. Her mouth was dry. She knew what she was about to say was going to be a lot for them both. "What if I want you as my partner? For life."

Lauren's eyes glistened. "Are you asking me to marry you?"

"I am," said Sam. "We've already lived together, so we know what we're getting into." She smiled. "I missed you every single day we were apart, and I've done nothing but wait for a sign to tell you how I felt about you. You being on this plane with me is that sign. I don't want to wait any longer."

"Then, yes. I'll marry you."

Sam kissed her.

Clapping followed from the woman seated across the aisle and from the flight attendant who'd been about to ask for their dinner order. "Congratulations."

Sam knew her cheeks were flaming red. "Thanks."

"I got a video," said the businessman a seat back on the window side. "Accidently." He shrugged. "Tell me where to send it."

Sam laid her forehead against the arm of the seat.

Lauren stroked her head. "Can't take it back now."

"Wouldn't think of it."

She returned to her own seat. Now she was going to be too excited to sleep on the flight.

Lauren settled back in her seat. "I've already queued a few shows I've wanted to watch, and I plan on taking a nice long nap before we arrive." She pulled a small packet from a bag of complimentary items. "Be aware, I will be wearing this moisturizing facemask halfway across the Pacific, so don't freak out if I look creepy."

Sam caught her eye. As seriously as she could sound, she said, "You'd look hot in anything."

Lauren blushed.

Sam settled into her seat and began the show on her screen. She glanced at Lauren's screen showing the same thing. This flight was going to be exceptionally long but for an entirely different reason.

How had she gotten so lucky? Her father was getting better every day. He even had a new girlfriend. She was playing a game she loved and getting paid for it. The love of her life had just accepted her proposal of marriage. And now she was flying over North America on her way to Korea, hoping to discover things about her heritage that she had never known.

Definitely the best St. Patrick's Day ever.

About the Author

Suzanne Lenoir is the author of the Valmora series of young adult fantasy novels from Bold Strokes Books. Her first novel, *A Talent Within*, was a 2024 GCLS Goldie Award finalist in both the debut novel and science fiction/fantasy categories.

Suzanne is a technophile, video gamer, and history buff. At the moment, you can find her listening to French 79, rewatching *Arcane*, and playing *Call of Duty*.

Find out more at SuzanneLenoir.com.

Books Available from Bold Strokes Books

Across the Enchanted Border by Crin Claxton. Magic, telepathy, swordsmanship, tyranny, and tenderness abound in a tale of two lands separated by the enchanted border. (978-1-63679-804-2)

Deep Cover by Kara A. McLeod. Running from your problems by pretending to be someone else only works if the person you're pretending to be doesn't have even bigger problems. (978-1-63679-808-0)

Good Game by Suzanne Lenoir. Even though Lauren has sworn off dating gamers, it's becoming hard to resist the multifaceted Sam. An opposites attract lesbian romance. (978-1-63679-764-9)

Innocence of the Maiden by Ileandra Young. Three powerful women. Two covens at war. One horrifying murder. When mighty and powerful witches begin to butt heads, who out there is strong enough to mediate? (978-1-63679-765-6)

Protection in Paradise by Julia Underwood. When arson forces them together, the flames between chief of police Eve Maguire and librarian Shaye Hayden aren't that easy to extinguish. (978-1-63679-847-9)

Too Forward by Krystina Rivers. Just as professional basketball player Jane May's career finally starts heating up, a new relationship with her team's brand consultant could derail the success and happiness she's struggled so long to find. (978-1-63679-717-5)

Worth Waiting For by Kristin Keppler. For Peyton and Hanna, reliving the past is painful, but looking back might be the only way to move forward. (978-1-63679-773-1)

Flowers and Gemstones by Alaina Erdell. Caught between past loves and present secrets, Hannah and Vanessa must each decide if the other is worth making difficult changes for a shot at happiness. (978-1-63679-745-8)

Foul Play by Erin Kaste. Music librarian Kirsten Lindquist knows someone is stalking the symphony musicians, but can she prove that a string of murders and suspicious accidents are connected, all without becoming a victim herself? (978-1-63679-689-5)

Hollywood Hearts by Toni Logan. What happens when an A-list actress falls for a paparazzo, having no idea her love interest is the one responsible for the photos in a troublesome tabloid scandal targeting her? (978-1-63679-695-6)

Ride It Out by Jenna Jarvis. When the COVID-19 lockdown traps Mick and Katy in situations they'd convinced themselves were temporary, they're forced to face what they really want from their lives, and who they want to share them with. (978-1-63679-709-0)

Scarlet Love by Gun Brooke. Felicienne de Montagne is content with her hybrid flowers and greenhouses—until she finds adventurer Puck Aston on her doorstep and realizes nothing will ever be the same. (978-1-63679-721-2)

The Hard Stuff by Ana Hartnett. When Hannah, the sales manager for a big liquor brand, moves to Alexandra's hometown and rivals her local distillery, sparks of friction and attraction fly. It turns out the liquor is the least of the hard stuff. (978-1-63679-599-7)

The Hunter and Her Witch by Rachel Sullivan. When an ex-witch-hunter falls for a witch, buried pasts are unearthed, and love is placed on trial. (978-1-63679-830-1)

Trustfall by Patricia Evans. Devri and Shiv never expect their feelings for each other to linger, but sometimes what you've always wanted has a way of leading you to who you've always needed. (978-1-63679-705-2)

All For Her: Forbidden Romance Novellas by Gun Brooke, J.J. Hale, Aurora Rey. Explore the angst and excitement of forbidden love few would dare in this heart-stopping novella collection. (978-1-63679-713-7)

Finding Harmony by CF Frizzell. Rock star Harper Cushing has to rearrange her grandmother's future and sell the family store out from under her, but she reassesses everything because Gram's helper, Frankie, could be offering the harmony her heart has been missing. (978-1-63679-741-0)

Gaze by Kris Bryant. Love at first sight is for dreamers, but the more time Lucky and Brianna spend together, the more they realize the chemistry of a gaze can make anything possible. (978-1-63679-711-3)

Laying of Hands by Patricia Evans. The mysterious new writing instructor at camp makes Grace Waters brave enough to wonder what would happen if she dared to write her own story. (978-1-63679-782-3)

Seducing the Widow by Jane Walsh. Former rival debutantes have a second chance at love after fifteen years apart when a spinster persuades her ex-lover to help save her family business. (978-1-63679-747-2)

The Naked Truth by Sandy Lowe. How far are Rowan and Genevieve willing to go and how much will they risk to make their most captivating and forbidden fantasies a reality? (978-1-63679-426-6)

The Roommate by Claire Forsythe. Jess Black's boyfriend is handsome and successful. That's why it comes as a shock when she meets a woman on the train who makes her pulse race. (978-1-63679-757-1)

www.ingramcontent.com/pod-product-compliance
Lightning Source LLC
Chambersburg PA
CBHW022000010726
47494CB00003B/819